CHASSIE WEST

"Chassie West has created a heroine human enough to appreciate a mother's hug, gutsy enough to solve a murder, and sensible enough to love Italian shoes. Bravissima!"
New York Times bestselling author Lisa Scottoline

"Edgar Award nominee Chassie West delivers mystery, suspense, and intrigue."
National Black Review

"West has a knack for creating colorful yet realistic characters and witty dialogue."
Publishers Weekly

"Chassie West immerses you in atmosphere."
Award-winning author Eileen Dreyer

"A delight to read."
Booked for Murder

bursting at the seams. . . .
nuances of the small town
hite South to a 't.' "
Review of Mystery

mystery is always cause for
cing in the streets. No one does
friend, the divine Ms. West!"
elen Chappell

Also by Chassie West

Killing Kin
Loss of Innocence
Sunrise

CHASSIE WEST

KILLER RICHES

AVON BOOKS
An Imprint of HarperCollinsPublishers

AVON BOOKS
An Imprint of HarperCollins*Publishers*
10 East 53rd Street
New York, New York 10022-5299

Copyright © 2001 by Chassie L. West
ISBN: 0-06-104391-5
www.avonbooks.com

First Avon Books paperback printing: April 2001

Avon Trademark Reg. U.S. Pat. Off. and in Other Countries, Marca Registrada, Hecho en U.S.A.
HarperCollins® is a trademark of HarperCollins Publishers Inc.

Printed in the U.S.A.

10 9 8 7 6 5 4 3 2 1

1

I DON'T CLAIM TO BE PSYCHIC, BUT AS SOON AS the phone rang, I knew it meant trouble. I could sense it, smell it, even though the ring was no different than usual, a raucous electronic bleat more like a Bronx raspberry than the jangle of a bell. And I'd been on edge most of the day, waiting for the call from Nunna, my foster mother, to let me know that she and her new husband, Walter, were back from their month-long honeymoon.

I glanced at my watch. Six-thirteen, later than I'd thought. I'd been packing with such single-mindedness that I'd lost track of time.

The phone rang again. I crossed the room to answer it, my cane thumping against the bare hardwood floors. I picked up the phone. "Nunna?"

"This ain't Nunna. Leigh Warren, right?" It was the voice of a stranger. Male. Caucasian.

"Yes. Who's this?"

"Don't you worry about it," he said, his voice hoarse, his breathing raspy, labored. "Why ain't you here where you're supposed to be? Everything's gone wrong and it's all your fault!" He began a coughing fit, the deep, phlegm-filled hack of a heavy smoker. "Now you listen, 'cause I'm not saying this twice. Since you ain't here, I'm takin' your granny and grandpap."

"What?" Who the hell was this?

"Right now they're okay," the voice continued. "Whether they stay that way is up to you. Do what I say and I'll turn 'em loose. Try something smart and you'll be planning their funeral. No cops, no feds. Nobody. Am I clear?"

Uneasiness slithered up my spine. "Look," I said. "You've obviously got the wrong number, because I have no grandparents. And if this is how you get your jollies, I suggest you see a therapist PDQ. Now—"

"Shut up! I don't give a shit whether they're blood kin or not, I've got 'em. Want me to read off their driver's licenses? Nunnally H. Layton. Nunnally. What the hell kinda name is that? Five-eleven. Hunnert and eighty pounds. This ain't no pipsqueak here, is she? Birth date June second, nineteen and twenty-five. Walter Lee Sturgis. Five-ten. Hunnert and sixty-five pounds. Birth date—"

"All that proves is that you have their licenses," I interrupted him, still resisting. "For all I know, they could have lost them somewhere or you could have stolen them. So why should I believe you? Let me speak to Nunna."

"You'll speak to her when I'm ready to let ya and if you don't shut your yap, I may just flush the little pink pill she been yammerin' on about taking at six o'clock right down the toilet. You ready to listen now?"

The only way he could know she took them at six A.M. and P.M. is if she told him. "Please, don't hurt them. What is it you want? I don't have much money, but—"

"Shut up, goddammit! I talk, you listen. Forget money. Money won't do me no good. All I want is what's owed me, what's mine. You got it, I want it. You bring it to me, or else!"

"Bring you what?" I yelled. "What is it you want?"

"My medal! It was supposed to be mine and I mean to get it!"

"Medal?" I swiveled on the crate, eyes scanning the knickknacks on the etagere, the paraphernalia on the walls. I made a rapid mental inventory of the flotsam in my jewelry box. Nothing remotely fit the description. "What medal? I don't know what you're talking about!"

"Bullshit! Either I get that medal or your folks are dead! I'll call you back."

"When?" I shouted. "What time?"

The response was a dial tone.

I slammed the phone down, picked it up again and punched 1, Nunna's number on speed dial. It rang and rang and rang. No answering machine for Nunnally Layton Sturgis. "If nobody answers," she told me, "anybody with a lick of sense will know that either I'm—I mean, we're— not home, or don't want to be bothered, and the reason's nobody's business but mine. I mean ours." Marrying again at seventy-five, she had yet to adjust to thinking of herself as plural as opposed to single. But I'd let the phone ring twenty times. If Nunna had been there, she'd have answered out of sheer aggravation.

I replaced the handset and sat, hog-tied with indecision. I had to do *something*. But what? Don't jump the gun, I told myself. It's a prank. It had to be. All I had to do was confirm it.

Grabbing my cane, I hurried to retrieve the black hole of a purse I'd left next door in 503, where I'd been bunking with my friend Janeece for the last couple of weeks. Rushing back to the apartment in which I'd lived for the last seven years, I rooted in my bag for my address book, so old that rubber bands had long since replaced the spiral binder. Flipping pages, I found the telephone number for Mrs.

Elias, Nunna's neighbor. I began to dial, then discon-
nected. I didn't dare tie up the line. If he called back and
the line was busy, no telling how he'd react. I'd have to use
my cell phone.

Mrs. Elias picked up on the first ring. "Yes, whaddaya
want?" Mrs. E. considered Mr. Bell's invention a nuisance
to be borne with rudeness.

"Hi, Mrs. Elias. This is Leigh Ann." Here in the North I
might be just plain Leigh. Down home in Sunrise, I was
Leigh Ann or the response would be "Who?"

"Leigh Ann, bless your time. Ain't this a nice surprise?
You married yet? That Dillon of yours won't wait forever,
don'tcha know."

There were no secrets in Sunrise. "No, ma'am, but it's
on again for next month. I'm just checking. Have Nunna
and Walter gotten back yet? I thought you might have seen
them drive up."

"Well, yes'm, I did. I'd been watching for them in that
big silver thing they wasted perfectly good money on."

I collapsed in relief, so happy that I'd checked down
home before making an idiot of myself.

"Coulda took a train or a bus if they needed a bathroom
close to hand," Mrs. E. rambled on. "But no, they—"

"What time was that, Mrs. Elias?"

"What time was what?" she asked.

God, give me strength. "What time did they get back?"

"Let's see now. Musta been around two. She didn't call
to let you know she was home? Tsk. I reckon she'll phone
you up when they get back."

In other words, they'd gone to return the Airstream and
were perfectly all right. "What time did they leave?"

"Couldn'ta been no more'n ten or fifteen minutes later.
Didn't even take their suitcases in. 'Course they might
have unloaded while I was on the phone. My oldest called

about then. Did I tell you he got a new job? He's assistant principal—"

It was break in or this could take the rest of the day. "Did you actually see them, Mrs. Elias? You saw them both go into the house and come out again?"

"Well, now I didn't say that I saw them go in, but by the time I went back to the window after I got off the phone with Robbie, that trailer thing was at the end of the street. Dern near clipped Martha's mailbox goin' around the corner too."

So it was possible that Walter might have brought Nunna home and then left to return the trailer without her. Still, she would have phoned.

"Mrs. E., would you please go next door and see if Nunna's there? If she is, ask her to call me immediately?"

"You think she might be sick or something? She must be not to ring you right off. I'll go right now. You want to hang on?"

"Call me from Nunna's," I suggested. "Just punch the two on her phone."

"All right. Poor Nunnally. Probably at death's door. I'd better get on over there in case she needs an ambulance." She banged down the phone, leaving me deaf in one ear for a couple of minutes. And I'd been in a panic for nothing.

I'd almost convinced myself of that by the time the phone rang, enough so that I expected to hear Nunna's voice. Unfortunately, it was Mrs Elias's.

"Leigh Ann, nobody's here. And I was right, they didn't leave their suitcases. Musta been powerful hungry though, because they ate. You should see this kitchen." She sounded scandalized. "All these dirty dishes in the sink. I thought Nunna was a better housekeeper than that. I'd straighten up for her, but I've got to get dressed. Auxiliary meeting, don'tcha know. Now don't you worry. I'm sure she'll call as soon as they get back. Say hello to Dillon for me." Never one to say goodbye, she slammed down the phone again.

My uneasiness returned. Unearthing my Sunrise directory from the box in which I'd packed it, I looked up the number for Aubrey's Wheels To Go and called them. Mr. and Mrs. Sturgis? No, they hadn't been by, but there'd be no reason for them to return, unless they were having trouble with the Airstream. It had not been rented, it had been purchased. Evidently Walter had future plans for life on the road.

I tried Walter's son, Monty, the current mayor of Sunrise, hoping he might have heard from his dad. Answering machines at his office and home declared him on vacation until Monday week, eight days from now.

Frustrated, I flipped through Sunrise's white pages, trying to figure out who else I could call. There were any number of places Nunna and Walter might have stopped. I got busy with my cell phone again and interrupted the dinners and newscasts of everyone I could think of who might have spotted my errant foster mother and her husband, trying not to alarm them. No one had. There was nothing I could do but wait for the next call. I just prayed it would be from Nunna and Walter.

Too antsy to sit still, I tackled another carton, watching the numbers on the digital clock flip at a slug's pace. I'd been at it all day, packing like a madwoman, cramming things into boxes with little regard for their fragility or tendency to wrinkle. If something didn't survive the move to Duck's condo, so be it. The point of the exercise was to get done as much as I could as quickly as I could, not because the wedding was imminent, but because I couldn't stand being in this apartment any longer.

There's nothing like returning from a few weeks away and walking in on a corpse growing mold in your kitchen to spoil a place for you. I had Duck, my sweet, levelheaded fiancé of a detective on the D.C. police force, to thank for that, even though technically it hadn't been his fault. Regardless, the memory of the remains of J. B. Thomas in my kitchen had ruined the apartment for me.

Granted, I might have moved in with Duck as I'd originally intended, but couldn't bring myself to do it, not yet. Both Nunna and Duck's mother assumed I was no stranger to Duck's bed, but neither would have approved of our living together without benefit of the "I do's" and "I wills," and I thought too much of those two grande dames to go against their wishes, especially Nunna's.

Technically my foster mother, Nunnally Layton Sturgis had taken me in after the death of my parents and had raised me as her own. I owed her everything. Walter was a recent addition to the equation, Nunna's high school sweetheart who'd returned to Sunrise as a retiree. They'd jumped the broom just last month. I'd never seen Nunna so happy. Now this. *Goddammit, why didn't the son of a bitch call?*

And what medal was he talking about? As a cop on the job, I'd been awarded a couple of commendations but that was it. The only medal I'd ever received had been for winning a spelling bee in the sixth grade and I'd lost that years ago, probably to Lila Mae Whittaker, the class kleptomaniac. Besides, who would kidnap a couple of senior citizens and demand a plastic disk the size of a quarter with "#1" stamped on it as ransom?

I was in the john, drying my hands, when the phone rang. Forgetting I'd left my cane in the living room, since I rarely needed it anymore, I spun around, yelped as pain under my kneecap reminded me that today, at least, I did. Hopping out to the hall, I grabbed the phone.

"What took ya so long?" he demanded. "You ain't trying to tape this, are ya?"

Why hadn't I, a former cop, thought of that? But this wasn't the job. This was personal, the woman in peril so close to my heart that I couldn't think straight.

"I was in the bathroom, okay?" I snarled, panting. Pain made me angry, and reckless. "I'm tired of this! If you've got my folks, let me speak to them. Either you put Nunna on the phone or I'm hanging up. You got that, buddy?"

"Okay, okay," he said. "That'll prove I'm not just blowing smoke. Then we talk business. I want what's mine."

I heard the receiver hit a hard surface, then his voice, gruff, muffled, yet threatening.

"Leigh Ann, baby?"

"Nunna." It was her. This wasn't a nasty joke, wasn't a bad dream. "Nunna, are you all right? And Walter?"

"We're fine. Listen, baby, there's nothing you can do to help us—"

"Got that right," her captor seconded from nearby.

"—so don't feel guilty about it," she said, rushing. "Marry your Duck and be happy. We'll be watching from heaven. And don't forget, everything you'll need for our final arrangements is in the bank."

"Hey, what the hell kinda talk is that?" the voice I was growing to hate shouted.

I heard Nunna's protest, Walter's muffled explanation, then the bastard returned to the phone.

"All right, you've talked to her. Bring me my medal or these old farts are history, understand? I don't care, see? They ain't nothing to me. Nothing." His speech had deteriorated to an unintelligible mumble.

I sat down, shivering. "Don't hurt them, please. You want a medal, I'll get one for you from somewhere. What kind? Just tell me."

The question seemed to anger him. "What do you mean, what kind? The Silver Star, that's what kind. And don't think you can just pick up one from some hock shop and I won't know the difference. I'll know his when I see it because one leg of it got bent in a accident. Turned a Jeep over on it. Cried like a baby over it, too. It shoulda been mine and they gave my medal to him."

"Him who?" I yelled.

"Your ol' man, that's 'him who'! Your lieutenant rich college-boy daddy!"

"What?" He couldn't be serious.

"It shoulda been mine. Wasn't my fault I couldn't carry that kid any further. Lieutenant rich boy comes back and gets him too. So they give him the medal. Had to hand out a certain number to blacks or it would look bad. It should'a been mine! You bring it to me. You bring it or these people are dead!"

"Look, my father's dead!" I said. "He and my mother died in a fire when I was five. Everything burned. There was nothing left, I swear to you! Nothing!"

"Took it home," he said, as if I hadn't spoken. "To his mama. Had to make her 'n everybody in the family proud of him, prove himself. His old lady, she's the one's got it. So you go get it."

He must not have heard me. "Listen to me, please. I was five when my parents died. I knew nothing about them, barely remember them. Some distant cousin of my mother's took me first, then a second family of cousins. Finally Nunna took me home with her. All the cousins have moved; we lost touch with them years ago."

He coughed. "Don't care. It's mine." He began another round of rambling, which I interrupted out of sheer desperation.

"Look, I'm trying to explain that I never knew anything about my father and his family."

"Lieutenant rich boy lookin' down his nose at me, showing off pictures of his sisters, his house, fishing with his old man on their boat, always throwing his family in our faces . . ." He sounded as if he was running out of breath and steam.

"Didn't you hear me?" I yelled. "I don't even know where my father was from!"

"Maryland, Delaware, one of those dinky little states. This old lady says you're smart, been to law school and all. That means you're smart enough to find my medal. You got one of those cell phones?"

"Yes. Why?"

"Number. What's the number?"

I couldn't remember, couldn't dredge it up from my memory bank. "Just a minute." As soon as I picked it up, the number popped into my head.

"All right," he said. "No more talk. You got a week. I'll call you on your cell number next Saturday and tell you where to leave the medal then. Call the cops on me, these folks are dead. I'm dyin,' so I got nothing to lose. You get my medal or your Nunna and her old man got seven more days to live."

2

"OKAY, MS. WARREN, LET'S GO OVER THIS AGAIN. What time did you get the first call?"

All right, I admit it. I had an attitude about the FBI, for no good reason. They had never interfered with a case I'd worked on during my years as a D.C. cop; in fact, I'd never even met anyone who worked in the building at Ninth and Pennsylvania Avenue. But I'd seen any number of agents—you can't avoid them in the nation's capital—and there was an air about them, an aura of perfection that set my teeth on edge.

But kidnapping is kidnapping, and whether I liked it or not, I needed their help. I had called them from Janeece's phone, had run it all down to them and had then waited, pacing the floor, for them to arrive. I had also tried to reach Duck, but was informed that Detective Dillon Kennedy was in a meeting somewhere. I couldn't even bawl on Janeece's shoulder. She was out looking for a dress for my wedding to the aforementioned turkey, since she'd appointed herself my maid/matron of honor, the ambivalence of the title due to the fact that she was between husbands. So I was in one hell of a state by the time the two agents and a couple of tech types got off the elevator.

To give them credit, albeit grudgingly, they came prepared. The tech types swept the interior of 501 wall to wall and pronounced me bug-free. I took the squeaky cleans next door to Janeece's while the techies did whatever it was they needed to do to trace and record the call if and when the maniac phoned again.

And ten minutes into the interview with the squeaky cleans, I realized that they knew more about me than I knew myself. I assume they'd had to satisfy themselves that I wasn't some nutcase yanking their chain.

All I knew about them was that the blond one with the crewcut, whose round face gave a first impression that he was pudgy when he really wasn't, was Special Agent Pinkleton. The other one, Special Agent Grayson, had the kind of boyish features that made him look like a high school hall monitor trying to play grown-up. One glance in those Scotch-brown eyes and I knew he was nobody's pushover. These guys were professionals. Still, I found myself resenting having to repeat the events for a second and third time.

"The phone rang at six-thirteen, and I know for a fact it was six-thirteen because I looked at my watch before I answered."

"And why is that again?" Grayson asked, his voice noncommittal yet somehow disbelieving in tone.

"Because I'd expected to hear from them earlier, that's why."

"You were concerned because you hadn't." Pinkleton, with one of those questions that sounded more like a statement.

"I was and I wasn't. I thought they might have stopped at a flea market outside of Sunrise, in which case there'd be no way to predict what time they'd get back."

"Where's this flea market?" Grayson asked, gold Cross pencil and leather-bound notebook at the ready.

I gave him the location and expressed a certainty that if

they'd gotten that far, Nunna wouldn't have been able to pass on it.

"Okay. The call. What did he say again?"

With a deep breath for patience, I went through it again, trying to repeat it verbatim, which was difficult, given the rambling nature of part of the nutbag's rampage. "He had a really nasty cough. Deep, full of phlegm, so I wasn't surprised when he told me he was dying. That's what scares me. That he has nothing to lose."

"Assuming he was being truthful about his intentions," Pinkleton said.

I bristled. "If you'd heard him, you'd have believed him. He's wacko. I tried to make him understand that I don't know squat about my parents, but he didn't care. He wants the medal and I've got a week to come up with it. So what happens now?"

They exchanged a look before Grayson spoke up. "Well, someone's trying to reach the local authorities in Sunrise—"

I groaned and his brows hitched toward his hairline. "Look, the local authority—singular—amounts to one elderly gentleman named Nehemiah Sheriff. He's smarter than he looks, but I'm not sure how much help he can be, working alone."

"Well, actually, contacting him is a courtesy," Grayson said. "Our agents in the field office will be in charge of the investigation at that end."

"Treat Chief Sheriff gingerly, then," I warned him. "He's as crusty as a loaf of stale bread and as territorial as a bull moose when it comes to Sunrise. But he's a good man and your agents would be well advised not to be patronizing. I mean that."

They exchanged another glance and Grayson nodded.

"I'll pass that along. We'll be working this from a number of angles. If we can trace their return trip, we can get a line on where your folks were intercepted and hopefully determine whether the kidnapper befriended them somewhere earlier, perhaps even traveled with them."

"I don't think that's how it happened," I said, recalling Mrs. Elias's description of Nunna's kitchen. "I'm pretty sure he was waiting for them at Nunna's."

Two pairs of eyes, laser-beam sharp, homed in on me. "Why do you think that?"

I related Mrs. Elias's dig about Nunna's lapse in housekeeping. "My foster mother would never leave dirty dishes in the sink. Never," I repeated, for emphasis.

"Are you sure about that?" Pinkleton asked. "They might have been tired or in a hurry to return the trailer."

"Look," I said, wanting to make sure they understood in no uncertain terms. "The Airstream was theirs, not a rental. That's beside the point. I lived with that woman from the time I was seven until I graduated from college. If Nunnally Layton had accidentally slashed an artery and was bleeding to hell and gone, she'd get those dishes done before she called the ambulance so they wouldn't see her kitchen in disarray. That's how she is. And the only way that guy could have taken her out of the house with the kitchen in that state was at gunpoint." That image floated behind my eyes. "Oh, God," I whispered.

"Don't worry. Keeping them alive is the only leverage he has," Grayson said, before removing a phone from his briefcase. He crossed to a far corner of the room and dialed. "We'll have someone check the house. If you're right, he had to have left fingerprints, or something that will help identify him. Grayson," he said into the phone, and turned his back.

"By the way, Ms. Warren, we'll need a copy of their

itinerary," Pinkleton said, effectively covering his partner's conversation.

"They didn't have one. They just drove until they got tired, or happened on someplace interesting. All I can give you are these postcards they sent." I handed over the ones I'd collected while waiting for them to arrive. "And don't waste your time trying to track them by a credit card. Nunna's death on credit. Walter probably purchased travelers' checks. I—"

"Hey, roomie! What the hell's goin' on in your place?" The key rattled in the lock and the door banged open to reveal Janeece struggling with an armload of shopping bags and a long garment swathed in plastic over one shoulder. "Throwing a party and didn't invite me? Well, I like that!" She strode into the room and stood, examining the suits with undisguised interest.

Grayson, still in the corner on the phone, turned, spotted Janeece, and promptly forgot whatever he'd been talking about. Pinkleton, googly-eyed, popped up out of his chair like a jack-in-the-box. Their reactions were understandable. You don't run into women like Janeece every day.

At six-seven in her spike heels, my statuesque neighbor towers above practically everybody, her hair piled high in an elaborate topknot, her skin the color of cappuccino. She is also built, stacked, phat, foxy, or fine, depending on the age of the male describing her, with more curves than a Six Flags roller coaster. Duck swore the Fourth District's traffic section kept a running tally of the number of rear-end collisions she'd caused just walking down the street.

At the moment, however, she seemed to be taking an inordinate amount of interest in Special Agent Pinkleton. Eyes narrowed, she squinted at him, bottom jaw unhinged. "Pinky?" she croaked. "Is it really you?"

"Mayella Holloway!" His voice climbed the scale, hov-

ering dangerously close to coloratura. "I don't believe it!"
At that point, Special Agent Pinkleton lost the remaining
vestiges of his professional cool. He grabbed Janeece in a
bear hug and performed a first—in my experience, anyway—lifting her right off her feet. She hugged back,
smothering him in shopping bags from Macy's, the combined howls and squeals of laughter bringing the techies
over to see what the fuss was about. Grayson ogled them,
his own aplomb momentarily shattered as well.

Pinkleton put her down. "Lord, Mayella, you look better
than a chili dog from Jake's! What are you doing here?" Inexplicably, he'd developed a Southern drawl, an echo of
the one I usually heard from Janeece in her more relaxed
moments.

"I live here, bozo! And man alive, did you fill out! Little
Marty Pinkleton! I don't believe it!" They stood grinning
at each other like idiots.

Janeece tossed her purchases onto the black leather recliner. "Pinky and I went to high school together," she said
to me. "Graduated the same year, the class dorks and the
class valedictorians. He was a short, skinny little white
dude. I was a tall, skinny little black chick, both of us on
the outside looking in. He wanted to join the FBI. Our
classmates—all thirty-two of them—practically rolled in
the aisles when they read that in our yearbook. I didn't volunteer anything for posterity. Hell, all I wanted was to put
on some weight. Who's your friend in the corner?" she
asked him.

Slowly the two agents began the metamorphosis to suits
again, although Pinkleton seemed to be having difficulty
making a full return trip. "That's Special Agent Robert
Grayson, a coworker," he said, with far less starch than
before.

"Agent? Coworker?" She looked from one to the other

and back. "You *are* with the FBI? Come on! Give me a break."

He removed his ID and held it up to her. And grinned. "Told ya I'd make it, didn't I?"

"Oh, my God, is this country in trouble," she said, and grabbed him in a hug again. "Pinky, I'm proud of you. I really am. Congratulations." Freeing him, she stepped back, a frown beginning to wrinkle her forehead. "But why are you here? What'd I do?"

I'd been so astonished by their reunion that I'd forgotten my own troubles. Now that I had someone here on my side, my dam began to crack. "Nunna and Walter have been kidnapped," I blurted. "Some crazy motherfucker's holding them and won't turn them loose until I find some goddamned silver medal awarded to my father which this maniac says should have been given to him, and he thinks my father's mother probably has it and I didn't even know he had a mother and I've got a week to find it or he says he'll kill Nunna and Walter because he's dying and has nothing to lose. If anything happens to them, I'll find him and kill him if it's the last thing I do!" Completely out of breath, I finished on a wail.

Janeece, murmuring "Oh, my God," again and again, sat down, arms wrapped around me like bands of steel. It was exactly what I needed. I buried my face in my hands and cried, only slightly embarrassed at coming apart in front of squeaky clean FBI agents.

"Pinky, the bathroom's through there," Janeece said, freeing one arm long enough to point. "Wet a washcloth for me, please."

I heard footsteps, running water, and shortly felt cold, soothing terrycloth against my face. Pinky had also returned with a roll of toilet tissue, but rather than blow my nose with an audience, I got up and retreated to the john.

I was an unholy mess. Repairing the damage would have taken an hour I couldn't spare, so I did the best I could. Returning, I was in the doorway of the living room when it hit me.

"Mayella?" I said. "Your first name's Mayella?" She signed everything "M. Janeece Holloway" but would never divulge what the initial stood for.

She glared at me. "You betcher ass, girlfriend, and if you tell a single soul, you are on my shit list forever."

Special Agent Pinkleton, who I would forever think of as just plain Pinky, flushed guiltily, realizing he'd let the cat out of the bag. "Sorry, May—" He broke it off, just in time. "What are you calling yourself now?"

"Janeece, my middle name, and don't you forget it. You okay now, honey?" she asked me, pushing me down onto the sofa.

"I'm fine. Thanks for the shoulder. What's been happening?"

Little appeared to have changed in my absence. The techies had retreated to 501 and Grayson was still on the phone, not talking though, just listening, his expression unreadable, although I could swear he was struggling to control a frown. I felt a chill. Something must have gone wrong somewhere.

"What's happened?" I asked again, when he'd hung up.

He rearranged his features into their previous plain vanilla mask. "Nothing concerning your foster mother," he said, trying for a soothing tone. "Just a computer glitch."

"What kind?" Janeece demanded. "I know from computers."

"An internal matter," Grayson said hurriedly. "Well, we'll get to work with what we have so far. There's a tap on your phones so we can run a trace if he calls again. And there'll be an agent on site too, just in case."

"In five-oh-one? Does that mean I'll need to stay there too?" I asked.

"Is that a problem?" Puzzled, they both stared at me. "It's obvious you're moving, but it is your apartment, isn't it?" Pinky asked.

I winced. "Yes, but—" I really didn't relish explaining about the corpse in my kitchen. "Look, this guy said he'd give me a week to retrieve the medal. So he doesn't expect me to be here. And when he does call next Saturday, he'll be calling me on my cell phone. So there's really no point in wasting manpower by having someone stay in my apartment. I have a lot of running around to do, trying to trace the cousins I lived with for a couple of months after my parents died. I just barely remember their names. If Nunna were available, she'd be able to help but—" I ground to a halt, suddenly overwhelmed by the enormity of my task.

"We hope to be able to assist you with that," Grayson said, seeming to pick his words with care. "We have access to databases nationwide. All we need is a little time. We'll be next door in your apartment for the next fifteen or twenty minutes. In the interim, we'd appreciate it if you'd jot down the names of your parents, the cousins you stayed with, anything you think of that might be helpful. The perpetrator mentioned Mrs. Sturgis's medication. We'll need the name of her physician so he can tell us what it was, in case she had to have it refilled during the trip. Just another way to track them."

"It's a stretch," Pinky said, "just something else our field agents can check."

I nodded, but I was certain Nunna would have taken enough to last her. A teacher during her working years, she was organized to a fault. Her image drifted through my memory, tall, her hair ivory-white as long as I could remember, her carriage erect, an imposing black queen.

And Walter, his face as wrinkle-free as it had been in his high school pictures, his skin the color of Nunna's Sunday morning biscuits. He was a handsome old dude and I'd grown to love him in a matter of days. He wasn't as vigorous as Nunna; arthritis had damaged his joints and he was on shaky ground without his cane, but all in all, there was no reason the two of them shouldn't have a good many years together. Unless I couldn't find my father's medal. That prospect plunged me into a momentary blue funk.

The suits disappeared next door and I got to work on the information they'd requested. I'd filled a lined pad with my vital statistics and everything but the size panties I wore by the time they came back.

"That last call you received," Grayson said without preamble, "was made from a cell phone belonging to Walter Sturgis. There were no roaming charges so whoever used it was still in the Asheville area. That would include Sunrise."

My spirits plummeted even further. "But the Great Smokies, the Blue Ridge, Pisgah National Forest aren't that far away. Have you any idea how many places he could hide them up there?"

"If that's where he's taken them," Pinky said. "He may well be in Sunrise somewhere."

"Are you kidding? Sunrise is so small you could fit it in six D.C. blocks. A stranger would stand out."

"Assuming anyone spotted him," Grayson said. "If he's hiding in the Airstream . . . Well, we'd better get going."

"Here's a card," Pinky said, "with the numbers where you can reach us, day or night. And we'll be back. If not us, another agent. But don't lose hope, Ms. Warren. It's early days yet."

I nodded again and kept my mouth shut. Early days with only six more to play around with.

"Pinky," Janeece said, blocking his path, one long fingernail in danger of puncturing a hole in his tie as she poked him in the chest, "this is my best friend, and her Nunna is one dynamite lady. I expect you and your buddy here to clear this mess up posthaste, you hear? You guys are supposed to be such hot shit, so prove it!"

Grayson looked insulted, but Pinky apparently took it in stride. "We will," he said solemnly. "That's a promise."

"All right, then." She stepped aside and opened the door.

He managed a smile for the two of us as he left. Grayson bobbed his head in a noncommittal farewell. "We'll be in touch."

Be still, my heart, I thought, then chided myself for my ingratitude. At this point, they were the only help I had. But from the time Grayson had used the phone, I had the distinct impression that he'd learned something he hadn't liked. Was he holding out on me? Suddenly, I didn't trust him, not one little bit.

"Babe."

I jerked awake. Duck knelt beside the sofa where I'd stretched out, intending to rest my eyes and calm my nerves. Evidently I'd fallen asleep instead. And it was light out now.

"What time is it? Has anyone called?" I sat up quickly, trying to make sense of the pinkish glow beyond the windows. It had been dark when the suits left.

"It's seven-thirty—"

"It's Sunday morning?" How could I have slept so long, so soundly? Levering myself to my feet, I reached for my cane, then discarded it. The knee felt okay. "I've got to check next door. There's an FBI agent in there—"

"I know." He pulled me back down. "And the phone's been quiet all night. Janeece tracked me down at Mom's and told me what happened. I got here as soon as I could but Janeece wouldn't let me wake you. I'm sorry you couldn't reach me yesterday. It was a shift from hell. How are you doing?"

"You don't want to know. Oh, God, Duck, it's so awful. Why Nunna and Walter? Why didn't he take me instead?"

"Think about it," Duck said, moving onto the couch beside me, and nestling me against his shoulder. He smelled good, like grass and woods after a spring rain. "This guy wants the medal. He had to do something to ensure you'd cooperate. Ergo, Miss Nunna and Walter. He had no other choice."

I pulled away to glare at him. "You sound like you're making excuses for him."

"Come on, babe, I'm talking logic, and you know it. I doubt seriously he'll hurt them."

"Unless I can't come up with that stupid medal," I said, settling against him again. "God, Duck, what am I going to do? I barely remember my parents, can't even remember what they looked like. All I have of my first five years are foggy images."

"Tell me about them," he urged, rubbing my forehead. "Maybe that'll help thin the fog."

I recognized that he was trying to give me something else to focus on. My initial reaction was to resist, as if to stop thinking about Nunna and Walter might bring bad luck. But not finding my father's family would bring them even worse luck. Besides, perhaps Duck was right. Perhaps talking about my folks would trigger a few memories.

"I'm pretty sure my dad was tall. I seem to recall having to throw my head way back to look up at him. I remember feeling safe from everything when he held me. He was invincible, Superman and all those guys rolled into one."

"Like me, you mean." Duck smiled down at me.

I knew he was kidding, but again, he was right. "Yes. Like you."

On the surface there was nothing particularly remarkable about Dillon Kennedy. He defined the word "average" when it came to height and weight and looks, a walnut-hued complexion, dark hair and eyes, smiley lips under a modest mustache still edging toward full growth after having been shaved off a couple of months before. Like I said, nothing special, just a basic black brother. Until you talked to him.

I'd never met anyone who didn't take to Duck immediately.

He drew people to him like iron filings to a magnet. Even the crooks he'd arrested liked him. He was a good cop and a smart one, with a quiet inner strength.

"Your mother?" he prodded me, nudging me back on track, thought-wise.

"All I remember is a disembodied smile, a pair of gentle hands on my forehead, and a scent, a soft floral perfume I've never been able to find on any counter. I got a whiff of it once years ago in Lord and Taylor. It sort of wafted past me on a current of air, and slammed me back to my childhood like a time machine. I searched and searched," I said, remembering my frustration, "but couldn't pinpoint who'd been wearing it. And Mom had a gold pendant she never took off. I remember the light catching the chain as she bent over to tuck me in at night. But that's it. That's all I have left of my mother."

Muted voices reverberated out in the hall and the door opened. Janeece swept in wearing a Sunday-go-to-meeting outfit, Special Agents Grayson and Pinky in her wake. "Oh, good, you're up," she said. "These guys want to talk to you again. Grayson, Pinky, meet Dillon Kennedy. He's Leigh Ann's intended. Duck, say howdy to real live FBI agents."

The menfolk shook hands all around, taking each other's measure in that dumb way guys do when they first meet.

"I'm with the Metropolitan Police," Duck said, "detective working out of the Sixth District. I know this is your show, but if there's any way I or the Department can help, all you have to do is say the word. Miss Nunna and Walter, they're very special people. They deserve the best we can do for them."

"Thanks," Grayson said, his tone surprisingly cordial. "We'll keep that in mind." Evidently the suits approved of the way Duck had framed his introduction because they seemed to loosen up a little. Or perhaps it was just the usual Duck magnetism, drawing them in.

"I'll be right back," I said, and excused myself to brush my teeth and throw some soap and water in the general direction of my body. A shower would have to wait. I ran a damp facecloth over my hair, fluffed out my cropped curls with my fingers, and dabbed on a light film of Janeece's Midnight Mauve lipstick before hightailing it back to the living room, hoping I hadn't missed anything of importance. Duck, noting the unfamiliar color, lifted one brow, then smiled his approval.

Janeece wasn't as subtle. "Midnight Mauve? It's you, girl. I'll go turn the coffee pot on high. Then I'm off to somebody's early service. Gotta go pray for Miss Nunna and Mr. Walter. Roomie, you know where the breakfast stuff is. The sandwich I made you last night is in the fridge too." She had tried to convince me to eat, but for once, I hadn't the stomach for it.

Duck sat back down beside me, and the suits settled in various chairs, looking oddly uneasy.

"What's wrong?" I demanded. "What have you found out?"

"Nothing," Pinky assured me, then added. "and that's the problem."

Grayson cleared his throat. in effect taking the floor. "What he means is that in order to help you, we'll need a few things clarified, that's all. According to the info you gave us, your full name is Leigh Ann Warren. Date of birth: twenty-four June, nineteen sixty-eight."

"Right. So?"

"Place of birth?" he asked.

"You know that already. Baltimore."

"Maryland," he said.

"Uh, right." I squinted at him, wondering if I'd overestimated the level of intelligence of this guy. No doubt there were probably other Baltimores in this country, but almost anyone would automatically assume that unless some other state was specified, this particular one was in Maryland.

Grayson made a checkmark in his little book. "And your father's name?"

"Why are you asking me this?" I demanded. "Wayne Warren. If he had a middle one, I don't know what it was. Same with my mother. Dad called her Peg, so I assume her name was Margaret. Her maiden name might have been Anderson but I'm not sure why I think that. That wasn't the last name of the cousins I stayed with right after the fire. I do remember they were relations on my mother's side. All that's on the paper I gave you. What's the point of all this?"

"Well." He scratched an ear. "It doesn't quite add up."

"What's that supposed to mean?" I asked.

He looked at Pinky, who must have decided enough was enough. He took the reins back. "One way to get a line on the kidnapper is to check your father's service record, find out when he was awarded the Silver Star, then determine the names of the others in his unit at that time and narrow them down until we have our man."

"Uh-huh." That's what I assumed they'd do.

"The problem is, none of the Wayne Warrens in the VA database could be your father. They're either too young, too old, Caucasian, or if deceased, did not die in Baltimore in 1973. That's also true of all the other Wayne Warrens we searched on. And let's just say that the files we access are pretty extensive."

This didn't make sense. How could I have mistaken my father's name?

"We came up blank on your mother's name too," Pinky continued. "Plenty of Margarets, Peg and Peggy Andersons, but none married to a Wayne Warren or with the date of death you specified."

"But—"

"The fire is on record," Grayson interrupted me. "However, your parents' names weren't on the lease of the apartment. Evidently they were subletting or living there at the pleasure of the principal tenant. Unfortunately that person is deceased, so we've hit a dead end."

"Well, hell," I said, exasperated. "If I have the names wrong—and I could swear I don't—check my birth certificate. I don't have a copy, but with the clout you guys have, pick up the phone and ask for what you need."

Pinky scrubbed a hand across his mouth. "We did that, Ms. Warren. There's no record of your birth in Baltimore or, for that matter, the state of Maryland. We've checked every database available to the Bureau. There's no record of the birth of a baby girl named Leigh Ann Warren on June twenty-fourth of sixty-eight or any other year in any state. No record of a Leigh Ann Warren, even overseas."

"In other words," Grayson said, "whoever you are, you aren't Leigh Ann Warren."

3

TOO STUNNED TO REACT, I COULD ONLY SIT
there and gawk at him.

Janeece, better at eavesdropping than any electronic
gizmo on the market, must have heard Grayson's bomb-
shell. She swept in from the kitchen like a hurricane bear-
ing down on the Florida Keys.

"You," she said, looking down on him, "need to go back
to FBI school. That woman's name is Leigh Ann Warren. If
you can't find her or her parents in your cute little databases, you aren't looking in the right places." Swiveling
around, she took aim at the other agent. "Pinky, Pinky,
Pinky. I had such high hopes for you. You let me down."
She came over, sat beside me, and crossed her long legs,
one spike-heeled foot jiggling in agitation.

Pinky's lips formed a sad smile. "Afraid not, May—I
mean, Janeece. We don't know who she is, just who she
isn't."

How could that be? My psyche reeled in shock, unable
to deal with it, because without my name, who was I? It
not only identified me and made me who I was, it grounded
me in the universe, linked me to the parents who'd given
me life. It was proof that I wasn't another Topsy, someone
who'd "just growed," an accident or freak of nature.

Not that I hadn't known the love and security a child needs in order to thrive. Nunna had supplied that and more. I couldn't love her more if she'd been my biological mother. But she wasn't. I'd had a mother and father who'd cherished me for the first five years of my life and who'd had no control over leaving me an orphan. The name I bore was evidence they'd existed. I was their monument, their legacy. Without Leigh Ann Warren, there were no Wayne and Margaret. Okay, it may not have made sense to anyone else, but it did to me.

Grayson and Pinky were robbing me of my birthright. Indignation yanked me back into the moment where the two of them and Janeece were still going around the mulberry bush about who I was or wasn't. Grayson seemed to have developed an attitude. It was a second before I realized he'd practically accused me of hiding something from them. In other words, lying.

I didn't like being called a liar. I have ethics, dammit. For the most part I'd managed to keep my code of right and wrong intact, with only a couple of Band-Aids required to cover the nicks and dents. So the smear on my character rankled.

I didn't get the impression that Pinky agreed with Grayson, but he'd been downright uncommunicative during this exchange, probably afraid that Janeece would skewer him if he said the wrong thing.

"In other words," Grayson said, "you're asking us to believe that you don't have anything that belonged to your father? You don't even have a picture of him?"

"Look, hotshot." Steam began rising from my collar. "I had just turned five when my parents died. I was outside playing whatever the hell five-year-olds played back in the early seventies. There was an explosion and the next thing I know, flames are shooting out the side of our building. I ran into the front hallway, screaming for my parents. I tried to get up the steps—we lived on the third floor—but the stairwell was already full of smoke. Then the policeman who lived on the first floor ran out of his apartment and grabbed me and carried me outside. Everything was gone. Everything. All I had left were the clothes on my back. How many times do I have to tell you that?"

Grayson looked extremely put out, as if the whole thing was my fault. I was beginning to dislike him. A lot.

Finally, Pinky, obviously more perceptive than his partner, came through. "We realize that this is very difficult for you, Ms. Warren, but you have to understand the problems this has presented. Our people have been working on this since your first call. That's why we kept you on the phone so long yesterday, so we could begin checking on your father immediately. We got nowhere. There's no record of payments for rent or utilities by Wayne or Margaret Warren at the Baltimore address you gave us. They must have paid the rent directly to the tenant they were subletting from. Even the phone was still in the tenant's name. It's as if your parents were hiding the fact that they lived there."

"That's crap," I said, my civility quotient exhausted. "We weren't squatters. Perhaps we hadn't been there all that long, or weren't going to be, I don't know. Perhaps the tenant asked Dad to leave the phone listed to him. You must have a crisscross from back then. Maybe you can find some of the tenants who lived there when we did."

"We're trying," Grayson said, clearly insulted that I might think it hadn't occurred to them. "It won't be easy. It's now a yuppie enclave."

Janeece snorted. "In other words, all the black folks who lived there have had to find cheaper digs elsewhere." The foot waggled even faster.

Grayson didn't turn a hair. "That's right. But we'll try to trace them anyway. It'll just take time."

I was about to scream that time was a luxury we didn't have, but Duck must have sensed it. He squeezed my hand to silence me and asked, "Any chance her folks might have been in a witness protection program?"

Pinky smiled. "We're looking into that too. There's got to be some way to get a line on your father."

Grayson cleared his throat. "There's always the chance that he might have been a deserter and was trying to cover his tracks."

The safety valve on my boiler failed. I found myself on my feet, ready to make scrambled eggs of his face. "My father was *not* a deserter! He was good and kind and brave!"

"How do you know?" Grayson asked. "According to what you've been telling us, you barely remember him."

He had me, but I didn't have to like it. I sat down again, wondering why the Fates were plotting against me.

"Please understand that we have to consider all scenarios," Pinky said. "Vietnam played hell with a lot of psyches, sent a lot of GIs over the edge. Your father may have been one of them." He shot a questioning gaze at Grayson, who shrugged, evidently a signal for Pinky to continue. "Unfortunately, that's not the only dead end we've run into."

I closed my eyes. "Let's have it. What else can't you find?"

"We haven't been able to come up with one bit of evidence that Mr. and Mrs. Sturgis are unaccounted for, much less have been abducted."

My eyes snapped open. "You mean they're all right? They're back home?"

"Negative." Grayson's impassive eyes raked my face. "The postcards they sent enabled us to plot several routes they might use on their return trip. With Mr. Sturgis's license plates, we've found the last few campgrounds at which they stopped. The most recent one was at Burky Park yesterday morning. According to some campers who are still there, they weren't ready to go home. They asked for directions to several other campsites. Those are pretty wide-ranging, some as far north as Virginia and as far south as Georgia."

"But they'd have called me to tell me that," I protested. "They knew I expected them back in Sunrise yesterday, that I'd worry if I didn't hear from them. And they did stop at home. Mrs. Elias saw them. But they didn't call me, so something or someone must have prevented them from doing it. He must have bustled them out of there as soon as they walked in."

Grayson looked superior. "They were there long enough to notify the post office and the *Sunrise Guardian* to hold everything another ten days. I doubt that would have been uppermost on their minds with a kidnapper in the house. It looks to us as if they were in a hurry to get under way again and simply forgot to phone you."

"That's enough," Duck said, using his cop voice. "Excuse me for butting in, but Leigh's right. One or the other of them would have called her to let her know about a change of plans."

"Someone did call her, using Mr. Sturgis's phone," Grayson said to Duck, his expression implacable.

I hit the ceiling. "The only calls I received yesterday were from the kidnapper and Mrs. Elias, using Nunna's phone. Are you implying that I made all this up?"

"We're not implying anything. Unfortunately, we have only your word that the call you received was from a kidnapper. And so far, it's all we have to go on, because there's no evidence at your foster mother's home either."

I was beginning to appreciate how victims in quicksand felt. "What—what about the dirty dishes? What about the mess in the kitchen?"

Pinky leaned forward, elbows on his knees. "It's not there any longer. Seems Mrs. Elias believes in the good neighbor policy. She did such a good job on that kitchen that practically the only prints left in it are hers. Otherwise, we found three sets of prints in the house. Since Mr. Sturgis was in the military years back, we were able to identify his, and yours, of course, because as a D.C. employee, yours are on record. There are none on file for Mrs. Sturgis, but since the third set of prints are practically everywhere else in the house, we assume they're hers."

"In other words," Grayson said, snatching the ball, "there's no evidence that it's been occupied by anyone else."

"And of course," I said, my temperature edging toward the danger zone again, "the intruder couldn't have worn gloves."

He bristled. "With your background, you must know he'd have left trace evidence somewhere, gloves or not. You said the caller was Caucasian. None of the hairs our techs collected were from a Caucasian."

"Then he was bald," I said, teeth clenched.

"Perhaps, but there's always body hair. And all the carpets are thick enough to hold footprints. Mrs. Elias says she didn't vacuum, yet there were only two sets of footprints in most of the rooms and an additional set in the rear bedroom. Comparing them with the tennis shoes in the closet, we're almost positive those footprints are yours."

I'd forgotten to pack my tennies, so he was right again, but I couldn't bring myself to say so. I was working up a full-fledged hatred for this guy.

Grayson plodded on. "Any intruder would have had to

leave fibers from any fabric he wore, dirt from his shoes, something. We found nothing that couldn't be attributed to Mr. and Mrs. Sturgis. Mrs. Elias, or you."

I had no comeback for him. As far as I was concerned, the dishes in the sink were all the proof I needed that an intruder had made himself at home. But that would carry no weight with the FBI.

"I wish I could explain all the anomalies, but I can't. And I have no way of proving that the call I received was from the kidnapper. Want me to take a polygraph test? Fine, bring on the leads. I don't know what else I can do."

"Neither do we, Ms. Warren," Pinky said, apologetically. "We'll continue to monitor your phones for now. And we haven't given up on identifying your father, you can be sure of that. But I have to tell you, unless the kidnapper calls before next Saturday, or the all-points on Mr. Sturgis's car pays off . . ." He seemed to have difficulty putting an end to his sentence. "Well." He stood up and wiggled the crimps out of his shoulders. "You have our numbers if you think of anything that might help. Janeece, you take care, hear? It was great seeing you again."

"Well, get used to it," she said grumpily, opening the door. "I'll be in your hair until Miss Nunna's home safe and sound, so warn your wife not to get her jaws tight when I call."

"No problem." Pinky grinned. "No wife, so call as much as you'd like. Nice to meet you, Kennedy. Get some rest, Ms. Warren. We'll be in touch."

I managed a lukewarm thanks.

Grayson looked back at me from the door. "Sorry. I didn't mean to upset you. I just thought it better that you see the big picture." He bobbed his head in farewell, held the door open for Pinky, and shot a rather pointed gaze at Duck. "Kennedy, it might be a good idea for you to know how things are set up next door, just in case. Shouldn't take but a minute. Ms. Holloway."

Duck hesitated, then gave my arm a squeeze before rising to his feet. "Be right back, babe." He followed them out.

Frustration charging my batteries, I got up and began to pace. "I swear, I'd give thirty days in jail to slap Grayson's face."

"Forget it." Janeece tossed me my cane. "He's just overcompensating for looking like he should be sitting in a high school math class or something. Pinky says he's really good, just needs to work on his bedside manner, so to speak."

"You trust Pinky?" I asked, intrigued at the way her lips curved when she said his name.

"Oh, yes." She leaned forward, effectively hiding her face as she adjusted the strap of her right shoe. "One of the reasons he was an outsider at Johnsson High was because he didn't give a shit about peer pressure. Everybody else was dressing alike, acting alike, smoking pot, trying to be hip. Pinky did things his way. He was so square, always wore slacks and shirts to school instead of jeans and athletic shoes. Took a lot of heat for it too. And he was a straight-A student but it didn't come easy for him. He worked hard for his grades. He was quiet, serious, focused. He was . . . just Pinky."

This was very interesting. Evidently there was more to her history with Pinky than I'd thought. I might pursue the subject later, but for the moment, I had too many other things pressing on me.

"You're going to be late for church," I reminded her. "Go on, Janeece. Looks like Walter and Nunna will need all the prayers they can get."

She looked torn. "You sure? I can stay if you want."

She waffled for a short while, more for show than anything else. Sunday services were important to Janeece. Never mind that she rarely worshipped at the same place twice. It was enough for her that she was there.

I shooed her out, where she almost collided with the agents on their way to the elevator. Duck stood outside my apartment door, watching them with frightening intensity. I knew my Duck. He was sorely pissed about something.

Spotting me, he wiped his face clear of his irritation. "You okay?" he asked, returning to Janeece's.

"Just peachy." I shut the door and turned to confront him. "So what was that all about?"

He managed to fake ignorance but I wasn't going for it. I stood and waited.

"Okay, okay, but you have to promise you won't go off the deep end. They wanted to know about the state of your . . . your mental health."

My jaw sagged. "Excuse me?"

"They knew about your depression after the shooting last year and wondered if having to leave the department because of your knee might be . . . well, causing emotional problems."

"Emotional problems?" A fiery red haze filtered over my eyes. "Emotional problems? I'll show them emotional problems!" I was halfway down the hall, headed for the elevator, before Duck caught me. I hadn't moved that fast since my pre-injury days.

Duck, his arms clamped around mine from behind to halt my progress, spoke softly, his voice as soothing as a full-body massage. "Leigh, Leigh, honey, calm down. Come on now. You promised you wouldn't blow up."

"No, I didn't." My jaw was so tightly clenched, it hurt. "I didn't promise anything. Now, let me go."

"Not until you give me your word you'll behave."

"I'm not some five-year-old having a temper tantrum," I

said, wondering if I could get away with stomping on his instep. "How *dare* they! I'm supposed to be fruity enough to make up Nunna's kidnapping? Is that what they think?"

"If they did, they don't anymore." He gave my ear a nibble, normally guaranteed to begin an entirely different sort of melting process. "I gave it to them in no uncertain terms. And I'm pretty sure they heard me. They're a little gun-shy, honey. They just wasted a lot of manpower on a case they'd been led to believe was a kidnapping and it wasn't. So they're tipping lightly and grasping at straws. That's all it was, the question about your mental state. A straw, one they can eliminate. Okay?"

The warmth and concern in those dark brown eyes were the tranquilizer I needed. "Okay."

"When's the last time you ate?" he asked, scrutinizing me closely.

I couldn't remember, and also couldn't argue with his reason for asking. Hunger tended to turn me into a bitch with an attitude. It didn't wholly account for my irascibility with the suits, but it had probably contributed.

"Lunch yesterday. I think. I'm not hungry."

Duck smiled. "Uh-huh. Come on, let's feed you." My hero.

He walked me back into 503's kitchen where he rifled the refrigerator, found the smoked turkey sandwich Janeece had fixed for me the evening before, and made a ham and Swiss for himself. He poured orange juice for me, and grabbed a cup of French Roast for himself. "Eat. No lip, no thinking, just chewing. Then we'll talk."

"About what?" I asked. Something was still bugging him. I'd known him too long not to recognize the symptoms—a distracted air, a certain abruptness about his movements.

"Later, babe. Eat."

I gazed across the table and reflected on how much I loved him, even though he persisted in calling me "babe," which I hated. I lit into the sandwich. Another of Janeece's many talents: she made a dynamite sandwich.

I finished it, made a second not nearly as good, even though I'd used the same ingredients, and felt human again.

Duck lounged in his chair, squirming occasionally to accommodate his rear to the molded seat bottom. The chairs were patently uncomfortable, faux Bauhaus and never meant to be occupied for longer than a couple of minutes at a time. Janeece called them the secret of her weight control. She could barely sit in them long enough to down a full meal.

"Okay, Duck," I said, stacking our plates in the sink, "give it up. Any time you can barely eat for thinking, you've been chewing on an idea."

He reached up and flicked something, probably mayo, from the corner of my upper lip, then slid his finger along my cheek. "Let me tell you about my earliest memories, Leigh. I remember opening a Christmas present from my dad, a digital watch with a pair of baseball bats on the strap, a watch for an adult. Mom shakes her head about it to this day because I was all of three years old at the time. But I remember it.

"I remember going to see him in the VA hospital, the first time I could associate a real, live human being with the daddy in the 'God blesses' I said every night. I was four then. I have a lot of memories like that, just snapshots of events. But the point is, I was less than five but they're almost as vivid now as they were then. Which makes me wonder why yours are so sketchy and why you've never tried to find out anything about your parents before now."

"I remember the day of the fire," I said, more protest than reminder.

"Because it was a very traumatic experience."

"And staying with the cousins," I added, "both sets. At the first place, I had a big room with dark, heavy furniture and drapes. It was not a room for a little kid. I slept with the covers over my head because all that darkness scared me. At the second place, I shared a room with Yvonne and Yvette. They were twins, older than I was. And there were boys, two of them in the family. I always felt like an outsider."

"That was a little later," Duck said, plowing through my defensiveness. "Think about it, Leigh. Tyler's four, yet she remembers Shaggy, and that dog died when she was two. All right, she's my niece and I think she's a peewee Einstein, but I'm trying to make a point."

"Which is?" I was inexplicably uncomfortable with this.

"Miss Nunna brags about how smart you were when you went to live with her—reading well, doing third grade arithmetic problems. You were seven by then. Yet you have no concrete memories of your life with your parents and I have to wonder why."

I had no answer for him. Had I packed them away in some hidden corner of my mind until the day it might not hurt as much to face them? Had I done such a good job of hiding them that I no longer recalled where I'd stashed them to begin with?

"I don't know the reason," I admitted, "and if you're suggesting a hypnotist or something, I'll consider it. But getting Nunna and Walter out of that maniac's clutches comes first."

He eyed me, his expression unreadable. "I wouldn't put it off, babe. It may help to clear up the question of your parents' identities."

I stiffened. "There is no question. My dad's name was

Wayne, my mother's was Margaret. Period. I remember that much."

"And if those were aliases?" he pressed gently.

I glared at him. "They weren't." I abandoned him to the kitchen and went next door to my apartment to check with the poor shnook left to monitor the phone, which, of course, rang just as I came in. I froze, a block of stone.

The agent, whose name I finally remembered was Underwood, gave me a tight smile of encouragement. "Come on, now. We can handle this together. Wait for me." He moved quickly to the extension the techs had installed.

I shook myself and crossed to the phone, watching for his signal.

"Okay. Now," he said. Together, we picked up our handsets and I said hello, sounding like a frightened two-year-old.

"Leigh Ann, what the hell is going on back home?"

I exhaled like a rapidly deflating balloon. "Monty!" Walter's son, honorable mayor of Sunrise. I signaled an okay to Underwood, and he hung up. "Lord, I'm so glad they were able to reach you!"

"If you mean the FBI, they reached me, all right, just in time. I was about to go parasailing. Leigh Ann, what in the world made you think Dad and Miss Nunna had been kidnapped?"

Late as usual, I detected his exasperation. "I don't think it, Monty, I know it. The kidnapper called me yesterday. He was waiting for them when they got home. He wants me—"

"Leigh Ann, honey," he interrupted, "somebody's playing a practical joke on you. A particularly nasty one, but still a joke. Dad and Miss Nunna are fine—at least they were when I talked to him last night."

"What?"

Reacting to my astonishment, Underwood picked up his phone again, curiosity brightening his eyes.

"You talked to your dad last night?" I asked. "What did he say? Did you call him or did he call you?"

"He called me, his usual Saturday night check-in. He'd promised to do that as long as he and Miss Nunna were on the road."

This made no sense. "Did he say where they were? How did he sound?"

"Tired. Said they'd covered a lot of miles yesterday. He was calling from Flat Rock. Those crazy old people are heading for the South Carolina coast, perhaps Charleston."

"Did he tell you they'd stopped in Sunrise?" I asked.

"Yes, but just long enough to get the mail, cancel delivery of the paper, things like that. They're fine, Leigh Ann. I'd tell you if I thought otherwise."

"They aren't, or I'd have heard from Nunna by now. Have you tried calling your father today?" I demanded.

"Of course, as soon as the FBI reached me. Dad didn't have the phone turned on, but he wouldn't, unless he planned to use it. I'm not worried." He sounded amused. Sympathetic, but still, amused.

"Fine," I snapped at him. "I'm worried enough for both of us. Did they tell you that the call from the kidnapper was made from your dad's phone, Monty? Do you have an explanation for that?"

His sigh was audible. "There's only one logical explanation. Someone's pirated the phone number. As soon as I can reach him, I'll have him report it, so he doesn't wind up paying for calls he didn't make. And I'll ask him to have Miss Nunna get in touch immediately. I've got to go, Leigh Ann, but stop worrying. Everything's fine. I'll talk to you later. Coming," he called to someone, and hung up.

Underwood did too, with a speculative gaze in my direction. "Well. Curiouser and curiouser."

"I guess you think it's a practical joke too," I said, slamming the receiver onto the cradle.

He shrugged one shoulder. "Looks more and more likely. Otherwise why would Mr. Sturgis have called at all? He wouldn't volunteer to a kidnapper an arrangement he'd made with his son to check in every Saturday. Failing to do it would be a red flag. It would also add more weight to your claim they'd been kidnapped. As it is . . ." He shrugged the other shoulder. Perhaps he couldn't manage both at one time.

Buffaloed, I went back to my bedroom, shut the door, and sat down on the bed to think. As far as I was concerned, the call from the kidnapper, the few things Nunna had said to me, her messed-up kitchen, and not hearing from her since were all the proof I needed that she and Walter were being held. I was certain, however, that Monty's reaction and the information he supplied the FBI would carry far more weight than any argument I had. It might even be enough to convince them to abort their investigation. They might continue to pursue the question of my identity and that of my parents, but only as an academic exercise. That left everything up to me.

I thought about what Duck had said. He was almost always right about things; sometimes it bugged me more than others. And I had to admit I'd found his observations disturbing, his questions ones I should have asked myself years ago. Yet I hadn't. Why? Was there something back there I didn't want to face?

I wasn't sure. It didn't matter one way or the other. The time had come for me to get off the pot. I had to find my father's hometown, his family, assuming there was any left, and a medal given to him before I was born. I had to. For Nunna and Walter. Even if no one but me believed they were in danger.

4

I DO NOT WANT TO BE HERE.

That refrain kept playing over and over in my head two hours later as I sat in my second Baltimore gas station, wrestling with a map that seemed to have a will of its own. Not only wouldn't it allow itself to be folded to a more manageable size without a fight, it wouldn't reveal the location of Lanchester Street. The coordinates were printed on the map but as far as I could tell, the street itself was not. If it was, I didn't see it and I was getting desperate.

Normally I have a pretty good sense of direction, but every time I'd been to Baltimore alone, I'd managed to get lost, and this trip was no exception. The simple route plotted for me off the Internet had not allowed for an accident on the Parkway and traffic being detoured onto roads for which I had no frame of reference. The directions I'd received at the first gas station had gotten me to the general area in which Lanchester was alleged to be, but for the life of me, I still couldn't find it. The attendant here was my last hope—and that dimmed when his response was a blank look.

"Lanchester? Never heard of that one. Wait a sec." He sprinted into the service bay, conferred with a mechanic patching a tire, and trotted back, looking very pleased with himself. "Off Lansing. Bud says if you home in on that church spire—that's two blocks over—you can't miss it."

Famous last words.

I left and headed in the general direction of the church steeple barely visible above the trees, but one-way traffic necessitated my going several blocks away from it before I could double back. Since I was so close to my goal, however, I could relax a little and ignore the unsettled feeling that had worked its way into the pit of my stomach the moment I'd decided to drive up here. And I couldn't make that voice in my head shut up. It kept whispering and whispering, like a tape in a loop. Endless play. *I do not want to be here. Go home before it's too late.*

All things considered, it was a good day to be lost. Baltimore and autumn made an attractive couple, the trees ablaze in burgundy reds and burnt oranges under a clear, azure sky, and air as crisp as shaved ice. In spite of my navigational problems and the fact that I'd had few occasions to make the forty-mile trip from D.C., I liked the little I knew of the city—the fierce pride of its ethnic enclaves, its first-class restaurants and arts venues, the community feel of its neighborhoods. When people asked where I was from, I usually answered, "Sunrise, by way of Baltimore," to acknowledge my fragile link with the city.

Yet I was here now only because there was no other route to finding out what I needed to know about my father. I'd never tried to revisit the area in which I'd lived, and until Duck had pointed that out to me, had never even considered it. Why? That was something else I needed to figure out. But first things first.

Closing in on the church from a block over, I could see that the figure on its peak was an angel blowing a trumpet. A chord sounded softly in some remote recess of my mind. Somehow I knew that sleeping cherubs nestled at the corners of the roof of the church, and there were two stained glass windows on one side of its double doors, one on the other. Rounding the corner confirmed it. Archangel Gabriel African Methodist Episcopal Church, exactly as I'd pictured it. I was certain, however, that the adjacent parking lot had at one time been a playground with swings, sliding board, and jungle gym. I could almost see myself tugging at the hand escorting me across the street, and seemed to remember being lifted to the spigot of the water fountain in a far corner of the lot, water splashing my face as I tried to master the art of slurping from the arcing stream. This wasn't Lanchester Street, but it had to be nearby. It was a quiet neighborhood, row houses on one side of the street with postage stamp–sized patches of closely cropped grass behind wrought-iron fences. Semi-detached houses on the other marched two-by-two the length of the block, relieved only by the driveway to the alley behind them.

Services at the church had apparently just ended. Worshippers, their complexions running the entire spectrum of browns, milled about on the sidewalks and meandered toward their cars. I circled the block a few times, waiting for more of the church traffic to dissipate, then pulled into a vacant spot at the curb. On impulse, I dug through the flotsam in the glove compartment until I found the disposable camera I'd bought during last month's foray to the mountains of western Maryland. Eight shots left.

Crossing to the other side of the street, I aimed the camera and snapped a picture of the church, advanced the film and aimed again. That's when I saw her, an elderly woman, resplendent in purple, exiting the massive double doors, a cane in one hand. A teenager came out behind her and helped her down the steps to the sidewalk, then walked her across the street to my side.

I'd been staring at her from the moment I saw her, because of her club foot. My mouth dropped open.

"Jenky."

The name had simply popped into my head. I didn't even realize I'd said it aloud until the woman's head snapped around to peer at me. Considering that I was some distance from her and she had to be flirting with eighty, I was surprised she'd heard me.

Squinting at me in the bright sunlight, she turned to face me. "What did you say?" It was a voice I'd expect from a far younger woman, rich, full-throated. And very, very familiar.

I started across to her. The closer I got, the more garbled my thoughts became. I didn't know this woman, did I? Her face ignited no memories.

"I'm sorry," I said. "I—" Stymied, I shut up.

"You called me Jenky." Her eyes, grayed with age, raked my features.

"Yes. I guess I did."

"Years ago, I used to mind a few neighborhood children. The youngest was a little girl who had trouble getting her tongue around my name, Jenkretton, back then. She called me Jenky. A sweet little thing. Lord, what was that child's name?"

"Leigh Ann Warren?"

Her eyes widened behind purple-framed bifocals. "Yes! That's you? Little Leigh, all grown up? I'll be. So you've finally come back to see old Jenky." A smile of sheer pleasure contributed a new set of creases to the dozens already etched on skin the color of cinnamon toast. "I declare, child, you're the image of your mother."

My breath snagged in my throat. No one had ever said that to me before. "I am?"

"Just like her. More chocolate in your color than she

had, but otherwise, just the same." She turned to her escort. "Melvin, meet one of my children from years ago. Leigh, this is Melvin Jones, my pastor's son."

"Ma'am." He bobbed his head at me with a distracted smile, then took her arm again. "I've got to get back to help Dad, Sister Varney. Why don't I walk you to your house and then you and your friend can visit together."

Jenky's pale eyes regarded me, questioning. "Can you visit for a while, have a cup of tea?"

A herd of Serengeti elephants couldn't have dragged me away. "I'd love to. I can see her home, Melvin."

His gaze slid down to the African walking stick I'd brought with me, in case I had to do a lot of walking. It was more decorative than utilitarian, a sop to my pride.

"It's okay," I assured him. "We'll manage."

His urgency to get under way must have outweighed whatever reservations he had about my reliability as an escort. "Thanks, ma'am. See you at prayer meeting, Sister Varney." He hurried back into the church.

"A nice boy," Jenky said, watching him, "but if they marketed his daddy's sermons, the sleeping pill industry would go right down the drain. Now, it's obvious why I use a cane. What's your excuse?" She nodded toward my walking stick.

I gave her a truncated version of my collision with the fire hydrant as we walked slowly to the second house.

"A policewoman," she said, beaming, as she unlocked the door. "Well, isn't that fine."

"Ex-policewoman, I'm afraid. The knee limits me to light duty. I tried a desk job for a short while, but sitting all day was pure torture. So for the moment I'm at loose ends." It didn't seem as painful to talk about as it had even a week ago. Perhaps I was finally beginning to accept my separation from the police department.

I looked around as she ushered me into the living room, dismayed that nothing about it rang any bells, not even the layout—two rooms on either side of a central hall with stairs that doglegged their way to the upper floor. From what I could see, it was simply but tastefully furnished with delicately flowered prints and chintz reminiscent of Laura Ashley. But I was willing to bet I'd never been in this house before.

"Sit, sit. Make yourself at home." She plumped a pillow on the sofa. "I'll put on the kettle. Then we can have a nice long talk." She awarded me a grandmotherly smile and disappeared into the hallway.

As she left the room, I realized that my memory of her was hazy, but for whatever reason, her disability was not. It also explained why when a third-floor resident of my apartment building with a similar problem had moved in, I felt strongly that I'd met her before. I hadn't, yet whenever I ran into her, the feeling persisted.

"We can chat until the thing whistles," Jenky said, returning from the kitchen. She lowered herself gingerly onto the easy chair adjacent to mine and arranged the folds of her skirt over her knees. "Now. Tell me what else you've been doing for the last—how long has it been? Twenty-five years?"

"Close to twenty-eight." I gave her a thumbnail sketch of my abbreviated stays with my cousins, my years in Sunrise, college, law school, and my decision to join the police force. "A case of acting on hero worship," I admitted. "Ever since the policeman who lived on the first floor carried me out of the building the day of the fire . . ."

A smile full of memories transformed her face. "Casper Evans. A good man. He's retired now, moved into some sort of nursing home. Someone shot him, left him a paraplegic. So sad."

A pang of sympathy for a brother officer wounded on the job sliced through me. He'd always been a hero to me. He deserved better.

I came out of my brown study to find my hostess gazing at me and shaking her head. "What is it?" I asked.

"Just remembering your mother. Such a sweet woman. And you're just like her."

She'd said it before, but my reaction was even stronger this time, my throat closing in on itself. "I can't tell you how much that means. I don't even remember what she looked like. My father either. In fact—"

"Poor baby," she said. pushing herself to her feet. "Well, maybe I can do something about that. Let me see now . . ." She crossed to a small bookcase full of photo albums and ran her fingers along the ones on the bottom shelf.

I sat up straight, my pulse racing. "You have a picture of my mother?"

"Probably this one," she muttered, removing the second from the end. "I use the green albums for all the pictures we took at our Memorial Day block parties. We still have them, you know. There it goes," she said, as a nerve-grating whistle sounded from the rear of the house. "Let's go back to the kitchen. That's where you used to spend most of your time with me anyway."

I followed her, the memory of her rolling gait becoming clearer. Once in her pink and white kitchen, with herbs in pots lining the window above the sink, I took a seat in the breakfast nook. "I don't remember this kitchen."

"No reason you should," Jenky said, pouring water into delicate pink and white porcelain cups. "I moved in here when I married Mr. Varney back in nineteen eighty-two. When you were here, I was over on Lanchester, two doors from where you used to live."

She'd handed me an opening on a silver platter, and I

grabbed it. "Where is Lanchester? I couldn't find it on the map."

The mischievous grin that creased her face was suddenly very familiar. "Come here, baby," she said, backing up to the sink. "Look out the window."

I got up and moved to her side. Beyond a charming backyard with a garden ablaze with orange and yellow chrysanthemums nestled against a chain-link fence was the alley. Directly opposite were the rear views of several semidetached homes.

Jenky chuckled. "There it is, more a court than a street. You get to it from that driveway two doors down. There used to be a sign, but Lord knows what happened to it. We can go right out the back door to get there, but let's have our tea first."

I racked my brain for a palatable excuse to skip the tea, then remembered the photo albums and went back to sit down.

After she'd set the breakfast nook table to her liking, she brought over the cups and slid onto the bench beside me. "Now," she said, opening the photo album. "You sip while I see if I can find you and your folks."

"Pictures of me too?"

"Of course, all the children and their parents, starting from the first block party back in nineteen sixty-eight." She looked up, her expression pensive. "It's a different crowd now, of course, different dynamics. Mostly young, white families over there since the city went in and spruced things up."

She went back to the album, flipping pages, the snapshots arranged and labeled with loving care. The names of the subjects and year the photos had been taken were typed on strips of paper and pasted below each photo, a project that must have taken hours.

I scanned the scenes, dismayed that neither the faces nor the homes in the background meant anything to me. Perhaps what I'd told Grayson was right; we may not have lived on Lanchester long enough for it to make an impression. Skipping over the late sixties, Jenky mumbled a roster of names to herself as she worked her way toward 1973.

"Here we are." Adjusting her bifocals, she patted the page. "You should be in here somewhere. Let me see." Her index finger, the nail glistening with a translucent lilac sheen, tap-tap-tapped from one photo to the next. I tried to shrug off mushrooming tension.

"Yes!" Her voice rang with triumph. "Wayne, Peg, and Leigh Warren, nineteen seventy-three. And here's one with just you—look at that smile! And here's that pretty mother of yours." She slid the book over in front of me.

I stared down at my image, a round-faced urchin, hair in poodle ears tied with big, floppy bows. A pudgy tummy strained the fabric of the sunsuit I wore, stains from the chocolate ice cream cone in my hand decorating the bodice. I felt no connection, nothing. The child was a stranger. She looked so secure in her world, so happy and blissfully unaware of how soon that security would end. I felt sad for her, nothing more.

I moved on to the photo of my mother. Jenky was right. Her deep-set eyes were mine, a slight tilt at the corners. Her face was mine as well, not quite oval, a high forehead under a fringe of mink-brown bangs. A long ponytail flowed over one shoulder, imbuing her with a girlish air and a seductive aura at the same time. Only our cheekbones were different. Mine weren't as prominent, buried under round cheeks that had never relinquished their hold on baby fat.

The mouth was the same, however, the corners curved in a semismile that Duck dubbed devilishly sweet, an oxymoron as far as I was concerned. I had my mom's nose too, on the long side and rather narrow. The primary difference between us was one Jenky had mentioned out on the street: Peg Warren was considerably lighter than I was, emphasis on considerably.

My mental processes skidded to a halt. I squinted at the snapshot, wishing I had a magnifier. "Jenky, was my mom white?"

Her reaction, a head-back, full-throated belly laugh that built to a volume I wouldn't have believed capable from a frame as slight as hers, did three things for me: one, made me feel like an idiot; two, assured me I'd asked a stupid question; and three, slammed open a window in my memory. I remembered the Jenky I'd known, not just the limp. She was the little woman with the big, big laugh that could be heard from several doors away.

"No, baby, Peg was just real bright. That's what we used to call it years ago when we were Negroes and colored and one of us had really light skin. She was real sensitive about it too. Used to wear African jewelry and dashikis, and those head wrap things, her way of letting folks know in no uncertain terms. Do you remember her now?"

I was tempted to lie, but what was the point? "Not really. I keep thinking there must be something wrong with me that I don't. My own mother."

"That's silly. You were so young. And you were small for your age. Wayne used to enjoy carrying you around. Said the day would come soon enough when you'd be too big for him to do it."

"I think I do remember that," I said and shifted my focus to the third photo, that of a tall, handsome man with the little girl straddling his shoulders, her hands covering his eyes, blinding him, their mouths wide with laughter. Those same hands made it impossible for me to tell what he really looked like, left no means of determining if I'd inherited any of his features. I did have him to thank for my coloring; on a police blotter he'd be described as having a medium complexion. He had long, muscular arms and legs. I couldn't say without reservation that I remembered him, but there was definitely a familiarity about him.

"Does this help?" Jenky asked, watching me intently.

"A little. Perhaps if his eyes weren't covered and I could see his whole face—"

"Oh, those eyes." Jenky's features softened, remembering. "So dark they practically sparkled. It was the first thing you noticed about him, those warm, laughing eyes."

For some reason, that didn't seem right. "You're sure? That his eyes were dark, I mean?"

"Not just dark, honey. Black like polished coal. In fact, I was talking about him with Grace, Casper's wife, not too long ago. That's the first thing she said when I mentioned your father, how she would remember those eyes as long as she lived."

I stared intently at the photo, mentally trying to paste Jenky's description of my dad's eyes under the mask of the small hands obscuring that portion of his face. It was like trying to force a jigsaw puzzle piece in a space in which it didn't belong. It wasn't quite right, just wouldn't fit. Yet I could imagine lighter eyes with little difficulty, a lighter brown or perhaps hazel. With that image, something cold and sinister slithered through my mind. And yet again, the coda: *I don't want to be here. Go home, girl, before it's too late. Run! Run!*

"Leigh, are you all right?"

I blinked. "Uh, yes." I couldn't sit still any longer, couldn't afford to waste any more time playing tea party. "Jenky, if you don't mind, I'd like to go see Lanchester Street now."

I sensed her regard as she examined my face. "Something's wrong, isn't there? How can I help, honey?"

"You already have, by showing me these." I forced a smile, willing her off the bench. Until she moved, I was hemmed in, unable to leave.

Her fingers lingered on the page for a moment before she pressed the lever to open the rings of the binder. Removing the page, she placed the photos into my hands. "You take them. Have copies made and bring them back when you can."

Touched by her generosity, I pressed the sheet to my chest. "Thank you, Jenky. I can't tell you how much this means."

"No need." Closing the album, she slid from the booth. "Do you need me to go with you?"

My first inclination was to say no. But considering how much the street was alleged to have changed, I might not recognize the site on which our building once stood. "I'd appreciate it."

I waited, camouflaging my impatience while she went in search of her keys and sunglasses. We left by the rear door, walked through her garden and out of the gate to the alley.

We had to make our way back to the access road I'd ignored earlier to get over to Lanchester, which turned out to be a cul-de-sac. As we walked along the street on which I'd lived as a child, I might as well have been a newcomer. The houses, most of them semidetached with deep front porches, struck no chords at all. A young woman, her middle bulging with a child to come, spotted us and stopped sweeping her porch long enough to wave.

"That's where I lived," Jenky said with a trace of nostalgia, indicating a house on my right. "We're getting close to your end of the block now."

A knot in my stomach tightened. I prepared myself to

search for some small landmark that might remind me of the building the fire had razed, perhaps a tree that had been a favorite, the shape of a yard. Instead, to my amazement, we were approaching a large, detached house, graceful, a three-story Victorian with an astonishing assortment of gables. I ogled it, mouth open. "It's still here!"

"Well, of course, honey. Why wouldn't it be?"

"I—I thought it was gone," I protested. "I thought it had burned to the ground!"

"No, no! The only damage was to the floor you lived on. They'd chopped it up so that there were two apartments on each level back then. Only one on each now."

"But I could swear I remember flames blasting out the upstairs window on the side closest to the street, then the rear one."

"Right, your living room and kitchen. There was talk of arson at first, but that didn't pan out."

I turned on her, a wispy tentacle of a memory undulating near the base of my brain. "They thought someone set it intentionally?"

"Just at first," she hurried to assure me. "They finally put it down to careless use of smoking materials while lighting the gas range, something like that."

"My parents smoked?" I asked. This too didn't feel quite right.

"Peg didn't, as far as I recall. Wayne would stoke up a cigar with my boys after a softball game over on the church playground. I can't say I remember seeing him with a cigarette, though. And I never smelled it in your apartment. That's why I was surprised when they came up with what they did."

Smoking materials. Perhaps pipe tobacco? I had no idea why that had popped into my head, but it meant something. The smell of a very specific brand, Dutch Treasure, had always made me nauseous. Was that reaction rooted in the cause of the fire? How could it be? I'd been outdoors when it started.

"Wait here for me, please, Jenky." We had halted two doors from the house and I started toward it again with an escalating sense of danger. It undulated around me, sent adrenaline coursing through my veins. There was no apparent reason for it. Nothing had changed. I could still hear the swish of the broom of the young woman sweeping her porch, and somewhere the melodious blend of choral voices singing the last movement of Beethoven's Ninth. I didn't want to be here, and some inner voice kept urging me: *Run! Run!* A child's voice. Mine?

There were two steps from street level to the sidewalk, eight to the front porch. I climbed them, stood gazing at the stained glass inset in the top half of the door. No wrought-iron grate like those of other homes on the block. Four mailboxes. Evidently the basement was rented as well as the upper floors.

On impulse, I tried the knob. The door was unlocked. Once beyond it, I saw that the tenants weren't as trusting as I'd supposed. A decorative but sturdy metal door blocked access to the units beyond, its lock the kind likely to delay a thief past a point worth the effort of breaking in.

I stood there, trying to remember how the inner hall had looked twenty-eight years before. Dark, I thought. Paneled. Mr. Evans had lived on the left side of the first floor; the identity of the tenant on the right escaped me. I could still see Mr. Evans practically bursting into the hallway, like a mocha-hued Superman.

All at once I was that beribboned little girl again, my throat burning, seared by the suffocating smoke roiling down the stairs from the upper floors. I remembered huddling near the bottom of the steps, coughing, eyes blinded with tears. Mr. Evans saw me, scooped me up, and deposited me outside on the grass. It seemed so real, as if a cog had slipped on the wheel of time.

Backing out of the door onto the porch, I groped for the banister and stumbled down onto the sidewalk. As if to banish the memory, I hurried to the end of the walkway and turned to look up at the windows of the third floor. Venetian blinds covered them, shielding the secrets of the tenants who lived there now. My gaze dropped to the windows of the second floor, then to the green-shuttered ones of the first. On the side near the rear, a sloping roof sheltered the entrance to the basement.

The universe tilted on its side again, spilling me onto that day again in a bizarre out-of-body experience. I saw the child I was sit up and scuttle on all fours to a point in the yard where she could look up at the angry, red flames shooting from the windows. She tried to scream for her parents, her voice no more than a raspy croak. She had tried so hard to get up those steps to warn them, save them. All they had to do was form a line and march outside, like she and the other children did when they had fire drills in nursery school. But the higher she'd climbed, the thicker the smoke. It had been so hard to breathe, so scary that she'd started back down again. They were still up there.

Neighbors came running and somewhere far, far away, a siren wailed. The other people from her building were coming out, Mr. Settles who lived on the third floor too. Mrs. Allison, second floor rear. But not her parents, not Wayne and Peg Warren. It was all her fault. She should have kept going, kept climbing to get to the third floor.

A police car slewed around the corner onto her street, lights flashing, siren blaring. The driver got out and stood, face taut with anxiety as he spoke into the mike of his radio. Someone tried to pick up the little girl, but she struggled out of the imprisoning arms. She had to stay right where she was, watch for her parents.

The day took on an otherworldly sheen, the air shimmering under the combined effect of the setting sun filtered through layers of acrid smoke. Then she saw him through her tears, the sight of him giving her the strength to push herself to her feet. He emerged from the big doors that flopped up and open from the basement, her father, safe and sound, like they said in the storybooks. Moving quickly, he stepped out and let the doors drop closed behind him.

"Daddy!" she cried. But her voice was barely audible. "Daddy!" She'd run toward him, had tried to scale the chain-link fence that protected Mrs. Allison's rose garden and kept stray dogs and children from the backyard and her precious fish pond. The fence was twice as tall as she was, not easy to climb. And her dad was heading for the trees that sheltered the rear of the house.

"Daddy, where's Mommy?" she yelled to him. "You didn't bring Mommy!"

He must have heard her this time because he hesitated at the edge of the grove of oaks and looked back at her. She froze in place, halfway over the fence, fingers locked in the chain metal.

"I tried, Daddy!" she'd croaked. "Honest! I couldn't get up the stairs!"

But he hadn't believed her. He couldn't have. Otherwise, why would he have glared at her—me—with such loathing? Perhaps it was because of the weird color the day had taken on, or the tears blurring my vision. But loathing is what I thought I'd seen as he'd fixed me in the cross hairs of eyes that had appeared to glow with a pale amber light. Then he'd disappeared through the trees, hurrying toward the alley.

The scenario in my head faded. The reality did not, leaving me weakened, breathless with horror. My father had survived the fire? He'd deserted my mother, had left her to burn to death? He'd abandoned me, had left me to be raised by whoever cared enough to take the trouble. I had to find him to save the life of the woman who had. And I would, no matter what it cost. Wayne Warren would pay.

5

FREEDLAND REHABILITATION AND NURSING CEN-
TER sat on a low rise overlooking the Baltimore beltway, a
single-story brick building with beautifully landscaped
grounds and broad walkways meandering through a host of
shade trees and neatly trimmed shrubbery. I'd found it
without a single wrong turn, a miraculous feat given my
emotional state. Even though I hadn't told Jenky what I
thought I remembered, she could see that the experience
had shaken me and had pleaded with me to wait before
seeing Casper Evans. I couldn't, for my sake and Nunna's.
Six days and counting.

I got out, trying to organize my thoughts as I trekked to
wide sliding doors. The receptionist, a young woman
whose expression gave me the impression she was going to
be cheerful if it killed her, told me I'd find Mr. Evans and
his wife in the west wing's TV lounge. I'd have preferred
to speak to him alone, but couldn't afford to wait for Mrs.
Evans to leave. She might be there all day.

"I haven't seen Mr. Evans since I was a kid," I said, "so
I'm not sure I'll recognize him."

"Look for Mrs. Evans instead," she said, lowering her
voice. "Her you can't miss. She's wearing a big red hat you
wouldn't believe, with a long feather sticking off one side."

Armed with that information, I made my way along the

cheery yellow corridor to the West Wing. The few residents I passed clung to metal railings along the walls, their progress requiring every bit of concentration and stamina they could muster.

The yellow corridor ended at a nurses' station. I had no trouble finding the lounge from there. It was football season, and the Baltimore Ravens were being rooted by a raucous group at the end of the spring green hallway on my right. I winced. Bad enough that with his wife there I'd have to compete with her for Mr. Evans's attention. Throw the football game into the mix and I was probably facing a lost cause.

The lounge was a pleasant surprise, all plate glass windows providing an unobstructed view of a manicured lawn around a garden that would be glorious come spring. Few were paying attention to the outdoors. Patients in wheelchairs and their guests were clustered in front of the biggest TV screen I'd ever seen. Fans sitting in the stadium couldn't have had a better view; the players were practically life-sized. When they went into a huddle, you felt as if you could almost reach out and pat a fanny for encouragement.

Not everyone was interested. A number of patients entertained visitors in conversation areas on the perimeter, holding court in big, upholstered chairs and sofas.

I spotted Mrs. Evans immediately. She sat in a quiet corner, head lowered as she talked with a man in a wheelchair, his back to me, the feather, at least a foot long, hovering dangerously near his face. One wrong move by either of them and not only would Mr. Evans be a paraplegic, he'd be blind as well.

I hated to interrupt them, but I had no choice. As I crossed to them, Mrs. Evans glanced up, saw me approaching and gazed at me, an odd expression in her eyes. Her husband, evidently seeing that something had distracted her, grasped the right wheel of his chair and spun around to face me. I stopped, stunned, because I recognized him. I *remembered* him. The only evidence that a quarter-plus of a century had passed was a sprinkling of gray at his temples. Otherwise, he'd changed very little. He still resembled the lanky young man who'd lived on the first floor of the building on Lanchester Street.

"Mrs. Evans, Mr. Evans, I'm sorry to disturb you but—" I began.

He held up a callused hand to silence me, lips parted, dark eyes raking my features. "Wait, wait. I know you from somewhere. I never forget a face. Can't walk, but the brain's still functioning. Give me a minute to think about this." He waggled a finger, gaze darting back through the years.

It took him less than the sixty seconds he'd requested. His jaw dropped, his broad chest rising in a gasp of astonishment.

"My God, it can't be! You're the little Warren girl." He snapped his fingers, apparently scanning some mental roster. "Peg and Warren's daughter! I'm sorry, baby, your name's gone."

"Leigh. Leigh Ann," I said, bowled over that he remembered me at all.

"Peg's little girl," Mrs. Evans murmured, her face clearing. "Of course. I lived down the street from you. You used to play with my baby brother, Tommy." She could see that I didn't remember him. Or her. "It's okay," she said, smiling. "It was a long time ago."

"Here, have a seat," Mr. Evans said, waving me toward a chair opposite. "I can't believe it. Little Leigh. You've turned into the spitting image of your mother. Lord, did I have a crush on her!"

"Oh?" His wife's brows disappeared under the brim of the hat.

He grinned. "You're the one who just said it was a long time ago. Besides, she was married." Then he sobered. "Your poor folks. Such a shame. What happened to you? I called Peg's cousin a good while later to—"

"You knew them?" I interrupted. "I need to get in touch with them."

"Can't help you there. Only reason I knew who to call back then was because I'd been introduced to the lady when she came to visit once. But the name's gone."

"Was her last name Anderson?"

He thought about it, shook his head. "I don't think so, but I honestly don't remember. Anyway, she told me you'd gone to live with a distant cousin of her husband's in one of the Carolinas, some little town I'd never heard of. Only reason I remember it was because I've got a niece with the same name: Dawn."

"Sunrise," I corrected him. I related my serendipitous rescue by Nunna. "The cousins already had four kids; Nunna took me. Nunnally Layton. I lived with her in North Carolina until I graduated from Howard University's School of Law. I passed the bar, then signed on with the D.C. Metropolitan Police. Because of you."

"Me?" Surprise registered across his youthful face.

"I never forgot how you blasted out of your apartment the day of the fire. There's a lot I don't remember, but I can still see you scooping me up and taking me outside. From that moment on, all I wanted to be was a cop and managed to live that dream for seven terrific years until I injured my knee. It's damaged beyond repair, so far as street duty's concerned, so I'm examining my options. I'm just sorry it took me so long to say thank you for saving my life and being my role model."

He lowered his head. "Well, sir. Me, your role model. Can you beat that?"

"Here, honey." Like magic, a pack of tissues appeared in Mrs. Evans's hand. He dabbed at tears in his eyes and grinned self-consciously.

We blew the next half hour indulging in cop talk, exchanging experiences, which included how he'd gotten shot. Mrs. Evans watched him anxiously, obviously concerned that talking about it might upset him. But I sensed that it made a difference that his listener was someone who'd patrolled the streets as he once had, someone who could relate, understand, and empathize in a way the ordinary civilian, even his wife, could not.

Once we'd run out of tales of the bizarre and ridiculous, I broached the subject that had brought me there. "Mr. Evans—"

"Casper," he interrupted. "And she's Grace." His wife smiled her agreement.

"Casper, then. I understand you identified my parents' bodies."

"Yes." The memory transformed his face. For the first time, he looked his fifty-odd years, creases deepening around his mouth and eyes. "I was the most logical person to do it. We hadn't known each other all that long, but Warren and I had gotten pretty tight."

That was something else I didn't remember.

"Casper, I wouldn't ask, but I have to know. What condition were their bodies in? I mean, there was no doubt who they were?"

The pain of the memory was reflected in his eyes. "None. There's no way to soft-pedal this, Leigh. They were burned beyond recognition, but I could tell who they were because of their jewelry: Warren's academy ring and that pendant your mother always wore. If it hadn't been for those . . ." He swallowed, unable to finish.

So I hadn't seen my father after the fire. It was the fantasy of a traumatized five-year-old trying to put her world to rights. But I had more questions to ask.

"I'm sorry to monopolize your visiting time, but—"

Grace patted my knee. "No problem, Leigh. I'm here practically every day. And this is such a nice surprise. Your mother was the sweetest lady. And talented. Your folks weren't in the neighborhood all that long, but your mom especially was a big hit with us girls. Miss Peggy could make anything on her sewing machine. She helped me make my dress for the senior prom. I'd forgotten that."

Sewing? A talent I hadn't inherited, that's for damned sure. And as much as I wanted to hear more about my mother, it was imperative that I focus on my dad.

"Casper, I need to find out as much as I can about my father—where he was from, whether he had any brothers and sisters, anything you remember."

He pursed his lips in thought. "Funny you should ask. You aren't the first wanting to know about Warren here recently."

My pulse took on jackhammer speed. "Who else has been asking about him? Please, it's important."

"Some white dude said he served with Warren in Vietnam."

I scooted forward on the cushion. "When? I mean, how long ago was he here?"

Supporting his weight on his arms, he shifted in his wheelchair. "He showed up—what, Grace?—a couple of months back, just before I moved here. Said he'd been talking to some other guy in his unit over at the VA hospital and Warren's name came up. They'd been doing the 'whatever happened to?' routine and the other guy said he'd picked up Warren in his cab years ago, but couldn't remember where he knew him from until after he'd dropped him off. Went back later to say hello, catch up on old times, but couldn't find his name on the mailboxes. The one who came to see me said he owed his life to your dad and decided to track him down to thank him. Somebody in the neighborhood told him to find me, that I might know where Warren was, since me and Grace lived there until a few years ago."

"Was there anything special about him, anything re-markable?" I asked, trying to avoid a leading question.

"The worst cough I ever heard. Sounded like he wasn't long for this world, if you ask me."

Bingo!

"What was his name?" I asked, breathing so shallowly I was light-headed.

He scratched an eyebrow. "John? No, Jim Jameson. Real intense dude, acted like he was on a mission, a real Holy Grail–type thing. When I told him Warren had died in the fire, he took it real hard, but he was relieved that at least you had survived. Turns out he hadn't even known about you before then, said you should hear firsthand what a brave man your dad had been. I passed along what little I knew and he left." He gazed at me with a suspicious-cop expression I knew too well. "The odd thing was that he had Warren's name wrong. When he first asked about him, I didn't know who he was talking about."

"What did he call him?" I asked, little sparks dancing before my eyes.

"Rich. Lieutenant Wayne Rich."

I closed my eyes, pulled in deep breaths. The maniac on the phone had practically dropped the name in my lap. "Your lieutenant rich college-boy daddy" he'd called him.

Wayne Rich. Was that my name, then? Leigh Ann Rich? It felt alien, as if it belonged to someone else.

"Now, let me say something here." Casper's tone had taken on a different timbre, as if he were treading carefully. "I got to thinking after the dude left. Warren never talked much about himself, never volunteered anything. There was this one day us guys were shooting the bull about how much harder times were when we were growing up." He grinned at Grace. 'I'll never forget it because that's the day I found out that Willie Shiner had the hots for you."

"What?" Grace snatched off her hat to reveal thick reddish-brown hair. "That slimeball?"

"It's also the day I decided I'd better make my move before he did. Anyhow," he said, to me again, "we got into one of those 'we were so poor that' contests, stuff about wearing our brothers' hand-me-downs, things like that. And Warren didn't open his mouth until somebody thought to ask. He said he never had the problem because he didn't have a brother, only sisters."

Sisters. So I might have aunts somewhere. "Did he say how many? Or where he'd grown up?"

"No, but I got the impression it was on the East Coast, on water, at that. He said something about how his hometown had been a target for the last hurricane that had come ashore, how it had practically washed his house away. Agnes? Or maybe Camille."

I was disappointed that he wasn't more specific.

"Another time he said that he didn't get along with his family and had cut them loose," Casper continued. "He said he'd just as soon not talk about it, and got real uptight, so I took the hint. Maybe he changed his name because of that. And he made a point of everybody calling him Warren, not Wayne. What's going on, Leigh? Why are you trying to find out about him after all this time?"

I'd planned to tell him anyway, so I did, feeling the tick of the clock with every word I used. "I've got until Saturday to find my father's family and hope to God they've got the stupid medal."

Casper shook his head, despair twisting his features. "Damn. I never gave a thought to all the questions he asked about you. It's my fault, Leigh. If I hadn't told him where you went to live . . ."

He was right, but there was no point in rubbing it in. "Please," I said. "Who'd have thought he had something this crazy in mind? Regardless, what you've told me should help convince the FBI that this whole thing isn't a figment of my imagination."

"Look, Leigh, you tell them to come see me. I'll lay it all out for them. I can give them his name, describe him down to the shoes he wore."

"Er, honey." Grace frowned, and leaned forward. "He may have lied about his name."

His head snapped around. "Say what?"

"When I came in and you introduced him, all you said was 'this is Jim,' and you told me why he'd come. When I picked up his coat to hand it to him, I saw his initials on an inside pocket: JGH. Just like Mr. Hammersmith, an old supervisor who used to monogram every shirt he owned. If you had mentioned his last name before, I'd have told you then."

Casper groaned. "I should have known. Something about him didn't sit right at the time, but I thought it was because he wore gloves he never took off. He kept his hands in his pockets most of the time. He'd apologized for not shaking mine when he came in, said his hands had gotten so messed up in 'Nam, they made most folks queasy. I understood, but you know cops. We get edgy when we can't see a dude's hands. I'm sorry, Leigh. I don't know what else to say."

It took me ten minutes to convince him he shouldn't feel guilty about his part in Jameson's scheme. By the time I left, I think he felt better. With Grace working on him, it wouldn't be long before he'd put things in perspective. In the interim, I'd contact a pair of federal agents of my acquaintance and say: Told ya, goddammit!

Then something occurred to me and I had to turn around, go back in, and sign in again.

"Forget something, honey?" Grace asked, as I approached.

"Yes, I did. The FBI told me there's no record of the deaths of Margaret and Wayne Warren. If you identified the bodies, how could that be? Wouldn't there have been something in the paper, an article about the fire, or their obituaries?"

Casper looked uncomfortable and didn't answer.

Grace, puzzled by his silence, jumped in to fill the void. "The papers did report it but said the identity of the victims was being withheld, pending notification of kin. After that, I never saw anything else about it. My mom did try to find out which funeral home handled the bodies. She called all over the city, but none of them knew anything."

Casper cleared his throat. "I'm ashamed to tell you, Leigh. Nobody ever claimed their bodies. Eventually, the city . . . took care of them."

"They buried them?" I felt something shrivel inside.

"Probably cremated them, then buried them wherever they did that kind of thing back then." He scrubbed a hand over his mouth. "I'm sorry, honey. I should have told you before, but . . . Well, to be honest, I was ashamed, because I meant to follow up on things. Warren was my buddy. I felt it was the least I could do. And I did at first, calling every couple of days to see if they'd found his folks. Then time passed and I got busy on the job and, well, the next thing I knew months had gone by. I checked and the city had done its thing. I don't know what I could have done to make a difference but I've felt bad about it ever since."

I thanked them again and hightailed it out of there so I could deal in solitude with the fact that my parents had been buried in a pauper's grave, another bit of the city's flotsam. I wondered if a record of where they were buried even existed. That, unfortunately, was a problem for another day. I had to deal with the information I had on hand, Casper's visitor and what might be my father's real name.

Using my cell phone, I called and got Special Agent Grayson, ran down what Casper had told me and where he could be found. Oddly enough, I got the impression that he wasn't really interested.

"Well," he said, drawing the word out, "we'll add that to the file, but there may be no need for further interviews."

"Excuse me?" I jerked upright and whacked my forehead against the sun visor I'd lowered to block the glare. "What do you mean, there may be no need? This man can describe the kidnapper! It has to be him. It's too much a coincidence for it not to be."

"Yes. Well." I could hear his bored sigh from forty miles away. "Pinkleton and I were on our way to see you. We'll give you an hour to get back and come around then."

"Why? What's happened?" I yelled, wasting valuable oxygen. Dial tones don't talk.

Tossing the phone into my bag, I burned rubber leaving the parking lot, played hell with the speed limits all the way back to D.C. and only got lost once.

They showed up at five twenty-five, their faces as stony as the ones on Mount Rushmore. Terrified that they had bad news about Nunna and Walter, I offered them seats and sat down myself before blurting, "Please. What's wrong? What's happened?"

"What's happened," Grayson said implacably, "is that Mr. and Mrs. Sturgis have been located near a campground in South Carolina and were interviewed by state troopers. They're fine."

For the first time in my experience, I understood the meaning of lighter-than-air. I felt like a helium-filled balloon. "Thank God!"

"Not only are they fine, they claim to have no idea why you'd think they'd been abducted."

"What?" My exhilaration was gone, my balloon pricked, shredded. "Wait. How'd all this happen? Did someone reach them by phone?"

"No. The state police talked to them in person."

I could barely talk, much less breathe. "You're saying they were pulled over, just like that? By someone in uniform? And now Jameson or whoever he is knows that I've called the police, even though he threatened to kill them if I did. That's what you're telling me?"

Grayson looked exasperated. "There is no Jameson, Ms. Warren, at least not with Mr. and Mrs. Sturgis. In fact, Mrs. Sturgis alleges to have tried to reach you a number of times since yesterday, but got no answer. She promised to call this evening after they've reached the coast."

He'd missed the point and I realized they were no longer listening to anything I had to say. I'd be wasting my time reminding them that Nunna knew I was staying with Janeece and would have tried calling here. Or that since she had indeed spoken to me when Jameson had called yesterday, my Nunna had lied to the state trooper. If Nunnaly Layton Sturgis had lied, she must have been forced to. And the suits had already made up their minds that the whole thing was a hoax. Nothing I said would change their opinion.

I pulled in a deep calming breath, shut my emotions in a box. I would not blow up, not scream at them, not find the automatic Janeece thought I didn't know she had and blow their fucking heads off.

"And Walter?" I asked.

"He's fine too. And yes, it was Mr. Sturgis. They checked, compared his photo with his driver's license. He was puzzled but very cooperative. The deputy we talked to was impressed how well he handles his disability."

Walter's arthritis could be debilitating at times but I'd never heard him complain. He too was a member of the cane users' brigade. That was beside the point. Walter had lied as well.

"And there was no one in the Airstream?"

"Nobody," Grayson said. "Not in it or under it. So I'd advise you to look to your friends for the culprit, Ms. Warren. Or your enemies. Whoever the practical joker is put us and the authorities in several states to a great deal of trouble and he will be held accountable for it. This was a waste of the taxpayers' money."

I nodded, determined to keep my cool, ride this out. "And the information I gave you about my father? And the man who came to see Mr. Evans?"

"Probably a coincidence, but we'll check on that," Pinky said, relenting a little, "just to clear up loose ends. We did unearth a report about the death of a couple in a fire in Baltimore about the time you said it happened. The problem was their identities were never confirmed. And there was no mention of a child."

"You mean, I didn't exist even then."

Grayson stood. "Don't worry, Ms. Warren. We'll get a hit on you and your folks eventually."

"The FBI always gets its man," I said.

Pinky heard the cynicism and flushed, but it sailed right over Grayson's head. He actually smiled for the first time and I considered splitting his lip. "Yes, ma'am, we do. Well, we'll be pulling back on our personnel, but we will keep the trace on your phones. If you find out anything else about your father, we'd appreciate your letting us know."

I nodded again, levered myself to my feet. "Thank you for everything. I'm sorry to have wasted your time."

"Just doing our job," Grayson said, and led the way out.

Pinky squeezed my arm as he passed. "Tell Janeece I'll be in touch." Grayson cleared his throat and Pinky took the hint.

I watched them until the agent in my apartment opened the door to let them in, then eased Janeece's door closed. Shutting myself in her bathroom in case she returned from whatever evening church service she'd graced with her presence, I lowered the lid of the toilet and sat perfectly still, so angry that I was afraid if I so much as moved a finger, I'd shatter all over the black and white marble tile.

I'm not sure how long it took before I regained control, and a semblance of sanity returned. The FBI's position was logical. They'd spoken to Walter, had seen Nunna, and both had claimed ignorance of any trouble. They'd checked the Airstream. Why should they spend any more manpower on this?

All right, I was on my own, back at the starting gate. I could count on only so much help from my friends. They had jobs, mortgages, and rent payments. Duck was in no position to do very much; he'd torn his britches when he'd walked off the job in August. Now that he was back, he had to toe the line or he wouldn't be a cop any longer. So it was up to me to do whatever was required to free Nunna and Walter.

I'd tried it by the book by calling the feds and had nothing to show for it but twenty-four wasted hours. I was on my own. So be it. And if I was going to save Nunna and Walter, I might as well start where I'd lost them to begin with: Sunrise.

6

I'D NEVER REALLY APPRECIATED THE MEANING of being caught by the short hairs until I tried to book the earliest flight I could manage to Asheville. Two hours and almost eight hundred dollars later, I boarded the plane and found my seat, so hot under the collar at what I considered airway robbery that the jet could have made the trip on my fury alone.

I rented a Chevy Cavalier at the Asheville airport and hit the road toward Sunrise, my anxiety level increasing by the mile. Would this be a waste of valuable time I could have spent in some other way? Doing what? And if the FBI had found nothing amiss at Nunna's, what made me think I could? They didn't know her, that's why. They hadn't lived with her for fourteen years, wouldn't know that Nunna did things just so. All they'd seen was a small, neat house with no sign that anyone had been there who didn't belong. But someone had to have been there. No way Nunna would have left dirty dishes in the sink. No way. One way or another, Jameson, or whatever his name was, was a damned sight smarter than anyone was giving him credit for being. And that was scary.

It was nearing midnight when I parked at the curb on the three-bedroom home on Sunset Road. Sunrise had long since rolled up the sidewalks for the night. In truth, there weren't that many sidewalks, and those the town had were in too poor a condition to be rolled. Concrete cost money, and if there's another thing my adopted hometown didn't have much of, it was greenbacks. At one point the year before, a mall had been planned in the hope of bringing in dollars from the surrounding area, and the economic future had seemed brighter for a while, depending on which side of town you lived on. But the new construction would have wiped out the cemetery where the black population had been buried since the year one, and my friends and neighbors had been far from happy about it. Since then the plans for the mall had bitten the dust. So Sunrise was still aging, poor, and proud. And, in spite of the circumstances, it was good to be home again.

I parked on the street and got out, pained at how dark and deserted Nunna's house seemed. If she'd been here, the porch light would be on until dawn. Mrs. Elias, on the other hand, considered that an extravagance and a waste of a perfectly good electricity, so her home was dark too. And with no streetlights, the whole block was as black as the bottom shaft of a coal mine. Lugging my overnight case, I hopped the ditch at the edge of the property and headed for the front porch. From behind the house, I heard a soft "woof." Hannibal, the ever-faithful and supremely ineffectual guard dog. I had one foot on the bottom step when a disembodied voice cut through the darkness.

"Halt! Po-lice! Move one muscle and you're air-conditioned!" Chief Nehemiah Sheriff.

I'd almost wet my pants. "Don't shoot, Mr. Sheriff! It's me, Leigh Ann."

The chief and sole member of the Sunrise constabulary moved from the inky depths of the porch like a ghost stepping out of the great beyond, his flashlight searing my eyeballs. "Hey, Leigh Ann. Sorry. Can't see doodly squat out here or I'd have recognized you. Thought maybe it was your perpetrator, though I don't know what he'd come back for. You all right?"

"As close to a coronary as I ever hope to get, you scared me so bad. What are you doing here?" I dug out my keys and he aimed the beam of the flashlight on the lock for me.

"Just keeping an eye on things," he said, following me inside once I'd turned on a lamp. He was his usual self, a little man and a contemporary of Nunna's, Barney Fife–thin, in full uniform as crisp as if it had just been snatched off an ironing board. "I sorta missed the excitement yesterday. I had to take the missus to Asheville for some tests and didn't get back until the FBI boys were leaving. Have you heard anything new?"

"Not a thing. Tests? Is she all right?"

Fear shadowed my old friend's eyes. "Don't know yet. They're poking and prodding her, you know how they do. She'll be fine. Could use a prayer or two, though."

"You've got them, Chief," I said, unable to think of him without her. Mrs. Sheriff had become one of my favorites last year. Her moral support had meant a great deal after I'd been maneuvered into helping her husband solve the murder of the corpse in the cemetery. As Mrs. Elias had commented, "That Missus Sheriff, she's one nice white lady, she is."

"I really appreciate your being here, under the circumstances," I said. "I mean, with your wife in the hospital."

He hitched up his pants with his elbows. "Nothing I can do in Asheville but get in the way. Take a look around first and then tell me how the hell all this came about."

Grateful for his thoughtfulness, I walked through the home in which I'd grown up, infuriated at the signs of invasion. Fingerprint medium still fouled tabletops, light switches, cabinet tops, and doors, any place a person might touch. An assortment of footprints marred the nap of the carpets. Nunna would have had a fit.

The kitchen, ordinarily bright and cheery, seemed gloomy and more dimly lit than usual. The reason was immediately apparent. The one-hundred-watt bulb in the overhead light had been replaced with a forty watt, a size Nunna used only on the front porch and nowhere else. I opened the pantry and found her stash of bulbs, batteries, and fuses. There was an unopened pack of hundred watts.

"Here's the first sign that the guy was here," I said, and explained the giveaway. "Nunna can't abide a dimly lit kitchen. She wouldn't be able to read. Her nightly routine is to sit at the table with a big mug of hot chocolate and read until she finishes drinking it. Then she goes to bed. That forty watt just wouldn't cut it."

Chief Sheriff stared up at the bulb, then leaned over the sink to examine the shade at the window. "Uh-huh. The missus bought a shade like this for the bathroom. Doesn't let a bit of light through. Push the curtains closed for insurance and nobody'd see a thing."

"And the field agents were here during the day," I pointed out. "Even if they were here after dark, they probably thought a low wattage bulb was used to save electricity."

The chief bobbed his head. "We'll leave it be for now and I'll get it to them tomorrow so they can dust it." He gave me a pleased smile. "It's good you came. We'll show those boys a thing or two. You notice anything else?"

Sadly, I didn't, at least not at first. There was nothing out of place, nothing obvious missing. I opened the back door and found Hannibal on the steps, tail a-swish. After my cursory back-of-the-ears-scratching session in greeting, he began snuffling against my hands and pockets, as if looking for a treat. And that was out of character for him.

Hannibal had always been as predictable in his habits as

the woman who'd adopted him. Once the sun went down, there'd be no sign of him. If a person he considered a friend came around after dark, his only acknowledgment of their presence would be to stick his head from under the back porch steps, give a soft bark to let you know he was there and on the job, and that would be the end of it. Let a stranger invade his territory and it would sound as if all the hounds of hell had been turned loose—still from under the porch. Yet here he was after midnight on the top step, not only bright-eyed and as bushy-tailed as it was possible for a part bassett to get, but clearly expecting to be given something edible. This behavior was new, assumed since Nunna and Walter had left.

Mrs. Elias was feeding him during their absence and Walter had personally deposited a case of dog food and an extra bowl on her back porch. In other words, she had no need to come in our house to prepare Hannibal's meals. Yet someone must have gotten him used to snacks after dark, someone he expected to use the rear door.

The chief had stuck his head out of the kitchen. "Land o' Goshen. Hannibal's up?"

I could have kissed him. My certainty that Jameson had spent time here might be written off by the suits as based on flimsy evidence, but I knew Hannibal well and so did the chief, since the hound had originally belonged to him. The chief's question lent validity to my suspicions, and after a discussion of its merits, we came to the same conclusion: someone, probably Jameson, had taught this old dog some new tricks.

Back in the house, I fixed hot chocolate for myself and brewed coffee for my old friend, who insisted on staying on until dawn.

"No point in my going home this late," he said, settling his narrow backside on one of Nunna's captain's chairs.

"Kinda lonely without the missus waiting to chew me out for overdoing." He yanked a handkerchief from a back pocket and blew his nose with a short-lived, embarrassed smile. "Now." He pulled himself erect, the professional lawman again. "Tell me everything that's happened from the git-go."

I ran it down for him, repeating Saturday's phone conversations and in the process, reexamined something Nunna had said. Excusing myself, I left to rifle the file drawer of the desk in the master bedroom. The contents of Nunna's "Important Papers" folder sent me rushing back to the kitchen.

"Nunna told me on the phone that if I needed help with arrangements, to go to the bank," I explained. "She had just said that there was nothing I could do for her and Walter, that they could die happy. So I took the comment about the bank to mean that's where I should look for her burial insurance policy. But it's in the bedroom with all her other policies. She must have meant something else."

"Can you sign to get into her box? I mean, with her being a married lady now . . ."

"All she did was have Walter add his name on the card," I said. "We discussed everything, the three of us and Monty, the need for new wills, advanced directives, things like that. If both Nunna and Walter are incapacitated at the same time and need someone to take action for them, Monty and I are to do it jointly. That's why this is so frustrating. As far as the FBI and Monty are concerned, there's no problem. I guess if I were in their shoes, I'd see it that way too. But I'm not in their shoes, I'm here, out on this limb alone."

"Not quite," Chief Sheriff said, his tone a mild rebuke. "I'm here, ain't I? Now, finish your chocolate and get some rest. We'll want to be there when Prissy unlocks the door of the bank. If you don't mind, I'll keep watch from the sofa. It's a mite chilly out yonder."

Grateful for his companionship and his unspoken acceptance that something had indeed happened to Nunna and Walter, I dug out a blanket and pillow for him and retired to my old room, taking comfort in its familiarity, but certain that I wouldn't be able to sleep. Right. I don't even remember pulling the covers over my shoulders.

I awoke to the smell of coffee brewing and sunlight streaming in the window. I had to pass on the Maxwell House, since there was no half-and-half in the refrigerator. I got what caffeine I could from a cup of tea, and we made a beeline for the bank.

The chief, who somehow managed to look perfectly rested, hung back as Priscilla Rooks, eyes bright with curiosity, directed me to an adjoining room where I could view the contents of the safe deposit box in privacy. I grabbed the chief by the arm and tugged him along with me. It was a tight fit, but I sat and he stood, and I opened the lid, feeling as if I was invading sacred territory.

Evidently Nunna had used the box to stash items she considered irreplaceable: a few pieces of jewelry that had belonged to her mother, my prize-winning elementary school essay, some coins Charlotte, her other foster daughter, had sent from Kenya, her birth certificate and marriage license, the tassel from the cap I'd worn when I graduated from high school. And in the very bottom, a letter addressed to Nunna.

At some point it had gotten wet. The ink had run, rendering the return address and cancellation illegible. I hated to open it, but nothing I'd seen so far was anything I could use in the present circumstances.

Sensing my hesitation, the chief said, "Might as well."

I removed the letter, unfolded it, scanned the contents,

and felt astonishment zip through my veins like bubbles of champagne. It was from the cousins I'd lived with before moving to Sunrise.

> *Dear Nunnally,*
>
> *We've thought about it and Sell and I agree it's safest if Leigh comes to live with you, since practically no one knows of your connection to us. We just hate giving her up, but I remember how frightened Peg was the last time I saw her, and the least we can do is protect her child the best we can. After losing one baby, I can understand how she feels. No one back home knows Leigh has been with us and never will. Even though taking her to Korea with us might seem the answer to the whole problem, the child has been through enough. She's still very fragile and the counselor agrees that having to adjust to a foreign country may be more than she can handle. Hopefully one day she'll understand that we're not rejecting her. The important thing now is to see that she's safe and nurtured and we know we can count on you to do that in Sunrise.*
>
> *Come as soon as you can, Nunnally. Plan to leave with her after dark. Sell will arrange everything. And thank you so much. Peg and Warren would be so grateful.*
>
> *Sincerely,*
> *Andy*

Completely buffaloed by what I'd read, I passed it to the chief without comment, then got up and left. I heard Mrs. Rooks call my name with alarm as I hit the front door, but

I couldn't stop. I needed air, sunlight, space, time to think if only for a moment or two. Outside I took aim for the nearest place where I could sit, the slatted bench in front of the barber shop two doors from the bank. Once there, I shut down, concentrated on essentials like breathing and remaining upright and not coming apart at the seams.

I'm not sure how long it was before the chief joined me. He perched on the edge of the bench, the letter and the envelope with the safe deposit key in his hand, and just sat, without a word, waiting for me to get it together.

It took a few minutes. Finally, after a sigh from deep within my soul, I could talk.

"I never told Nunna," I said, "but all this time I thought the cousins let her take me because they didn't want me or couldn't afford to keep me. They already had four and it sounds like there was a fifth who died. But that . . ." I jerked my head toward the letter. "That says they did want to keep me. Here it is, twenty-five years later, and finding that out means so much."

The chief tsked, as if I should know better. "Childhood hurts never heal. I'm seventy-seven but I can still get blubbery over a dog of mine we had to shoot when I was just a little tyke. Had rabies. It was a long time before I could forgive my pap. But that's not all that letter says, Leigh Ann. Those folk were trying to protect you."

"Yes, but from what? Why was my mom so frightened? What had happened to make everyone feel I was in danger?"

"And what's it got to do with what's happened to Nunna and Walter?" the chief asked.

"Nothing, directly. I think it was the only clue she could give me to help me trace the cousins. If Andy and my mother were related, she might remember where my father was from. I guess Sell was her husband, but I don't remember their last name, and the return address is too blurred to read. And why would they be going to Korea?"

"Probably in the service," the chief said. "My nephew was stationed there for a while. Said he almost froze his peach pits off, it was so cold. Well, why don't you put this away and think about it." He placed the letter and key in my hand. "You may be able to remember more about them now that they're uppermost on your mind again."

That wasn't quite true since Nunna's predicament occupied the top tier, but I understood what he meant.

"I didn't ask last night," the chief continued, "but how long will you be in town?"

"I should probably get to the airport by four-thirty or quarter of five. Why?"

"Because I could use some help polling store owners, see if anybody remembers a stranger in town. You willing?"

It was barely nine-thirty, so I had no excuse for turning him down. Besides, it wasn't as if it would take that long; this wasn't Fifth Avenue.

"I'll take this side," I said, "so I can get breakfast at the diner. I missed seeing Maudine when I was here for Nunna's wedding."

"Good idea. I've got a taste for some scrapple or maybe liver pudding. Make Fred's your last stop and I'll meet you there. And if folks want to know why you're asking about a stranger, make up something. Tell 'em I was expecting someone and figure they got lost. And tell Maudine to heat up some scrapple for me."

Scrapple. The very mention of it made my mouth water. It wasn't the kind of thing you found in every D.C. supermarket. I shoved it to the back of my mind and began with Drop-In Shoppin', fielding questions and flat-out lying about how the newlyweds were doing from one end of the commercial section to the other. No one remembered seeing a stranger or a man who didn't belong. There was only one road in and out of Sunrise. To get to Nunna's one had to pass three-quarters of the business establishments to get to Sunset Road, so it was probably safe to assume that Jameson had arrived after closing time.

By the last store on my side of the strip, what little energy I had was gone and the prospect of breakfast at Fred's Diner was as welcome as a five-course meal after a six-day fast.

"Leigh Ann! How ya been?" Maudine, a big, blond Valkyrie of a woman, greeted me like a long-lost sister. She hugged me with one arm, hoisting an almost empty coffee pot out of the way with her free hand. The aroma of country ham and baked bread wafted from her uniform and hair. She smelled so good I was ready to bite her.

"Grab a stool, girl," she said, scooting behind the counter and grabbing a cup and saucer for me. "I'm so sorry I missed the wedding. I had to go to settlement that day, and I was scared if I rescheduled, Fred's wife would change her mind. This place is mine now, ya know." She beamed with pride, her porcelain complexion positively glowing.

"Oh, Maudine, that's terrific," I said, and meant it. Considering the hardscrabble childhood she'd survived, she had every right to crow. "Are you going to change the name of the place?"

She shook her head and the yard-long braid nestled against her more than ample bosom jiggled back and forth. "I wouldn't do that to this town. There's been a Fred's Diner since my no-account daddy was a pup. So Fred's it'll stay. What'll it be?" she asked, filling my cup.

I ordered for myself and the chief, who I saw waiting to cross the street, then took a moment to greet the regulars whose backsides warmed stools and benches at breakfast time five days a week.

"Maudine, have you seen someone you couldn't account for in the last few weeks?" I asked softly, proprieties completed. "A white man, middle-aged, with a really bad cough?"

"Sure have. Mornin,' Mr. Sheriff." She filled a cup for him.

"When?" he asked, so sharply that Maudine regarded him with undisguised curiosity.

"One night a while back, I don't remember exactly when. Came in as I was about to close up. Ordered coffee, decaf, and used four sugars. Makes me sick to think about it. Only served him to begin with because he was a friend of yours, Leigh Ann."

"Mine?" I almost choked on outrage.

"Well, I assumed he was. He thought you still lived here. I told him you didn't, and suggested he get your address and phone number from Miss Nunna. Did he get you?"

"Yes. He did." I concentrated on adding cream to my cup, determined to keep a steady hand.

"Maudine," Mr. Sheriff said, "I need to talk to you a few minutes. When's your break?"

She snorted. "Owners don't take breaks. Sorry, Chief, but it'll have to wait until the breakfast crowd clears out."

I excused myself and took refuge in the ladies' room, needing a minute alone again. So Jameson had simply followed up on what little he'd learned from Casper and had found Sunrise, and Maudine had pointed him to Nunna. I didn't blame either of them. But it was still frightening to see how easy my friends had made it for the man, and his bad luck that I no longer lived here. Or more accurately, Nunna's and Walter's. At least I now had more ammunition to aim at Pinky and Grayson.

Breakfast was ready when I returned to the counter. Maudine kept eyeing me worriedly, but I decided to leave it to Mr. Sheriff to tell her as much as he thought she needed to know. I managed to eat about a quarter of the scrapple, eggs, and grits, a dead giveaway that I was not myself, as far as Maudine was concerned, but it was all I could handle.

The chief, on the other hand, cleaned his plate and finished the biscuit I hadn't been able to touch, ordered an additional waffle, and drowned it in maple syrup.

I couldn't sit still any longer. I told Mr. Sheriff I'd walk home and see him later.

He told Maudine he'd be right back and went outside with me. "You all right, Leigh Ann?"

"I guess. I just need to move, do something. What will you tell Maudine?"

He allowed as how he felt he could trust her with the whole story. "What I want to do mostly is get a good description of the son of a bitch," he said. "If this doesn't convince the government boys that there's a problem, they're idiots. What are you gonna do now?"

I shrugged, feeling helpless. "I don't know. Clean the house, maybe. I'd hate for Nunna to see it the way it looks now. Shouldn't you be leaving for the hospital soon?"

He made a face. "After I talk to Maudine, I guess. Why don't you stop and talk to Betty Elias? See if she noticed anything unusual. Let me know what she says. Here's my cell phone number. If I don't answer, call the house and leave a message. I hope to get back before you leave, but if I don't, you call me, keep me up on what's goin' on, you hear? Don't care what time it is, you call me."

He fixed me with a gaze filled with warmth and concern, and if we hadn't been outdoors with half the street watching, I'd have hugged him, but tongues would have been wagging for weeks. "I'll call. I promise."

"Good." He patted my arm. "By the way, you found yourself a new job yet? Did you sign on with that insurance fellow you told me about at the reception?" Since Duck and I had been on the outs when Nunna got married, the chief and his wife had made a point to see that I wasn't alone during the ceremony or afterward.

"I decided against the insurance agency," I said. "I could practice law, but my heart wouldn't be in it. Duck keeps telling me to take my time and think about it. I'm still betwixt and between. A cop is all I've ever wanted to be."

He nodded with understanding, then tipped his head to one side, slate-gray eyes riveted on mine. "I said it before, I'll say it again. You can always come home, Leigh Ann. I'd be honored to work alongside of you."

I thought, to hell with it, leaned over, and kissed his parchment-thin cheek. "That's the nicest compliment I've received in a long time, Mr. Sheriff. I'll keep it in mind."

"See you do," he said, and went back in to his cooling waffle.

The trek home, uphill all the way, wasn't such a hot idea. By the time I reached Nunna's block, I was overheated, winded, and wet, perspiration streaming. The knee, which I'd long since begun to think of as an entity unto itself, was cussing loud and long. Unless I gave it a rest and a good soaking before it was time to leave for the airport, I'd need a wheelchair, if not at Asheville's, definitely when I changed planes in Charlotte.

I hesitated as I trudged by Mrs. Elias's, and had the matter decided for me. She came out, head tied in a scarf, about to engage in her daily midmorning ritual: sweeping the porch, whether it needed it or not.

"Leigh Ann! I declare! Is that your car yonder? I thought yours was tan."

I gave up. It would be foolish not to talk to her anyway. "Good morning," I said, and limped my way to her front steps.

"You're ailin.'" She squinted at my leg. I wasn't sure what she expected to see under my slacks.

I found out. Despite my protests, she pulled me inside to her bathroom, argued my slacks down around my ankles, and began slathering my knee with the smelliest concoction on God's green earth.

"Holy smokes!" I exclaimed. One didn't swear around Betty Elias. "What in the world is that stuff?"

"Never you mind. All you need to know is that it does the trick. You'll get used to the smell 'fore long. Did you ever hear from Nunna?"

"Yes." I looked down at the top of her head as she worked on me. The scarf was askew, exposing a bald spot surrounded by wispy gray hair, and I realized I'd never seen her without her head covered. "I just came down to make sure the house was all right."

"You mean after all those men finished tromping in and out," she said, turning to wash her hands. "Leigh Ann, I know everybody thinks I'm a nosy, gossipy old woman and I have to admit they're mostly right. But one thing I've learned in my seventy-one years is when to keep my eyes open and my mouth shut. And I know something's wrong. So you might as well tell me. What the hell is going on?"

Shocked speechless by her slip, I focused on the knee. It was a losing battle and I knew it.

"Mrs. Elias, I want your word that you'll keep what I tell you to yourself, unless and until Mr. Sheriff says otherwise."

"My hand to God," she said solemnly. "What's happened to Nunna?"

So I told her and consoled her when she began to cry. After pulling up my slacks, I went with her back to her living room and sat with her until she'd regained control.

She wiped her eyes on her apron and wrung her hands. "It's all my fault," she said. "That man stopped by here Wednesday morning, I think it was. Said he'd knocked on Nunna's door, but no one answered. He wanted to know when she'd be back."

Somehow I knew what was coming and prepared to listen without comment. "And . . . ?"

"And I told him, Leigh Ann," she wailed, tears starting anew. "I talked my fool head off about the wedding and the crazy honeymoon they went on and when they'd be getting in, everything. I get lonesome, don'tcha see. The boys can't come home like they used to, and Mr. Elias has been dead so long I don't half think about him anymore. And this man seemed so nice, had good manners, talked to me like I was somebody. He was company, Leigh Ann. Sick, too. Worst cough I ever heard. And something was wrong with his hands. He wore gloves and begged my pardon for not taking them off. Said they'd gotten messed up in the war."

"How long did he stay?" I asked quietly.

She sniffed and wiped. "An hour, maybe. Then he left."

"Driving? Did you see his car?"

"Yes, it was black, one of those SUV things that sit up high. Nice and clean too."

I filed that to tell Mr. Sheriff.

"Do you hate me, Leigh Ann?" The plea in her voice was heart-rending.

"No," I said, because I didn't. "I won't even mention it to Nunna. I'll let you do that." Sorry, but I couldn't let her off scot-free. "Now, did you tell all that to the FBI agents?"

She stared at me, bloodshot eyes stretched wide. "They

really were government men? Oh, Lordy. I didn't believe them. They were wearin' coveralls, not suits like on TV. And I didn't like their attitude."

"What do you mean?"

"They came over and asked me about going in next door, made it sound like I was trespassing or something, even though I told them I had a key and you'd asked me to go. So I didn't tell them anything but exactly what they asked."

I wished she'd been as reticent with Jameson, but saw no point in saying it.

"What should I do, Leigh Ann?" she asked. "Is it too late to talk to the government men?"

"Best to start with Mr. Sheriff," I said. "He'll be in touch with you. Tell him everything you've told me and he'll decide whether to ask the agents to come back. Before I forget, did you see any sign that there was someone in the house this week?"

"No, indeed. If I had, I'd have called Nehemiah. I'm so sorry, baby. I did everything ass-backwards."

"If we did things right all the time," I said, getting up, "we'd be perfect, and nobody would be able to stand us. I'd better get on home now. The house is a mess."

"Let me help," she pleaded. "That'll make up for a little."

I agreed only because I wasn't certain I could finish in time to leave for the airport. But I had to admit, the knee felt better.

As I waited for Mrs. Elias to check to be sure she'd turned off her stove, I noticed the rack of keys mounted beside the front door. Nunna's key was plainly marked on a cardboard tag in big red letters.

"Was Jameson ever alone in your living room Wednesday morning?" I asked, when she joined me at the door.

She thought about it. "When I used the water closet,

and then again when I went to find my address book to see if I had your number. I didn't. At least he didn't get that from me."

But if he'd come prepared, he might have managed to make a copy of Nunna's key. I didn't have the heart to ask if the key has been missing at any point. I'd pass that along to Mr. Sheriff to do, then realized Jameson needn't have made a copy. Mrs. Elias left with me and when I reminded her that she hadn't locked up, I had my answer.

"You been in the big city too long," she said with a rueful smile. "Don't nobody lock their doors during the day."

Nice, safe, friendly little Sunrise, the very reason I cherished it, couldn't have been more helpful to Jameson. They'd practically given the man a key to the town. And there was nothing I could say.

Together, Mrs. Elias and I got the place in order. I managed a hot soak in the tub while she prepared a meal for me and ran my slacks through the laundry. But the putrid-smelling stuff had worked. The knee felt fine. I caught a nap on the connecting flight to Reagan National and disembarked with an idea I wished I'd thought of on Saturday. The FBI might have their databases, but I had something even better: Plato dePriest.

7

THE DOORBELL WASN'T REALLY A DOORBELL, SO I had graduated from a series of discreet taps through knocks to toe-jamming kicks before I heard any signs of life from inside the trim brick house on P Street. Granted, 11:04 P.M. might be a little late for dropping in on normal people, but the resident to be rousted was anything but normal.

"Who is it?" Plato dePriest's muffled voice filtered through the series of pick-proof locks that decorated a door thick enough to guard Fort Knox. He knew damned well who it was. The camera behind the button of the doorbell had a lens that covered a hundred and eighty degrees.

"Leigh Warren," I said anyway. "Open up, Plato."

Silence. Then: "You got a warrant?"

"Want I should go get one?" I asked. He wasn't serious. It was a routine he enjoyed to point out the fact that, for the moment anyway, he had the upper hand.

"Wait a sec." The clunks of disengaging deadbolts, hasps, and Charlie bars was like something in a comedy routine. After a full thirty seconds, the door opened a couple of inches and a pale blue bloodshot eye peered at me. "You alone?"

"No. I brought the Sixth Army with me. Cut the crap, Plato. I need your help."

The eye sparkled. "Moi? The hacker who with allegedly nefarious intent allegedly invaded the sacred files of the highest echelons of the government? I'm honored." The door opened wide and he stepped back with a courtly bow.

I went in and, as usual, felt claustrophobia wrap its suffocating tentacles around my shoulders. On my way there, I'd sworn I'd keep my opinion to myself, but I couldn't help it. "Jesus, Plato! How can you live like this?"

His living room, larger by half than my whole apartment, was a rabbit warren of piles of newspaper, magazines, and computer catalogs stacked to his ten-foot ceilings, a fire hazard waiting patiently for a spark.

"Live like what?" He looked around, blinking myopically, his glasses a tiara atop a mop of Mississippi mud–brown curls. "What's the matter with it?"

Hopeless, I thought. "Never mind. You got any place I can sit down?"

"Oh. Sure. Come on back. She needs my help! Boy, what a kick!"

I followed as closely on his slippered heels as I dared through the labyrinth of stacks, afraid that if I lost sight of him, it would take me half an hour to find his computer room. I'd been here on a number of occasions and each time the route had changed. It was not my imagination. Plato, aged thirty-one going on twelve, was obscenely rich, Einstein-brilliant, and as squirrelly as a tree full of acorns. He was a hypochondriac, obsessive-compulsive, agoraphobic, and anmeophobic, which I'd never heard of until I met him. Once I found out it was an extreme fear of winds and drafts, I suspected I knew when he'd discovered it was yet another problem for him, since because of his agoraphobia, he almost never went out.

As screwy as he was, Plato was also incredibly naive, a genuinely sweet guy whose love of puzzles had been stuffing his bank account since he'd designed his first computer game at age fourteen. More recently his fascination with puzzles had very nearly cost him what little freedom he had. As far as he was concerned, working his way into the computer files of the military and a number of intelligence organizations was simply another puzzle-solving exercise. The only thing that kept him out of jail was the fact that after each invasion he left a set of codes to be used to ensure no one else would be able to get in the way he had, and included his name and number in case they had any questions. To Plato's way of thinking, he'd performed a patriotic duty, and was highly incensed to find he was considered a threat to national security. His future had looked grim until a couple of unorthodox thinkers on a high enough level realized that, in light of what he'd accomplished, this particular screwball amounted to a national treasure the government would be well advised to mine— and monitor. As a result, Plato now answered to an unspecified agency and was in hog heaven, with only one assignment expected of him: invade as many federal computer systems as he could and design a method to make them as impenetrable as possible.

There were only a handful of civilians aware of this and the only reason I was one of them was that a couple of years before, I'd responded to a call to assist a lockout in the middle of a January snowstorm. I'd shown up, Slim Jim in hand, prepared to open someone's car door for them, and found instead a nearly hysterical and hypothermic Plato on the front stoop of his house. He'd stepped out to get the newspaper normally brought in by the cook and a gust of wind had slammed the door shut behind him. The forty-five minutes spent in my cruiser while we waited for a locksmith had launched the beginning of our bizarre friendship, and I was now one of few who could drop by unannounced, but only because I'd been a cop and was also considered computer illiterate enough to be deemed trustworthy.

Plato's workroom was windowless, with banks of computers lining three walls; printers, scanners, fax machines, and other buzzing mechanisms I couldn't identify arranged along a fourth. The room was soundproof and shielded. The computers were shielded as well, the monitor screens polarized in such a way that unless you were directly in front of them, they appeared blank. The proceeds from a number of well-known computer games and software programs he had designed had paid for the house, its renovation, and every piece of equipment Plato used. He wasn't as rich as Bill Gates but could certainly afford to live in Gates's neighborhood if he'd wanted to.

"Uh, let's see." He knocked a stack of printouts onto the floor to clear a chair for me and flopped down onto his own ergonomic throne on wheels. "Hey, no cane. Knee must be better, huh?"

Surprised that he'd noticed, I allowed as how it was coming along, albeit slowly, and got right to the point. "Look, Plato, I need you to do a search for me."

His eyes lit up like Roman candles. "Yeah? Hey-hey-hey! What's the subject?"

"My father."

"No shit." Patting the top of his head, he found his glasses and settled them on the bridge of his nose. "Well, okay, but why?"

Plato was one of the few people with whom I was willing to share the whole story, beginning to end. He listened, his face a kaleidoscope of emotions. "Whoa!" he said, when I'd finished. "That's some really heavy shit. By Saturday, huh? Uh—what's today?"

I closed my eyes. "Monday, Plato. Night. In an hour it'll be Tuesday, okay?"

"Wow! Guess we'd better get to it, then." With one foot, he sent himself backward across the room to a computer at the end of a row. "Got a suggestion, though. Instead of searching on your father's name, makes more sense to start with yours."

"Why?" I asked, scooting my chair next to his.

"Your father could be Wayne No-Middle-Name Rich, Warren No-Middle-Name Rich, Wayne Warren Rich or Warren Wayne Rich. Plus we have no year of birth for him. Even guessing, ask for all those combinations of names born between, say, nineteen thirty-eight to forty-eight and we'll probably get hundreds of hits. We don't have time to figure out which one he might have been. So let's assume you were originally named Leigh Ann Rich. When's your birthday supposed to be?"

I told him but the question rattled me. It had never occurred to me that I might not have been born on the date I'd been celebrating for thirty-three years. That was even more unnerving than the possibility that I wasn't Leigh Ann Warren.

"Okay." Plato grinned, eyes still glittering. "That means I need to get into—"

Cutting him off, I said, "Don't tell me, just do it. I feel like such a hypocrite by asking for your help. This is illegal, for God's sake!"

He hummed, considering it. "Maybe, maybe not. I've sorta got carte blanche to do this kind of thing—"

"For a specific purpose," I reminded him, "not for anybody who walks in off the street wanting to find out when Auntie Maybelle kicked the bucket in Minot, South Dakota."

"North," he corrected me, with a "gotcha!" smile.

"Plato." I gripped his upper arms. "This is serious. No more playing around. You know I wouldn't be here if I wasn't desperate."

The smile faded. "Yeah. I do know. And I wouldn't do this for anybody else either. But I figure I owe you."

"For what?" I asked, puzzled.

He looked me full in the face, scanning my features. "For treating me like a regular person instead of a freak," he said softly. "For making me feel like a normal Joe. Now let's have some fun." He pushed the sleeves of his sweatshirt up to his elbows, wiggled his fingers with theatrical flair, and attacked the keyboard.

Even sitting beside him, I couldn't see what was happening on his monitor. I moved behind him, and was confronted by lines and lines of type scrolling upward at such blinding speed, it made me dizzy. I got up and nudged the chair to his side again, watching in frustration as he typed, grunted, typed again, shook his head, and swore under his breath. He was in his element, tackling a puzzle, and within a minute had probably forgotten I was there. It was the longest few hours I'd ever spent.

Leigh Ann Rich turned out to be a dud. He tried spelling my first name with two E's, tried my middle name with an E, even tried Rich with an E. No hits came close.

Finally, nearing ulcer country, I said, "What else sounds close? Ridge? No, he said 'rich college boy.' All right, how about R-I-T-C-H."

Plato peered at me over his glasses. "That's reaching, but what the hell. While I'm doing that, let's order a pizza. I'm starving. There's a menu from the all-night place on the bulletin board in the kitchen."

I wasn't used to pizza this late but Mrs. Elias's beef stew

and my four-hundred-dollar bag of peanuts on the plane back had long since been digested. I started toward the door before pulling up short. "Er, how do I get to the kitchen?"

He'd already begun typing and didn't turn around. "Take a right, pass two stacks, then another right."

"Right, two stacks, right," I mumbled, wondering if I'd ever see him again. I'd found the kitchen, which, to my astonishment, resembled something out of *Architectural Digest*, when I heard him whoop.

"BINGO!" he shouted. "Leigh, get in here!"

Pizza menu in hand, I hurried back. "You got a hit? You found it? I mean, me?"

He was on his feet, boogying in front of the computer. "Looka there!" he shouted, reaching for my hand. "All your parents did was change your name a little bit. Lee Anderson Ritch, born June 24, 1968 at Walter Reed, Washington, D.C. Father, Wayne Warren Ritch. Mother-" He pointed. "Look at that! Margaret Anderson Rich! Your mom was a Rich and married a Ritch! Isn't that rich?" He chortled, pleased with himself, and grabbed me in a bear hug. As far as I could remember, it was the first time he'd ever touched me.

I hugged back, so weak with relief that it was just as well I had someone to hold on to. "Plato, you're a genuis."

"Hey, we aren't done yet," he said, pushing me to arm's length. "Got to find out about your old man now. Let's celebrate with the pizza. You call while I print this out. I want thin crust, a big one, with *everything!* Use the phone in the kitchen. There's money in the Fred Flintstone cookie jar on the counter. Hot damn!" He turned back to the computer.

I sprinted to the kitchen, ordered the pizza with everything for Plato and one with pepperoni for myself. Under

other circumstances, I'd have satisfied myself with a slice
or two of his, but nothing, not even gratitude, could induce
me to eat anchovies.

So that's who I was, I mused. Lee Anderson Ritch. Anderson was obviously a family name. Which might explain
why the cousin who'd written the letter was called Andy.
Or perhaps her name was Andrea. I still couldn't remember.

When I rejoined him in the workroom, I found Plato sitting, fingers idle, a stunned expression on his long, angular
face.

"Something wrong?" I asked.

He swiveled around, blinking as if he had sand in his
eyes. A pink tongue made a round trip over his top lip, then
the bottom. "That hit. It wasn't you."

"What?" I lowered myself onto one knee and looked at
the monitor. "It had to be. There I am, Leigh Ann—" I ran
out of words, getting his point. It was my first and middle
names on the screen, not the Lee Anderson I'd seen before.
"I don't understand."

He swallowed. "See, what happened, I searched on
Ritch with a T on your birthday. I guess I was so excited, I
didn't notice a couple of things. The first was that number
in the corner that tells you how many hits the search engine
found. Or this either." He pointed. Sex: M. "So I checked
the second hit. This one here, that's you, Leigh Ann Ritch.
The first one has to be . . . well, your brother."

I snorted. "Plato, puh-leeze!"

"Nothing else computes. Same date, same parents. You,
good buddy, have a twin."

Flabbergasted, I dropped back onto my butt. "A twin? A
twin brother?"

His head bobbed up and down, unruly curls flopping in
all directions. "See for yourself. Here's the one I pulled up
first. Definitely a boy. It just didn't register."

"A twin brother," I said again, still unable to digest it. "What could have happened to him? As long as I can remember, there's been just me. Perhaps he died right after he was born." And perhaps Andy had been referring to the child my parents had lost, instead of one of her own and I'd misinterpreted it.

"Let me see what I can find." He began pounding the keyboard, fingers flying. I watched, completely mystified by what he was doing. Eventually, he shrugged. "Nothing. So he may be alive somewhere. No, he couldn't be. No Social Security number."

The name divulged no more hits.

As tempting as it was to let him pursue it further, I didn't want him to get sidetracked. "We'd better get back to my father."

"Yeah. Okay." He pursed his lips in thought. No finger wiggling this time. He stood, stretched, arms to the ceiling, lowered and shook them, then sat down, hard. I'd seen him go through this routine before. Plato was about to engage in what he called "some serious computing."

Several hours later in the darkest leg of the night, I left with a file folder that laid out what little he'd been able to find out about Wayne Warren Ritch. I had my father's date and place of birth, his parents' names and their address. Now all I had to do was locate the town in which they lived, which, to my astonishment, was in Maryland, just as Jameson had said. I would go there, introduce myself, explain my problem, and hope to hell they, one, believed that I was who I said I was, and two, had the medal. If they weren't receptive, I would have to improvise, but one way or the other, I'd do what I had to to free Nunna and Walter. I could only hope that in the process, I'd get to the bottom of a few other pieces of unfinished business—for instance, what had happened to my brother.

One way or the other, I had to find out whether my father had survived the fire and if he had, why he'd walked away, abandoning me, and leaving my mother to burn to death in that third-floor apartment, along with the poor unidentified stranger who'd died up there with her, wearing my dad's ring.

"Ourland? Where the hell is Ourland?" Duck, pacing the width of my living room, watched as I unpacked boxes in search of clothes I hadn't thought I'd need for a while. "I've checked every map I have. I've searched the maps on the Net. It doesn't exist."

"Then why," I asked, nibbling at the last bit of patience in my emotional larder, "are Dr. and Mrs. Wayne M. Ritch listed at an address there?"

"Maybe it's a typo." Janeece was perched in a lotus position on a stack of boxes I'd already finished raiding. "I mean, anything's possible. Search on my parents' address and the street is spelled wrong."

"Well, Plato's working on it. If anyone can find it, he can."

Duck, who had mixed feelings about my hacker friend, grunted. "Breaking how many laws in the process? All right, all right," he said, reacting to the dirty look I shot at him, "you had no choice. But I still say give the information to the feds and let them—"

"Do what?" I demanded, turning on him. "There is no kidnapping, remember? The feds think some friend of mine is laughing his fool head off over the practical joke he played on me. Even after they find out Jameson was in Sunrise, that probably won't be enough to convince them because they think Nunna and Walter are having a high old time on a South Carolina campground. Never mind that I know Nunna's voice when I hear it. Never mind that I know the kind of man Walter is. He wouldn't lie to the authorities to save his own life, but he damned sure would to save Nunna's."

"Then why not try to check out campgrounds down there first?" Duck asked. "There couldn't be that many. I mean, the island's not that big."

"Someone's doing that for me, a friend of Nunna's who lives in Sun City, near Hilton Head. She's contacting buddies all over the state to help her look. I gave her Walter's license plate number. And she's got sense enough not to do anything that'll put anybody in danger."

"Famous last words," Duck grumbled. "I still think—"

The ringing of the phone cut him off. We all froze, staring at it. Finally Janeece reached over to pick it up and extended it to me. I didn't breathe again until I heard Plato's voice.

"Bingo, again, Leigh! I found it! Well, sort of."

"What does sort of mean, Plato?" I asked, nudging a carton close enough to sit on. "Did you find Ourland or not? Where is it?"

Duck sprinted down the hall to my bedroom to pick up the extension.

"Well, that's the thing," Plato said. "I didn't find it on a map but I got a hit when I did a run of the mill search. It's a small black enclave south of Annapolis."

"You aren't talking about Highland Beach, are you?" I asked.

"No. This Web site mentions Highland Beach as being seven years older than Ourland, and points out the similarities between them, so we're talking about two different places."

I knew Highland Beach well enough, a residential community on the Chesapeake rich with African-American history. Founded by a son of Frederick Douglass, it claimed properties that had been passed down from one generation to the next for over a hundred years. If Ourland was close to the same size, that would simplify matters. The smaller the place, the easier it would be to find my grandparents. I stumbled over the thought, blown away by the novelty of the whole idea.

"Where exactly is it?" I asked Plato.

"Well, see, that's the problem. What I found was one of those 'This Is Our Family' type Web sites designed by an Amalie Ritch. Gotta be related to you somehow. She lives in Ourland, and put up a history of the place as one of her links. Pretty interesting stuff, actually. But she doesn't pinpoint the exact location."

"What's the URL?" I asked, grabbing a pad and pencil. I scribbled as he rattled it off and passed it to Janeece, who knew exactly what I wanted. She climbed off her perch and left to power up her laptop and printer.

I thanked Plato, and after promising to keep him informed, hung up.

Duck sauntered in from the bedroom, his body language betraying tension uncharacteristic of him. "So you're still going?"

I wrapped my arms around his waist and buried my nose in his shirtfront. "Duck, what's wrong? How can you even ask?"

He sighed, his forearms propped on my shoulders. "Because I can't help you, can't take leave to go with you, can't do squat. And I'm worried. There's no way to know what you're walking into. Your dad was estranged from his family and the letter from your cousin talks about how scared your mother was and the need to protect you. You yourself suggested that may have been the reason your father wasn't using his real name. His family may have been the problem."

"What, you figure they may be the black Mafia of the mid-Atlantic or something?" I asked, trying to inject a bit of humor into the moment.

Duck wasn't going for it. "I almost wish they were. Then your going would be out of the question. I had our people check their names in CIC, but nothing shows. Leigh, let's get married. Tomorrow. First thing in the morning."

"What?" I let him go, looked up at him in astonishment at this unexpected twist.

"We have the license and I can call in some favors, find someone who'd perform the ceremony downtown or wherever you want. Janeece can stand up for you and Eddie'll be my best man. Come on, Leigh. Why not?"

I nudged him away, not wanting to be touched. "You know why. I want Nunna there. She's my mother of the bride, and I want her with me in the room, wherever that is, when I get married." Easing off the box, I put some distance between us, searching for some logic for this turn of events. "Don't tell me you figure that if you became my husband tomorrow, you'd be able to tell me not to go to Ourland and I wouldn't."

His lips smiled, but his eyes didn't. "That big a fool I'm not. But I wish you wouldn't, honey. I wish you'd hire a PI to do this for you. I'd even foot the bill."

I'd considered it earlier today, for about two and an eighth seconds. "This involves family, Duck, family I didn't even know I had. Along with getting the medal, I want to meet them, find out why my father cut them out of his life, find out a lot of things. I have to go. I have to."

He regarded me soberly. "I know. I won't fight you on this. I have no right, considering what I put you through while I was searching for my dad. The thing is, it took me eight long years to admit how I felt about you. And I remember how empty I felt when we broke up. I'm scared. I don't want to lose you, Leigh. And I've got a bad feeling about this, really bad."

One of the annoying things about Dillon Upshur Kennedy was his hunches. He didn't have them that often, but I had never known him to be wrong. Never. He wasn't this time either.

8

THE ONLY REASON I LEFT LATER THAT MORNING knowing the general vicinity in which to look for Ourland was because of the link in the Web site Plato found. Even then, it took a bit of digging and improvising to fill in the gaps, since the history of the town, while colorful and informative about its origins, seemed intentionally vague about its location. Even reading between the lines, all we could determine was that it had been settled in 1900 by two black families of distant cousins, and was south of Annapolis on the Chesapeake Bay.

"The Chesapeake. Big wow," Janeece had grumbled. "I count twenty place names on this map between Annapolis and Point Lookout at the southernmost tip of the western shore. That doesn't include all the little towns too small to waste the ink. The Chesapeake, for God's sake."

Hit by a moment of inspiration, I blurted, "Waco. Waco Brockman!"

Duck's eyes glittered. "Smart girl," he said, grabbing Janeece's phone book. "He's on the bay in his boat every Sunday, knows it from one end to the other."

Waco, once Duck tracked him down, claimed the most he could contribute was a small café he'd seen from his boat. "The sign above the door says Ourland Eatery, but I haven't heard of a town with that name. Don't remember precisely where it is but it's about a block off the water."

So after an anxious night on Janeece's lumpy sofa, and a call to Mr. Sheriff to keep him up-to-date, I set off with Waco's general directions printed in twenty-four-point type. Two hours later I had blown a quarter of a tank of gas scouring eight communities along the shore. Turning east from Route 2 onto yet another road with no name, I headed in the general direction of a dot on the map called Umber Shores, promising myself that if this next community was a bust, I'd get a soda from somewhere, park as close to the water as I could, and eat the cheese and crackers I'd grabbed as an afterthought. The complaints from my empty stomach sounded like summer thunder.

The vista beyond my windshield was, however, anything but encouraging, since the only buildings along this route were the rusting corpses of a few small warehouses. From the looks of them, whatever businesses had used the corrugated buildings had either moved or gone belly-up years ago. At the end of the industrial area, trees closed in on the road, sort of a forest primeval, blocking the daylight and plunging the area into a dusk-dark gloom I found even more unsettling. I kept going, becoming more and more uneasy at finding no signs of human habitation back here and deciding that it might be a smart idea to turn around at the first opportunity. There was no way to do it on this narrow two-lane stretch without using the shoulders, both of which looked mud-soft and treacherous.

About then my cell phone chirped. I slowed, one eye on my rearview mirror as I dug the phone out of my bag, my heart banging against my rib cage. It was Janeece.

"Hey, girl," she said, sounding frazzled. "Forgot my stuff for aerobics and had to come back and get them. Any luck yet?"

"No. Eight towns down, a hundred more to go."

"I'll keep my fingers crossed. Lookit, I checked to see if you had any messages. Mrs. Franklin called from Sun City. No sign of the Airstream yet. Some of the old biddies are checking campgrounds, the others are calling motels to if Miss Nunna and Mr. Walter are registered. They're having a high old time playing detective." She ran down, out of breath. "Did you get all that?"

I told her I had and she was off the phone before I could thank her. I wasn't surprised that Mrs. Franklin and her friends had come up empty. Jameson might be a first-class nutcase but he was also smart. And now that he knew I'd called the authorities, he was certain to have changed the license plates on Walter's car. He may have even ditched the Airstream somewhere. I could only pray that he hadn't harmed Nunna or Walter to pay me back for being the good citizen.

I speeded up, anxious to find a spot to turn around, when without warning, my surroundings changed. The woods became sparse, allowing sunlight again. Directly ahead stretching toward the near horizon and framed by a vibrant palette of autumn-hued trees, a warm gray triangle of water shimmered beneath a clear blue sky. The bay. Hallelujah.

The road ended abruptly in a cul-de-sac, spokes branching onto residential streets, if the few roofs visible among the flame-bright trees were any indication. Directly in front of me now was an unobstructed view of the Chesapeake, the Bay Bridge off in the distance, so far away it resembled a mirage. The shoreline ahead was an expanse of a warm beige sand that seemed to fit perfectly with the autumn color scheme. A parade of piers jutted out over the water, dozens of gulls standing sentry on the railings.

To my right a small ramshackle house was set off the end of the cul-de-sac by itself, its weathered siding pockmarked with flaking paint, tiles missing from its roof. It wasn't until I started around the cul-de-sac that I spotted the pickup parked in back, Beedle's Roofing painted on the door. A rangy young man was maneuvering a ladder into position, the first sign of life I'd seen since leaving the highway.

Relieved, I eased over the crumbling curb onto solid ground and got out, leaving the engine running. "Excuse me," I called, "what is this place?"

He squinted at me. "Mary's," he said, as if surprised I didn't know. "You just gettin' here? You're kinda late for lunch. Everybody left for the exhibit hall maybe fifteen-twenty minutes ago."

"Excuse me?"

"If you've got a voucher that says lunch at the Ourland Eatery, you're too late." He grinned, a flash of white teeth against deep chocolate skin. "Mary's a stickler for folks being on time. You go in there, she's gonna take your head off."

I discarded all the unnecessary details he'd given me, including the fact that he thought I was part of some group or other, and homed in on the important.

"*This* is the Ourland Eatery?" I swiveled around to scrutinize the ramshackle edifice. People actually ate in there?

He grinned again. "Don't let its looks fool you. Mary lost her sign out front and half the roof, thanks to the last tropical storm. That's why I'm here. Nothing wrong with the inside, though. She still makes the best potato salad in Ourland. Parking lot's around back."

I couldn't believe it. I'd hit the mother lode. "Thanks," I called, got back under the wheel, and drove the car around behind the diner, grabbing my cheese crackers off the seat before getting out.

Opening the door of the diner, I stepped inside and

kicked myself in the fanny for judging books by covers. The exterior may have been a wreck but the inside was bright, worn but clean, and so redolent of the chicken roasting on a rotisserie behind the counter that I salivated on the spot.

The place was small, four booths and five diminutive tables, a half-dozen stools flanking the counter. Hand-printed menus were tacked to the wall in the booths. There wasn't a soul in sight.

"Hello?"

A door in the rear slammed open, whacking the wall behind it. "We're closed!" A burly woman of indiscriminate age with biceps like a Redskin defensive tackle burst in, forehead terraced with frown wrinkles. "Who the hell are you? Never mind, I don't want to know. If you're with the cultural heritage group, you're too late. It says right there on the schedule." She slapped a pamphlet on the counter. "Lunch eleven-thirty to twelve-thirty. And if you're selling something, I'm not buying, so am-scray."

I held up my hands in a gesture of surrender. "I'm sorry. I didn't realize you were closed. The door was unlocked."

"The door's always unlocked during the day." Just as I was about to explain that I was not with the cultural heritage group, she cut me off. "What's that you got?" She leaned over the counter, eyeing my cheese crackers with suspicion. "You swipe something from back of here?"

"No, no. I came in with these, honest. It's my lunch. I was hoping to get a soda or something."

"Oh," she said, subsiding, then looked vaguely insulted. "You call that lunch?" She hesitated, then jerked her head toward a stool. "Hell, might as well sit down. You'll have to make do with a sandwich. Ham salad, chicken salad, or tuna salad?"

I swallowed, mouth flooding again. "Chicken, please.

Uh—your roofer said you make the best potato salad in Ourland."

She made a face and turned away, but not before I'd caught a gleam of pleasure in her eyes. "I guess you're saying you want some of that too, huh?"

"Please."

Five minutes later, cheese crackers forgotten, I was ripping into the best damned chicken and potato salad I'd ever had, bar none, and said so.

She rolled her eyes. "I've made better. The name's Mary Castle."

I gave her my name and sacrificed one hand long enough to shake hers before getting back down to business, using it as a cover to figure out what I could learn from her.

She actually grinned. "You were hungry, huh? Enjoy. You know, you look familiar. Have you been around here before?"

With my mouth full, all I could do was shake my head, and moan in pure ecstasy, not purely for effect. This was very good food.

Evidently deciding such appreciation warranted a moment or two of her time, she came around and nabbed a stool, propping her massive forearms on the counter.

"I've never been to this part of the shore," I managed, feeling an obligation to be social. "It's beautiful, and so peaceful. I could park my butt on one of those piers and just sit all day. And," I added, seeking verification, "I don't even know where I am."

Mary chuckled. "Where you are depends on who you ask. Most call it Umber Shores, because of the color of our sand, don'tcha know. If you run into a Ritch—that's R-I-T-C-H, mind you—it's Ourland. 'Course, you aren't all that likely to run into a Ritch-with-a-T on this side of town."

"This place is big enough to have sides?"

"No, but they got 'em anyway, physical, philosophical, and social. Makes for interesting fireworks."

Stifling an urge to shout with joy that I'd reached my destination, and my grandparents were somewhere within spitting distance, I dedicated a few more minutes to the potato salad, gathering my thoughts. It would help to find out more about the place and its dynamics before bearding the Ritches in their den.

"So what's wrong with this side of town?" I asked. "I mean since you mentioned that I wouldn't run into the Ritches-with-a-T around here?"

"Well, I guess if you're with the cultural heritage bunch, you oughta get a true picture of the place. Nothing wrong with the town geographically. The Ritches tend to keep to themselves, is all. They live on the east side in their compound, don't associate much with the west siders unless it's business. The younger generation will come in here now and again. Neutral territory, as it were. But the sign on the post outside their gate says 'No Trespassing,' and by God, they mean it. Miss Elizabeth, she's the matriarch, don't take kindly to unexpected visitors and her sister, Miss Ruthie, has been known to take a potshot at you and ask which side you belong to later."

Which did not bode well, considering what I had to do.

"And you're a west sider?" I asked.

"Me? Uh-uh. It's where I live, but I've only been here fifteen years so that makes me an outsider. My say doesn't count and that's fine with me. As long as they eat my chicken and dumplings—"

"You make dumplings too?" I was momentarily distracted.

"—and whatever else is on the menu, they can go on not speaking to one another."

The Ourland history on the Web site, what there was of

it, had hinted at some sort of divisiveness in the town, but since all I'd wanted to know was where it was, I hadn't paid much attention to it. Evidently it was something to take seriously.

"What's the problem here?" I asked, chasing a bit of celery across the plate.

"Don't know and don't care." She snorted, her disgust evident. "Nobody talks about it. They may not even remember, it started so long ago. Whatever happened, they've been dragging their animosity around behind them ever since. Must have been pretty bad for the west siders to decide they didn't want to be known as Ourland anymore."

This was getting me nowhere. "Look," I said, deciding to lay it on the table, "I need to see the Ritch family about something important, and—"

Mary cut me off. "Important to you or important to them?"

"Well . . ."

"Elizabeth Ritch is only interested in advancing her own agenda, so if it doesn't benefit her, don't waste your time. The only people who get past that front gate are the black history and cultural heritage groups touring the town's oldest houses." She reached over and removed a brochure from a pile near the cash register. Scanning it, she nodded. "The next tour's tomorrow. If you can help her get her place onto the National Registry, she just might grant you a royal audience. Otherwise forget it. Where's your voucher? I gotta get dinner ready."

She had me. "I don't have one. How much do I owe you?"

Slipping off the stool, she wrote out a receipt. "Six-thirty. The registration material you'll get has vouchers for meals. Bring your lunch voucher back when you come for dinner and I'll refund your money."

She waited and watched while I dug seven-fifty from my wallet, then rang it up, pocketing the change.

"Which way to the Ritch house?" I asked.

Head tilted to one side, she stared at me. "You're serious, aren't you? Well, don't say I didn't warn you. Take North Star Road off the circle out there for about a half a mile, then the first right. You won't get any further than their gate. If you do, I hope you've got a bulletproof vest." With that, she departed for the kitchen.

As soon as she left I swiped a brochure and made tracks. I wasn't sure I'd need it, but just in case . . .

Driving through Umber Shores/Ourland was enlightening. The homes I could see through the trees ran the gamut—cabin-sized to large, decades old to newish A-frames, signs out front advertising the year of construction, several dating from the early 1900s. A slow-moving creek was visible behind a few, and most of the houses backing onto it, whether new or old, had private piers, boats secured to their pilings, everything from small runabouts to miniature yachts. In other words, money. To embrace this kind of serenity, one had to have a nice chunk of change to pay for it. And this is where my father had grown up? It had never occurred to me that I might have roots in the black bourgeoisie. I wasn't sure how I felt about that.

I almost missed the first right, since at first glance, it looked more like a driveway than a street. The sign, however, said "Ritch Road." I made the turn and prayed I wouldn't meet any oncoming traffic. There wasn't room for two of anything on four wheels going in opposite directions. There were a couple of pull-offs, just in case, but they all looked like places to get well and truly stuck.

The road wound through uninterrupted woods for so long that I was wondering how much farther I'd have to go when after rounding a deep bend, I found myself about to collide with an imposing wrought-iron gate at least six feet in height. I skidded to a halt, my front bumper a kiss away from wearing that elaborate grillwork like a cowcatcher.

After a moment to allow my heart to regain a more normal rhythm, I got out. A wrought-iron fence extended deep into the woods as far as I could see. The sign on the brick pillar to the left of the gate: "Ritch." Nice understated lettering embedded in the concrete cap. The sign on the right? "Private Property, No Trespassing." Big thick letters, all capitals. I guess they wanted to make certain you got the point.

Closing the car door, I went in search of a bell or intercom. Couldn't find it. There had to be something or how did the touring groups let someone know they'd arrived? The answer was provided by the gatehouse, easy to miss because it was brick, an extension of the pillar it sat behind. Its Dutch doors were closed. Terrific.

So I yelled. "Hello? Anyone in there?"

Silence.

I yelled a couple of more times, shook the locked gate in frustration. Same response. Shit, shit, shit. I surveyed the surroundings. I had to get beyond this gate.

The fence, perhaps seven feet in height, seemed more forbidding than the gate, which I might be able to scale, except I'd probably stab myself in the rear on the arrow-shaped thingamajigums on top. Perhaps the brick pillars were a better idea. After a moment for strategy and plotting, I returned to the car and with a heck of a lot of forward and reversing, managed to park it parallel to the fence, with the front just clear of the gate. They might get me for trespassing, but they wouldn't be able to accuse me of blocking the damned entrance.

I locked the car, looped the straps of my purse around

my neck, and climbed up onto the hood. Grateful that I'd worn slacks, I hauled, hoisted, and pulled myself up onto the cement cap atop the brick pillar. It was neither pretty nor ladylike, but I got up there. Stepping onto the roof of the gatehouse, I sat and scooted toward the edge. The ground seemed a long way down without the hood of a car under me. I rolled over, my bottom half dangling, positioned my hands at the roof's overhang, and slowly, the muscles of my arms trembling with strain, lowered myself to the ground.

Breathing as if I'd just run a four-minute mile, I leaned against the corner of the little brick enclosure, eyes closed for a few minutes as I tried to pull myself together. The trip over the fence must have been more demanding than I'd thought. It had affected my brain. I could swear I smelled peanut butter.

Once various body parts felt as if they'd function normally again, I stood up straight, opened my eyes, and found the barrel of a twelve-gauge shotgun an eighth of an inch from the end of my nose. The top half of the Dutch doors was open, the pungent aroma of peanut butter much more pervasive. Inside the gatehouse on the other end of the shotgun, the last of a sandwich disappearing into the corner of her mouth, was a white-haired, roly-poly old lady, hazel eyes aglitter with malice. She took a moment to swallow, then said, "Oh, goody. Haven't shot me a trespasser in a long, long time, but I'm gonna shoot me one today."

Now I've been on the receiving end on a bullet once. I've been aimed at and missed a couple of times. But there's nothing like having the barrel of a gun, no matter what kind, practically glued to the end of your nose to make you take the whole business seriously. I mean, the individual holding it is right there in your face, in this instance near enough that I could smell the peanut butter on her breath. Things can't get more up close and personal than that.

And I didn't even have the luxury of getting mad about it. Mary had warned me and if she hadn't, the sign outside the gate certainly had. I was trespassing and, therefore, dead meat unless I did some super-fast talking.

"Whoa!" I said, raising my hands in surrender. "Don't shoot, okay?"

She grinned. "Why not?"

"How about because I'm a really nice person who likes babies and animals and wouldn't ordinarily break the law but had to because the lives of two people who mean the world to me are depending on my speaking to Elizabeth Ritch. Is that you?"

She emitted a cackle. "You don't know when you're well off. If I'd been Lizzie, you'd be dead by now. I'm Ruth, her sister. You look familiar. Who are you, anyway?"

I took a deep breath, immensely relieved to be alive to do it. "My name is Leigh Warren. Elizabeth Ritch is my grandmother."

She didn't miss a beat. "Yeah, right. Sorry, dearie, you'll have to do better than that. No way is Lizzie your grandmother. Her daughter Beth lived right here until the day she died last year and she probably died a virgin. I'm eighty-two and have yet to see a star in the east, so you can't be Beth's child. Her other daughter, Rachel Ann, had a hysterectomy longer ago than you are old. Sorta rules you out there, too. That's it. So whose child do you claim to be?"

"Her son's. I'm Wayne's daughter, Wayne's and Margaret's."

That shut her up. Every bit of blood drained from her round face. She scanned my features intently and slowly,

slowly lowered the shotgun. She believed me. I saw it in her eyes.

But all she said was, "Oh, Lordy." No inflection. No hint of emotion.

"My parents died when I was five. And I need to talk to my grandmother as soon as possible."

"About what?"

"I need to retrieve a medal awarded to my father when he was in the military."

She tucked the shotgun in a corner of the gatehouse and said, "Forget it. In the first place Lizzie's not here and won't be back until late. In the second, I doubt seriously she has whatever you're talking about, and even if she had it, she wouldn't give it to you."

"Why?" I demanded.

"Because it was Warren's and you're his daughter. I'm sorry—Leigh, you said?—but you might as well hear it now. He was dead to Lizzie long before he died. She wiped him and any evidence of his existence out of her sight and out of her mind probably way before you were born. She hasn't mentioned his name since. My sister doesn't do things by halves."

"But why?" I asked again. "What did he do?"

She hesitated, her lips pressed into a straight line. "Well, I guess you have a right to know. Your daddy dear was a tomcat, romancing two women at the same time. One of them, Faye, must have issued an ultimatum. There was an argument. People heard them but couldn't figure out where their voices were coming from. She kept insisting that he marry her or else. The end result was that she jumped—or was pushed—from the church tower. However it happened, it split this town in two. That's why if you cross to the other side of North Star, you're not in Ourland anymore. As far as everyone's concerned, your father was a murderer, Leigh. He left a lot of devastation in his wake and Lizzie never forgave him for it."

"But—"

"Don't waste your breath," she said. "It makes no difference all this happened before you were born, you're Warren's and Margaret's child, and Lizzie's not going to see you. Anybody else around here know who you are?" I shook my head, in too much turmoil to respond. "Good. I'm gonna open that gate. I would advise you to take your fanny back wherever you came from before folks get curious about you. It's not as if the people behind this fence are the only ones Warren hurt so badly. There's Frances and Bonita. I don't know how they lived through it."

A strange emotional fatigue and despair had set in, to such an extent that it took a good deal of energy to ask, "Why? Who are they?"

She frowned. "You really don't know, do you? I guess it's not the kind of thing your parents would talk about over dinner." After a deep breath, she paused. "There were four of them. Frances, Bonita, Peg, and Faye, all bright girls, each prettier than the one before."

"Peg? My mother was from Ourland, too?"

"Of course! Faye was the youngest, a real stunner, and smart as a whip. She was the one Lizzie was counting on to be her daughter-in-law. And Faye was the one Warren took advantage of. Faye was the one found on the ground beneath the tower. That's right," she said, as the realization hit me between the eyes. "The woman whose life your father destroyed was your aunt, your mother's baby sister. And if Frances and Bonita have memories anywhere near as long as Lizzie's, you're about as welcome in this town as the plague."

9

I LEFT AND DID WHAT I USUALLY DO WHEN I'M TOO
zoned out to think straight. I drove, in this instance up and
down, in and out of the streets of Umber Shores, primarily
because I was in no shape to head for the highway again.
The fifteen-mile-an-hour speed limit was about all I could
handle.

I wound up back on the waterfront where I claimed a
few feet of a bench on one of the piers and just sat, letting
the breezes off the Chesapeake blow all the confused
thoughts from between my ears. The implications of what
I'd been told were devastating.

For as long as I could remember, I'd cherished the vague
images and memories of my parents. It had helped me con-
struct a picture of loving caring people. Was that a fairy
tale, the desperate fantasy of an orphaned child? Or was
the phantom memory of my father leaving the scene of the
fire rooted in a side of him I'd seen during my few years
with him, a side I'd chosen to forget?

I listened to the voices of Jenky, of Casper and Grace in
my head, heard the affection in their intonations as they'd
talked about my parents. They'd been neighbors, close
friends. Casper had worn a badge, and cops were good at
sizing up people. Their lives depended on it. He'd recognized that there were areas of my father's life that were off-

limits, but he'd still liked him, appeared to have trusted him. So who was I going to believe?

But as important as that was to me, it had to take a back-seat to my reason for being here. I had to talk to my grandmother, find out once and for all whether she had the medal. Nothing Ruth said had changed that. There was only one way into that house to see Elizabeth Ritch without getting shot: tag along with the cultural heritage folks. I spent a few minutes looking over the brochure I'd swiped from the diner, relieved to see that this wasn't a formal organization after all. Twice a week Ourland opened its doors to those interested in tracing their roots and researching historical sites attributed to African Americans. That made it easier for me. I could pass myself off as someone who'd just boarded the cultural heritage train. Time to get moving.

The rhythmic sound of nails being pounded had been an intrusive undercurrent to the whisper of wind and the slap of bay water against the pilings. The roofer was still at work. Walking to the diner, I stood back far enough for him to see me.

"Hi up there," I called.

He peered down, shading his eyes against the blinding sunlight. "Yes, ma'am?"

"Where did you say the black cultural heritage group was meeting?"

"You haven't found them yet? Exhibit hall. Straight up North Star just the other side of Market. You can't miss it. It's the only building with a bell tower."

I thanked him and made my way to my car, wondering if it was the same tower from which my Aunt Faye had jumped. Or was pushed, as Ruth had so blatantly suggested. That would be one of the drawbacks in dealing with a town of this size. Everywhere I turned I'd be running into a piece of my family's tainted history. If it colored their view of everything they did, that was their problem. I was determined not to make it mine.

Finding the exhibit hall meant retracing part of the route I'd taken to get to Ritch Road. A Land Rover, only the third vehicle I'd encountered since my arrival, approached, its signal blinking, its nose veering right into my path as the driver began the turn onto Ritch. His focus appeared to be on something on the passenger seat, certainly not on where he was going. In other words, he was about to T-bone me.

He glanced up at the last minute, just as I slammed on my brakes and hit the horn. His reflexes were good, thank God. He braked too, stopping with perhaps the depth of a bird dropping between us. He pantomimed flicking sweat from his brow and mouthed "Sorry." He completed the turn, slowed for a second to extend an arm from the window and wave, an additional apology, I assume. Then he was gone, swallowed up among the trees. I slumped in my seat, wrestling with a case of bloodred road rage. If that idiot had hit me, I'd have been out of commission indefinitely. As crazy as Jameson must be, Lord knows how he'd have reacted. My legs were still shaking when I finally got under way again.

The residential section was interrupted by one long block of commercial establishments, stop signs at each end of it serving as the beginning and end of Market Street, after which it became North Star again. I cataloged businesses as I passed, seeing everything from a barber and beauty shop to a fitness center and a lot in between. From all appearances, the community need not go beyond town limits for run-of-the-mill supplies. Unless the year-round population was larger than I'd thought, I found it surprising that these businesses could survive.

The roofer was right; there was no way to miss the exhibit hall. It sat on the corner where Market ended and North Star resumed, a white clapboard edifice that had started life as a church in 1902. I parked out front, opened the double doors to the foyer, and was immediately assailed by that close, faintly musty smell characteristic of old, old wooden buildings. There wasn't a soul in sight, so I picked up a registration form from a bow-legged mahogany table to see how much this business would cost me. Seventy-five dollars?

I blanched, appalled, until I saw that this included a room for a night, two lunches, dinner tonight and breakfast tomorrow. But when I'd left home, it hadn't occurred to me I'd be away overnight. If I went back to D.C. for a change of clothes, I'd be looking at a good two-plus hours' round trip. I would also have to face Duck, who would argue against my returning, and I was in no mood to listen. I'd seen a dress shop in the business section. If I could get a change of underwear and perhaps another top for tomorrow, I could survive. I filled out the registration form and a check, then wondered what to do with it since there was no one to take it.

Just then a tiny little woman burst through the doors from the inner sanctum, eyes wide when she spotted me. "Lord, child, I didn't know anyone was here. Your mom's—" She stopped, looked confused. "I'm sorry. I thought you were someone else. May I help you?"

I explained why I was there and that I was so late, I wasn't certain I'd be allowed to join.

She chuckled, her face clearing a little. "Anybody's welcome, but you just missed lunch. I'll need to see a driver's license," she said, looking over my check, then added, "Oh, dear. You've paid enough for a room but the boardinghouse where everyone else is staying is full. You'll have to stay at the Shores Inn outside town, assuming they have a vacancy."

She began jotting down the number of my license, taking one long, last look at the photo before returning it to me. "Do you have any kinfolk here? I declare, you favor a couple of people I could name."

"Well," I said, smiling, "you know what they say, that we all look alike."

She chuckled. "In this case, there's more than a grain of truth there. You go join the others and I'll check the motel for you. It isn't fancy, but it's clean and the service is good. Here's your registration packet and meal vouchers."

She handed me a navy folder full of pamphlets and lists of resources—genealogical societies, Web sites, lists of African-American communities to be researched. I took a badge, wrote my name on it, slapped it to my breast pocket, and pushed through the double doors to the sanctuary.

It spoke of simpler times. No stained glass windows, just double-hung six over six. No decorative elements or religious symbols, just plain white walls that served as the background for poster boards filled top to bottom with Ourland/Umber Shores family trees and photographs. A long utility table stood against the rear wall, with urns of coffee and hot water, and plates containing crumbs. A stray chocolate chip on the plastic tablecloth was the only clue to cookies long gone.

Watching my approach were a dozen people, the youngest probably in her mid-teens, the others twenty to eighty, two of them of the Caucasian persuasion, sitting in a circle and chatting with animation, coffee cups and paper plates balanced on their knees. Apparently their common interest and the few hours they'd spent together today had been enough to help them bond. I grabbed a chair from the stack in the corner and joined the circle, momentarily interrupting their conversations and feeling like an interloper.

But the blue folder under my arm was all the invitation I needed. The fact that I had come made me welcome. Most were deeply into genealogy. I felt vaguely hypocritical since after my conversation with Ruth, I had little interest in Ourland or the branches of my family tree. But these people were serious. Most had been at it for years.

Things went fairly smoothly until I was asked to explain how I'd become interested in researching African-American history. After thinking fast, I began my explanation with what I felt was a lie, then realized that it was anything but.

"I'm getting married next month," I said, "and if I'm fortunate enough to have children, I want them to know from whence they came, so to speak, show them how rich our heritage is."

Mrs. Lawrence, who called herself the facilitator, and had the demeanor of a first grade teacher, beamed at me as if I was her prized pupil. "Excellent, Leigh. You've come to the right place. Now, class—I mean, friends—this is free time until dinner at the Eatery promptly at six. Leigh, some of us are driving up to Highland Beach to the Frederick Douglass Museum, if you'd like to join us."

I hated to leave the group so early in the game, but I'd been there before, and I had to check on my room for the night and buy the change of undies for tomorrow. I agreed to meet them at the Eatery. But the little woman who'd promised to call the motel was nowhere to be found. I decided to give her a few minutes and use the time to get a good look at the exhibits.

The displays were cleverly done, amounting to a history of Ourland/Umber Shores sans narrative. There were ten family trees, many names appearing on more than one

since there'd been a lot of intermarriage. If the original set-
tlers had been cousins, I hoped someone had kept track of
how closely related some of these unions had been or the
resulting children must have had interesting problems.

The photographs were fascinating, a few dating back to
the turn of the twentieth century, a tintype quality to them.
The poses were stiff and formal, the garb their Sunday
finest, solemn dark gazes riveted on the camera. Toward
the late thirties, the clothes became less dressy, attitudes
more natural. Family groupings grew as generation after
generation was added to the photos and as other faces
aged, then disappeared. The final space on the extreme
right end was filled with pictures of previous summer gath-
erings taken at the beginning of each decade starting in
1940. And at the bottom, centered under the panels, long
enough to extend beneath six of them, was a panoramic
shot of all the families together taken in the summer of
2000. So they'd obviously managed to bury the hatchet for
this one occasion every ten years.

I walked back to the Rich family tree and found my
mother's name and those of her sisters. Frances was the
oldest, my mother the third of the four, all born two years
apart. I pulled out the complimentary lined pad and copied
the information from my mother's—and my, I reminded
myself—family tree, bemused by the number of names
straight out of the Bible and almost choked on a great-
great-great uncle named Deuteronomy. That trend appeared to have petered out by the forties, replaced by film
stars of the era. Certainly my mother and aunts fell into
that category.

One panel over from the family tree the Rich photos
were displayed. I searched for and found Mom's face and
those of her sisters. Ruth had been right; they had been very
attractive young women, all on the pale end of the tan color

chart, my mother the lightest, Faye the darkest, but not by much. Someone had written "The Four-in-Ones" across the corner of one of the shots and its meaning was clear. There was no mistaking their sisterhood, neither in their features and hair, nor in the attitudes caught by the camera. They were always together, stairsteps in height, arms around shoulders, waists, or necks; in a couple, fingers entwined, their physical proximity to one another revealing how close they'd been from their earliest ages on up.

There were no photos of them after the mid-sixties, only those of other branches of the Rich family. It was as if all four of the Rich girls had simply disappeared. This alone was testament to the damage my father had allegedly done. The Four-in-Ones had been no more.

It was time to deal with the Ritches-with-a-T, who'd apparently taken "Be fruitful and multiply" seriously during the earlier generations. There'd been no fewer than nine children on each limb and those who'd lived to adulthood had been prolific as well, begatting between six and ten offspring. Evidently I was up to my yin-yang with cousins. No wonder the Ritch compound consumed a good half of the acreage around here.

I worked my way down from top to those born in the thirties. My father had been one of six, three of which had died in infancy. That was all there was of him on the tree. Just his name and date of birth. Wayne Warren Ritch. August 1, 1938. No wife. No children. So what was I? Chopped liver?

Dutifully, I copied the names of my grandparents and those who had come before. At least there were no more Deuteronomies, just a bumper crop of Waynes in each generation and one Waynetta, named for my great-great-granddaddy. Then, sidestepping to the adjoining panel, I found my father's pictures, a little surprised that they were still there. There weren't many, and it took some hunting to find him among all the rest of the Ritches his age, the majority of them boys. He was never alone, always captured with other children and young people, whether sisters or cousins, I couldn't be sure.

The last photo in which my father appeared was one taken at his high school graduation. He and a dozen others in white caps and gowns posed with wide grins under a banner that read "Ourland Academy, Class of 1956." I was longing for a magnifying glass when I felt the hairs at the nape of my neck begin to twitch. I was not alone.

I swiveled around. The room was empty. One of the double doors to the foyer, however, moved gently back and forth on its hinges. Relieved that the registrar had returned, I retrieved my purse from the floor and went out to the foyer. Empty. No registrar. Nothing. Correction, not quite nothing. An aroma lingered in the air, an additional scent overlaying that of Essence of Old Building. Tobacco.

More accurately, Dutch Treasure pipe tobacco, a brand to which I'd reacted badly years before. I'd been a freshman at Howard University in D.C., in conference with a faculty adviser. He'd come in from the hall, the aroma of his pipe tobacco a miasma surrounding him like an aura. A tin of it sat on his desk and he'd packed his pipe while we talked. The smell of it had made my stomach churn. I'd barely managed to sit through our meeting without throwing up.

I remembered it distinctly because I couldn't understand why it had affected me in that manner. I'd been around pipe smokers before, our next-door neighbor in Sunrise, for one, my hometown best friend, Sheryl's, father as well. Walter had smoked a pipe until Nunna had told him she wasn't about to marry any man dumb enough to suck on burning weeds. Yet none of those had made me feel sick. It was this one particular brand and a fleeting association with someone I'd known at some point. Someone . . . not nice. Unpleasant. I couldn't remember who it was then and couldn't now. Even as I stood there thinking about it, the odor weakened and was gone.

I opened the front doors and looked outside. There were a few pedestrians on Market in the next block, all female. The only car in the immediate vicinity was mine and none was starting up nearby. Yet someone, a male, had just left, I was certain of it. I darted in the little alcove off the foyer that served as a coatroom and catchall. Nothing there other than a coat rack with metal hangers and several boxes of brochures and lined pads.

The coat rack blocked a door. Access to the infamous bell tower? I peered at the old-fashioned doorknob. Undisturbed dust, no fingerprints or smudges. Whoever had looked in at me seemed to have disappeared in a puff of smoke. Literally. But he had been there. My instincts told me so. Those same instincts had kept me alive as a cop so I was not about to ignore them now. It was time to get out of there. I got.

Shopping turned out to be easy. The selection of underwear in the little dress shop on Market was limited but since I wasn't interested in raise-his-temperature skimpies, what they had was fine. I bought a winter-white turtleneck to wear the next day and, succumbing to an impulse uncharacteristic of me, asked them to hold a black and teal sweat suit until I could check my bank balance. Promising to pick it up before they closed this evening or before noon tomorrow at the latest, I left.

From there I found my way to the Shores Inn, which turned out to be a charmer, small, intimate, with none of the cookie-cutter appearance of national chains, the decor somewhere between country-cute and nautical. It was clearly a family-run enterprise, with photos of sepia-toned parents and children adorning the mantel of a working fireplace in the lobby, some I thought I'd seen in the exhibit hall. The youngster behind the desk, one of the faces beaming from the mantel, appeared to be young enough to put a strain on Maryland's child labor laws.

To my relief, she was expecting me, and after overseeing my registration, handed me the keys to number two in the Chesapeake Wing, on the ground floor nearest the lobby. It was simple, clean, with a pink and sea green color scheme and wallpaper chock-a-block with seashells. Sandpipers scurried across the bathroom tile. No doubt about it; they wanted you to know the bay was nearby.

I freshened up and, tired of the growing ache in my left shoulder, dumped all but necessities from my purse, eliminating several pounds of weight, including the tacky vinyl case full of photos and my two credit cards. The latter I slipped into my wallet.

I still had a couple of hours before dinner, so I called the banking line, checked my balances, and transferred the cost of the sweat suit from my savings account. Next I left carefully worded messages for Duck and Janeece, letting them know I'd be gone overnight but omitting the phone number of the motel. With Duck in his knight-in-shining-armor mode, he might just show up. If either of them needed me, they could reach me on my cellular. As could Jameson.

I stretched across the bed to concoct a strategy for my confrontation with Elizabeth Ritch tomorrow, and woke up with a squawk of horror an hour and a forty-five minutes later. I had to hustle to get to the diner on time and arrived just as the rest of the group were being seated. The rush was worth it, the evening meal fantastic: a savory bouillabaisse with the biggest mussels I'd ever seen, a fresh green salad with homemade dressing and rolls the size of a compact disc. Dessert and coffee, it was announced, were waiting for us back at the exhibit hall.

Mary Castle shanghaied me as I was about to leave. "You owe me a voucher for lunch today and I owe you a refund," she said, rather more loudly than I thought warranted. "Need to talk to you," she added under her breath.

She waited until the others had left and nudged me toward an empty table in the corner. "How'd you make out at the Ritches?" she asked softly.

"Almost got shot. I hopped the fence."

"You didn't." Incredulous, she looked at me with new respect. "After I warned you?"

"Ruth Ritch caught me and booted me out. So I'm going back tomorrow for the tour. I've got to talk to Elizabeth."

"Well, that explains whose ass you stuck the burr up," Mary said, arms folded across her chest. "See, if you're back there at a certain spot in the kitchen, you catch practically everything said by whoever's at that corner table over there whether you want to or not. I heard a couple of guys talking. One was describing a woman in your group and you're the only one it fits. He was saying he thought he recognized you and if he was right, you meant trouble. I had several orders backed up and by the time I was free, they were gone. My nephew's waiting tables, but he's new in town and didn't know them. Lemme give you your refund before I forget." She barreled her way to the cash register.

"I'm not here to make trouble," I said, following with the voucher from the registration material. "All I want is to talk to Elizabeth Ritch and leave with what I came here for."

"It ain't money, is it?" Her brown eyes bored a hole through me.

"No. Look, Mary, you might as well know. I'm Elizabeth Ritch's granddaughter."

The astonishment on her face was almost comical. "Get outta here!"

"I hope to by tomorrow. She may have a medal awarded to my father in Vietnam. I need it. I've got to have it. That's all I want from her."

"Well, if that don't beat all," she said, taking inventory of my features. "You sure as hell were a deep, dark secret. I bet that guy figures you're some distant relation come to demand a piece of the Ritch family pie. They got plenty of money, most of it in land. It wouldn't be the first time things got nasty over which plat belonged to which member of the family. And that compound of theirs is worth millions. They ain't likely to parcel off a sliver to somebody's love child without a fight."

Temper tugged at the reins. "I'm a love child all right, I just also happen to be legitimate. My father was the only son of Wayne and Elizabeth Ritch, and he and my mother were well and truly married. I'm not interested in their money, their land, or in establishing any family ties. All I want is the medal and I'm outta here."

Mary removed money from the till, minus the tip, placing each bill and coin in my hand as if I thought she might cheat me. "Well, I hope you get it. And I'll keep what you've told me to myself. Nobody's business but yours. But you be careful. These people take family matters seriously."

So did I. And the only family I cared about were Nunna and Walter.

Back at the exhibit hall, everyone was clustered around Hal, a law clerk in the group who'd brought his laptop and a portable printer, and was demonstrating all the bells and whistles in a new genealogy software package. I watched for a while, then drifted to the exhibits again, feasting on photos of my mother instead of German chocolate cake and vanilla ice cream.

It wasn't long before I'd reached my limit. There were only two choices here: hover around the family trees and people I'd never get to know, or hover around Hal and his laptop with the others. In no mood for either, I decided to call it a night, begging off with the universal cop-out: a headache. I had to be prepared for every possible scenario that might crop up tomorrow when I'd meet Elizabeth Ritch and I couldn't plan for it here. And the dress shop would close in a few minutes.

The group was so engrossed in Hal's demonstration, I doubt my goodnight even registered.

Once outside, however, I changed my mind about picking up the sweat suit. An ambulance, a couple of police cruisers and an attendant crowd of onlookers blocked the middle of Market. It was hard to tell what had happened and I didn't want to know. I went back to the motel.

To my surprise, the parking lot at the Shores Inn was full. A sign dangled in the window of the lobby. "Welcome A-Phi-A!" That stopped me cold. Duck was an Alpha. Was this a frat meeting Duck would normally be attending? Was that sneaky bastard waiting for me in my room?

I unlocked the door, went through it as if serving a search warrant. No Duck. I pulled the first half of one great sigh of relief, my breath snagging on the exhale. Backing toward the door, I sniffed twice, three times. I could have sworn I'd caught a whiff of that damned pipe tobacco again. I didn't smell it now. Still, before I closed the door to the parking lot, I checked the bathroom. No particular odor there, just the same sandpipers skittering atop the tiles. Feeling silly, I shut and locked myself in, got rid of my shoes, and turned on the hot water in the tub. While it filled, I stripped, removed the labels from tomorrow's sweater, opened the top drawer of the dresser for the comb. And stopped breathing. Again.

Someone had been in the drawer. Not that I'd arranged things so neatly that I could detect if something had been moved so much as an inch, but I distinctly remembered closing and engaging the snap of the tacky vinyl case from which I'd removed my credit cards. It was now open. And it wasn't so full of pictures and business cards that the clasp would come undone by itself.

Using a pencil, I flipped through the plastic sleeves one by one. Library card, photos of Duck, Nunna, Nunna and Walter, Duck's sister with her husband and daughter, Tyler. Voter registration card, union card. Everything seemed untouched but I would expect them to be. There'd been nothing of value left in it.

At the last sleeve, I had to revise my opinion. Something was missing after all: the only decent photo of myself I felt comfortable enough to carry, and the snapshots Jenky had given me of my mother, and my father holding me on his shoulders. They'd been loose, tucked in back until I could get copies of them.

I checked a second time, but there was no need. Wayne, Margaret, and Leigh Ann Warren were gone.

"I swear to you, Ms. Warren, the only people who can get into the rooms are the housekeeping staff—my mom and two of her sisters." The poor kid at the registration desk, tears streaming down her cheeks, seemed to be taking the theft personally. "And the manager, of course, my cousin Jon. Oh, and Uncle Pete, he's maintenance, but he's . . ."

She hesitated, but evidently couldn't think fast enough to come up with a lie. "He's in the hospital, drying out. Mom and my aunts left at six."

"Who takes care of security?" I asked gently.

"Uncle Kevin's company rents out guards and we use one of them. He patrols the parking lot, but he doesn't have a key to the rooms. If something comes up and he needs one, he has to get it from whoever's working the front desk. And he hasn't tonight."

Jon, the cousin/manager/temporary maintenance man was working the cash bar for the Alphas' meeting, and had been overseeing the kitchen staff since four. Alerted about the theft, he dashed into the lobby and skidded to a stop at the counter.

"Trina, honey, stop blubbering, okay? I'll handle this." He turned to me, and in the blink of an eye lost the mantle of concerned family member and slipped into the role of manager.

"Jon Ritch," he said smoothly and extended a hand. "You are . . ."

"Leigh Warren. I'm in room two, Chesapeake Wing. Are you a Rich like rolling in money or Ritch-with-a-T?" As if it mattered. Either way he was a cousin.

He grinned, and dimples appeared. "You've been in Ourland, or perhaps Umber Shores. Or both. And I'm both too, technically speaking. My dad's a Ritch-with-a-T but I've got a double-great-uncle who was a Rich-without-a-T. Let me take a look at your room," he said, and with a hand on my elbow, led me from the lobby to the Chesapeake wing.

Something told me he was good at his job. Easy to look at too, a little over six feet; a cocoa complexion under dark, curly hair, and a slash of smooth black brows over deep-set brown eyes. And a plain gold band, ring finger, left hand. Not that I was interested, I assured myself.

"Door looks okay," he said, examining the lock and the frame with a penlight.

"There's no evidence it was jimmied," I said. "I just spent the last seven years wearing a badge," I explained, "so you'll have to forgive me if I lapse into cop-speak."

He backed up a step, surprised. And alarmed? I asked myself. I detected a tension that hadn't been there before. "Terrific. Your being with the police, I mean. I hope you won't be insulted if I ask if there's any chance you might not have closed this securely when you left."

Smooth, I thought. "Not at all. I closed it and checked to be sure it was locked. It's habit. Whoever came in used a key."

He sobered even more, a tautness working its way around his mouth. "Or picked the lock," he said tersely. "He—or she—couldn't have used one of our keys. Definitely not." He shook his head, as if to punctuate the point. "We keep rigid control over our keys. And our track record is a hell of a lot better than most. There have only been two break-ins since we took over from the previous owner and in both cases, the doors were jimmied. Let's go in."

He removed a key from his pocket. "Skeleton," he said, shoving it into the lock. Pushing the door open, he restrained me with one arm, then stepped inside. I'd left the lights on. "Well, at least he didn't trash the room." As I'd done moments before, he checked the bathroom. "Okay in here too. So, what was taken?"

"Three photographs from my card case," I said, crossing to the dresser drawer, still open.

"Three . . . Are you kidding me?" He stared at me, incredulous. "Just pictures? No money or credit cards?"

I turned to face him. "I'd taken the credit cards out of the case before I left. And under other circumstances, I might not have realized the pictures were gone. But I'd closed the thing after I removed the credit cards. One was a picture of myself and I'd only had the other two a few days. They were important to me, irreplaceable, the only photos I had of my parents."

Stressed as I was, I might have imagined it, but I could swear I saw something flash in his eyes, a nanosecond's betrayal of a new awareness. "Your parents," he said.

"Yes. They died in a fire when I was a kid. There was nothing left. A neighbor who'd known us back then happened to have pictures of them and she let me borrow them day before yesterday. I put them in the card case and now they're not there. And by the way, I could swear I detected the odor of pipe tobacco when I first opened the door."

He stood there for a moment, forehead ridged with a frown, gaze fixed on me but definitely not seeing me. "I don't get it. Why would . . . ?" He shook his head. "Well, guess we'd better report this."

At that, I stopped to think, knowing firsthand how the local constabulary would feel about having their time tied up and writing a report on the theft of three photographs and nothing else. It would have been worth the aggravation to me, but not to them. They might even go so far as to dust for prints if I insisted and question anyone with access to the rooms, but I doubted it would do much good. Anyone with half a brain would have used gloves. So to Jon Ritch's relief, I told him to forget it. Something in the air, however, told me he would not.

Even with a chair wedged against the door of the room, I spent a restless night, weighed down under an information overload and trying unsuccessfully to prevent it from blurring my focus. I could follow up on what I'd learned about my parents any time. It was imperative that I keep my goal in mind. Things would have been so much simpler if any Silver Star would do, but the bent arm Jameson had described made that impossible. Even if I could get my hands on one, there was no way to know which arm had been mangled in the accident he'd described. I finally dropped off after three and dreamed of searching for Nunna through a suffocating fog of pipe tobacco. I'd fought my way through it and had her in my sights when the sound of the phone filtered through and woke me.

I squinted at the clock radio, so disoriented that I wasn't certain whether it was four-thirty in the morning or afternoon. Groping for the phone, I sat up, cleared my throat, and answered.

The voice that responded woke me completely. Male, I thought, but I couldn't be sure.

"This is the only warning you're gonna get. Go back where you came from or else."

10

THE CALL, WHICH SUCCESSFULLY RUINED ANY chance that I could go back to sleep, gave additional weight to Mary Castle's warning, I mused, as I sat in the exhibit hall later, unable to focus on the discussion of the parallels between Highland Beach, where they'd gone the day before, and Ourland.

My appearance in this town had upset somebody's applecart. I just wasn't sure why. The fact that I was the granddaughter of Wayne and Elizabeth Ritch was not common knowledge. Even if it were, it might keep tongues wagging for a while but that's about all it was worth.

Granted also, my presence might tickle the memory of a few old-timers and dredge up a rehash of the death of my Aunt Faye, but I was thirty-two. Aunt Faye had died before my parents were married. How many people here then were still around? And aside from the immediate families involved, why should anyone else give a kitty? I was stumped, but I was also on the alert. Anyone so curious about me that they'd invade my room and swipe snapshots of me and my parents—

My thoughts screeched to a halt. Was that the purpose of the theft, to get rid of any proof that I was the daughter of Wayne and Margaret Ritch? Possible. If that had been the motive, the dummy had failed. I had the printouts Plato had made for me. Or did I?

I grabbed the manila folder from my purse. It had been in the drawer last night, but it hadn't occurred to me to check it. Flipping through the sheets, my stomach dropped into a black hole. The information on my birth, the data on my father, was gone.

"Something wrong?" Mr. Brinkley, an elderly flirt, leaned forward, in danger of losing the plate of melon slices on his lap.

"Just realized I lost something." I took a few deep breaths to calm down. Plato could always pull together another set. But the goal of the thief was now clear. It would be a hell of a lot more difficult to prove my heritage without those sheets in hand. And I didn't have time to go back to D.C. If I did, I'd miss the tour scheduled to begin in an hour. And I'd already learned the folly of hopping fences. I'd have to bull my way through the encounter to come.

Whatever appetite I'd had was gone. I nibbled on a corn muffin, drank orange juice and coffee, and downed a couple of aspirin to calm the headache—a real one—I felt hovering around the edges. I poured myself another cup of coffee and grimaced when I saw that the container of creamer was empty. This amounted to a major crisis. Black coffee did unpleasant things to my GI tract.

"They probably got some in the kitchen back there," Mr. Brinkley said, pouring himself a refill. "Through that door there. See if they got any muffins left. Those are some good muffins." He plopped an ample rear end on a chair.

Accepting the role of creamer and muffin retriever with good grace, I placed a lid on my cup and stashed it behind the urn. The kitchen was through a door to the left of the dais, a recent addition, from the looks of it, squeezed into a hallway that led to a rear exit. The aroma of baked goods still lingered in the air.

There was a phone on the wall next to the back door, which reminded me that I should check in with the dress shop. With the business card the sales clerk had given me in hand, I called, got an answering machine, and left a message saying I'd be in today and hung up, hoping that would satisfy them.

Checking the tiny refrigerator under the counter was an exercise in futility. Soft drinks, spring water, orange juice, but no creamer. I opened an overhead cabinet in hopes of finding some of the powdered stuff. No luck there either but a big box from a bakery yielded one big blueberry muffin still faintly warm and smelling heavenly.

All the blueberry muffins had been snatched up by the time I'd gotten to the breakfast buffet table. Temptation cavorted behind my eyes. I could stash the thing in a purse and Mr. Brinkley would never know. But I would. Feeling martyred, I snatched a paper towel from the roll above the sink and set the muffin on it. I was opening the lower cabinets in search of the trash can for the empty box when someone bumped against the back door. Reacting like a kid caught with the cookie jar, I closed the cabinet and grabbed the muffin, about to beat a hasty retreat into the sanctuary when I heard the door open.

"Tracy Leigh Hanover! What are you doing here? The doctor said—"

I turned around. An attractive woman, middle-aged at a guess, stood one foot inside, one outside, her arms cradling an enormous gift basket of fruit. She stared at me. "You. Aren't. Tracy."

"Uh—no." I wasn't certain of the reason for the gap between words, but figured she deserved a response. "I hope you don't mind my rifling the kitchen, but—"

"Who are you?" she cut me off and stepped inside. Her eyes, an intriguing shade of dark gray, had widened to the size of the pilfered muffin. There was something familiar about her. I'd probably seen her picture in the exhibit hall somewhere.

"Leigh Warren," I said. "I'm with the cultural heritage group. We ran out of creamer—"

"No. I mean, who are your people? Your parents." She sounded winded, as if she'd just run a race.

I hesitated, but no matter the consequences, I would not deny my parents. "My mother's name was Margaret," I said. "Margaret Anderson Rich. My father—"

The basket of fruit slipped from her arms and she hit the floor as if poleaxed, out cold.

I tossed the muffin on the counter and, dodging apples and oranges caroming off one another like balls on a pool table, knelt beside the woman and felt for a pulse. It was regular and strong and she appeared to have no trouble breathing. Scratch a coronary. Perhaps a stroke?

I peeled back an eyelid. She slapped at my hand and said, "Stop that." With a groan, she sat up, her back against the door, and shook her head. "Brother! Haven't done that in a coon's age. What—?" She blinked, then focused on me. "Oh, my God. Peg's daughter. I don't believe it." She tucked a finger under my chin, turned my face to the side, and chuckled, even as tears glistened in her eyes. "You're a Rich, no doubt about that. You and my daughter are built just alike. Look at the two of you from the back and I wouldn't be able to tell which was which. I'm your Aunt Bonita, by the way. We had no idea Peg had had a child. How in the world did you find us?"

I hated to burst her balloon, but there was no point in lying. "To be honest, I was searching for my father's family. I didn't realize that my mother came from Ourland until yesterday. So meeting you is a bonus I hadn't anticipated."

"Peg's dead, isn't she?" she asked abruptly.

The question brought me up short. "She and my father died twenty-seven years ago. I guess I thought you knew."

"I knew it in here," she said, palm to her chest. "We'd have heard from her otherwise. Twenty-seven years ago? Warren too?"

"In a fire."

She closed her eyes, her face a mask of grief. "Oh, my God. Poor Peg." She pulled herself together with effort. "Well. At least you survived. You must have been just a baby. How old are you? Wait. Help me up. There's no point in your having to tell everything twice. You might as well come meet your Aunt Frances and get it over with."

I didn't particularly care for the way she'd phrased that but there were more pressing concerns. "I'll have to come back," I said, helping her to her feet. "The tour of homes begins in a few minutes and it's important that I go."

"That's easy enough to fix. Do me a favor and pick up this fruit while I tell Rowena to wait for you." She strode from the kitchen, clearly recovered.

I rescued the apples and oranges, dumped them in one side of the double sink and rinsed them off. After drying my hands, I retrieved the blueberry muffin and took it out to Mr. Brinkley. Up on the dais, my aunt and Mrs. Lawrence were engaged in an animated discussion, which ended when the latter spotted me and gawked until Aunt Bonita reached up and closed the woman's mouth for her.

"We won't be long, I promise," she said, and with one hand extended toward me, stepped off the dais. "Come on, child."

She sounded just like Nunna. I followed her through the kitchen and out the back door.

"How far are we going?" I asked.

"Right here," she said, leading me across the rear yard of a small white house next door. "Frannie just dropped by, but she lives in the old home place down on the bay. This is mine. Raised four kids and a lot of dogs and cats under this roof. Frannie!" she called, opening the screen door and towing me across the back porch to the entrance to her kitchen.

"What are you yelling about?" a voice, much like Bonita's, demanded. The woman who swept into the room was tall and spare, her angular features set in consternation. Gray hair nestled at her temples; the rest was dark, a lustrous mahogany mass piled atop her head with an assortment of combs. She was very light, her complexion so pale a tan that I realized for the first time that the European twig on the family tree wasn't quite as far removed as I had thought. Dark gray eyes regarded me with an expression I found hard to read.

"Who's this?" she asked, a stillness about her.

"Peg's daughter, uh . . ." She turned to me, laughing. "I passed out on you before you got to tell me your name."

"Leigh Ann Warren."

"She named you Leigh." Her voice thickened. "After our mother. Leigh, this is your Aunt Frances. Look at her, Frannie! When I first saw her, I thought she was Tracy, they're so much alike from the back."

"I'm told I look like my mother," I said, hoping for confirmation from those who'd been closest to her.

Frances, who hadn't moved, shook her head. "No. She doesn't look like Margaret. She looks like Faye."

It was evidently a new thought for Bonita. Once again, she did the finger under the chin bit, moving my head from side to side. "My God, you're right," she said softly. "Not that there's no resemblance to Peg," she added hurriedly, as if she sensed how important it was to me. "There is, there is. But of the four of us, Peg and Faye looked more alike and you're just like Faye. A little darker, like Warren, but otherwise, you're Faye."

"No!" Frances's voice was hard, cold. "She's not Faye. Faye's dead, remember? Laid to rest under a concrete slab in the cemetery thanks to this girl's father, the *bastard*!" Spittle sprayed from her lips and she wiped a hand across them, regaining her composure with difficulty. "I'm sorry. I know it's not your fault. That doesn't change anything. You're Peg's and Warren's child. You may be welcome in Bonita's home but you will not be welcome in mine. I'll be leaving for the hospital in a few minutes, Nita. If you're riding with me, you'd better get cracking." Without a backward glance, she left the room.

Bonita slumped in a chair. "I'm sorry, Leigh. You have to understand, our mother was sick for a long time before she died, so Frannie practically raised Faye. Hell, she practically raised all of us. But Faye was her favorite, her baby. And she's never gotten over the way she died. Maybe I can talk her around, but I doubt it."

"Don't, please," I said. "It's obvious I bring back painful memories for her. Besides, I'm only here today. I'd better go. The others are waiting and you and your sister can go to the hospital."

She nodded, her hair, a shade lighter but worn every bit as haphazardly as her older sister's, bounced with the movement of her head. "Yes. We're hoping Tracy will be released today."

"I'm sorry. Nothing serious, I hope." I mean, what else do you say?

"No, thank God. A broken ankle, some bumps and bruises. If she hadn't jumped, Lord knows what shape she'd be in today."

I couldn't help it: I had to ask. "What happened?"

"Hit and run, some idiot speeding on Market. Fortunately, she saw the car coming at the last minute and vaulted out of the way. It clipped her foot as it went by, but it could have been so much worse."

Uneasiness tickled the back of my neck with a feather touch. "When was this?"

"Last night. Not sure of the time, but it was after dark."

The thought that occurred to me was too bizarre to take seriously. So why did I? Because I'd been on the receiving end of double-takes ever since I'd arrived. Even the little lady who'd handled my registration with the group had thought I was someone else when she'd first seen me. Now I understood why. Was there a possibility that in the poorly lit one block stretch of Market Street, Tracy had been mistaken for me? It was something to be considered, but not now, not with my meeting with Elizabeth Ritch dangling over my head a la the sword of Damocles.

"Do come back," Bonita pleaded, gripping my hand in a vise. "I want you to meet Tracy and my other kids. You're blood kin and you should get to know the other members of your family. Peg would want that, I'm sure she would. And we want to get to know you too."

The best I could do was agree to return as soon as I could. I had no idea when I would see the end of my current crisis or, for that matter, how it would end. If I had to go to Sunrise or points south to deliver the medal, there was no way to tell how long I'd be gone.

Bonita got up and walked with me to the door. She waited and watched until I was back at the exhibit hall. I returned to the group feeling a little better. At least one member of the family had welcomed me. Now it was time to deal with one who definitely wouldn't.

We straggled through two Ourland homes built in 1901, the pride of the original residents in what they had accomplished preserved in the furnishings and faded photographs on the walls. For the first time, the name they'd chosen for their settlement took on meaning it hadn't before. Regardless, I could barely wait to get to my grandparents' home.

The minivans chartered for the tours stopped at the gate of the Ritch compound, the driver of the first tapping the horn to announce our arrival. I'd made certain to take a backseat where the windows appeared so dark from the outside that it would be difficult for someone looking in to see faces clearly. Once beyond this point, I was halfway home free.

I didn't recognize the youngster who sprinted to open the gate, but he wore the stamp of the Ritches; I could see traces of Ruth across his forehead and jawline. He also bore a faint resemblance to Jon, the manager of Shores Inn. Another cousin, I reminded myself.

The minivans crawled ahead and progressed down a long twisting driveway bordered by stately evergreens still rich with color despite the late fall. We'd traveled quite a distance before I spotted the first house. Small, compact, and old it was not. Three stories high and contemporary in the extreme, it proved to be an exception. Most of the other homes were on the order of others I'd seen in town, medium-sized ranchers and unpretentious cottages nestled among the trees, a few elevated to permit parking beneath. There were a number of homes on our left, set back among the trees, but the choice locations were on the right nearest the Bay. By the time we'd passed the seventh one, I began to wonder how much waterfront acreage the Ritches owned. Considering what I'd seen to that point, we were talking a pot load of money.

The vans turned right into a crushed stone driveway. Leaning forward in my seat, I peered through the front window. No way this could be anything other than the home from whence the rest had sprung. Three stories of white clapboard Victoriana sat on stout brick pillars so tall that there was a clear view of the water from under the house, interrupted only by the wide span of a good dozen and a half steps to the porch. Each of the upper floors was slightly smaller than the one beneath, stacked like a wedding cake. There was a minimum of gingerbread and froufrou, but the widow's walk around the third-floor roof lent the house a regal air, a broad-beamed dowager queen sitting comfortably on her throne. Despite this, there was nothing pretentious about it. It was simply a big, old house, with porches around each floor. The grounds around it were immaculate. Someone here was a serious gardener.

We dismounted and climbed the steps, and Mrs. Lawrence, stout leader both literally and figuratively, looked around to be certain all her charges were in tow. She pulled a lever and somewhere inside a bell jangled. Almost immediately, the door opened and another young Ritch in turn-of-the-twentieth-century dress welcomed us, stepping aside to let us in.

She introduced herself as Amalie Ritch and with the polish of a professional, led us through the house, her patter smooth and well-delivered, but with a spontaneity that revealed her pleasure and pride in sharing this bit of history. This was the designer of the Web site Plato had stumbled upon, and older than I'd first thought, probably a college student.

The interior was more museum than home, the furnishings and appointments an antique collector's dream. There had to be two kitchens. The one we went through contained several generations of stoves and food storage units that had served the family over the years, from a squat pot-bellied number, a stick of wood protruding from its gaping maw, to a gleaming black Franklin that brought tears to Mr. Brinkley's eyes. Leesha, the group's teenager, gaped at the four-door ice chests and the thirties' model refrigerator with the cooling unit on top. And Mr. Brinkley's attempts to enlighten her to the sheer joy of sitting and listening to programs on the old model radios reduced even me, as on edge as I was, to hysterical laughter.

"But there's no picture!" she exclaimed, flummoxed. "What did you look at?"

Mr. Brinkley shook his head and gave up.

The tour ended and there'd been no sign of any other member of the family. That left me with little choice. As the group began to leave, I stopped to speak to our guide.

"Amalie, I need to speak to . . . Mrs. Elizabeth Ritch. It's very important or I wouldn't ask. Is she here?"

Amalie regarded me warily. "Yes, but she wasn't feeling well today; that's why I stood in for her. If you'd like to leave your name and number, I'm sure she'd call you when she's feeling better."

"Leigh," Mrs. Lawrence called from the door.

"Don't worry about me," I said, refusing to be deterred. "I'll call a cab and meet you later."

"Uh—ah," Amalie was stammering. "I'm sorry, but you'll have to go. I told you Aunt Liz can't see you."

I didn't want to bully the young woman. She was caught in the middle and I knew how that felt. But I also wasn't leaving until I'd done what I'd come here to do.

"Listen to me, Amalie." I kept my voice low, unthreatening. "I must speak to your aunt. It's a matter of life and death and I'm not exaggerating. Either you take me to her or I go looking in each and every room in this house until I find her. You can call the police to have me arrested if you like but by the time they get here I'll have tracked her down. I'm that desperate, Amalie. So which is it gonna be?"

Evidently she saw the determination in my eyes and opted for the lesser of two evils. "Okay, but she's gonna kill me. If she doesn't, Grandma will. She warned me something like this might happen. Come on." She headed for the steps to the second floor.

"Your grandmother wouldn't be Ruth, would she?"

Startled, she looked around, almost tripping on the hem of her long dress. "You know my gran?"

"We've met." I left it at that. I also suspected that the selfsame gran had arranged for someone other than Elizabeth to handle our tour today.

The room to which Amalie led me was at the very end of the hall on the front. She opened the door and I stepped into a symphony in organza. The rest of the house might be a museum but Elizabeth's room was hers, and it was obvious she'd had her fill of antiques. The furnishings and decor were strictly twentieth-century Thomasville, her choice of colors a cool blue and white, the decor so utterly feminine that I doubted her husband slept in here with her.

"Amalie? They're gone? Just a minute. One more stitch and I'm done. I'm so sorry you had to cut class to do this. There was no good reason I couldn't have conducted the tour myself."

Amalie cleared her throat nervously. The woman who peered around the arm of the high-backed easy chair in front of the window and then stood up, dropping her needlework to the floor, was every bit as regal as her home. With hair whiter than her curtains, she stared at me with eerily light eyes. Other than the color of her hair, she resembled her sister, minus thirty or so pounds. Short, almost delicate, she was slender, her skin the color of burnished bronze, her posture erect.

She frowned. I could see her searching her memory bank, trying to place the name my features had dredged up. "And you are?"

I glanced at Amalie and decided it was up to Elizabeth whether she remained in the room. "I'm Leigh Warren, the daughter of Wayne and Margaret . . . Ritch." It was time to stop fooling around with assumed names.

"Who?" Amalie asked.

Elizabeth stiffened, her breath whistling between her teeth.

"Leave us, Amalie," she ordered, her gaze never leaving my face.

"Yes, ma'am." From the submissive quality of her voice, I could almost envision Amalie bobbing a curtsy before I heard the door close quietly behind me.

"So." My grandmother didn't move. Neither did I. "How old are you?"

Why was everyone so interested in my age? "Thirty-two."

"Hmmm. How do I know you're who you say you are?"

"Because you're looking at me and you see your son's complexion, the shape of my mother's face and that of her sister, Faye. You also see the slightest hint of your widow's peak above my forehead. And before you reach the wrong conclusion, I am not here to be welcomed into the bosom of this family."

"I'm happy to hear it because you certainly wouldn't be."

"I'm aware of that. Ruth told me as much."

Her jaw dropped. "Ruth knew you were here?"

So I'd misread the situation. My sneaky great-aunt had not told her sister why she wanted her granddaughter to conduct the tour today. And I'd spilled the beans, tattled on Ruth. Tough.

"I met her yesterday when I tried to see you. She let me know how matters stand. Fine. When I leave here today, you will be happy to hear that I won't be back."

"Then why did you come?" she asked, her tone colder than dry ice.

"As much as it pains me, I'm here to ask you for the Silver Star my father was awarded in Vietnam. The only reason I need it is because some insane man who served with him has kidnapped the woman who raised me after my parents died. He isn't asking for money," I said, forestalling her attempt to interrupt me. "All he wants is that medal. He feels it should have been awarded to him rather than my father. He's dying. He's given me until Saturday to get it or he says he'll kill my foster mother and her husband. Whatever your feelings about my father, if you have it, I'm pleading with you to give it to me. I'm trying to save two lives."

She was silent, hands folded at her waist. "That's quite a story."

"Hearing it is a hell of a lot easier than living it," I said, short on patience. "If you doubt my word, I can give you the names and phone numbers of the FBI agents I reported it to." It was a gamble, but one worth risking.

"That won't be necessary," my grandmother said, and walked back to her easy chair, swiveling it around. She sat down. "I'm sorry to tell you I won't be able to help you."

Not believing for an instant that she was sorry, I asked, "You destroyed it?"

"No. I'm afraid your kidnapper is deluded. Your father was in the service, the air force to be specific. But contrary to what you've been told, he never served in Vietnam. He never left the country, unless you're one of those who considers the Pentagon a country unto itself. He was there for a while, and in Hawaii. He never saw combat. So I'm sorry—Leigh, is it? I have no medal to give you because as far as I know, Warren never received one."

11

I MADE IT TO THE PORCH AND DOWN THE FRONT
stairs before I collapsed on the bottom step in defeat. I had
assumed that the "lieutenant rich college-boy" Jameson
had borne a grudge against all these years had been my father. I hadn't even asked the man which branch of the service he'd been in. I'd assumed army, forgetting that there
were lieutenants in other branches as well. I'd been stupid
and now Nunna and Walter would die.

I'd bungled everything.

"Well, good morning. Need some help?"

Startled that I hadn't heard anyone approach, I looked
up into the face of the best-looking old dude I'd seen in a
long time. Tall and rangy with skin the color of cocoa, he
gazed down at me with eyes so dark they sparkled like spit-
shined shoes. Mesmerized by them, I lost my train of
thought for a moment before my brain finally reengaged.

"Uh—good morning. I'm not trespassing, honest." I
pushed myself to my feet. "I'm supposed to meet a cab at
the gate. They said it would be a while so I guess I can start
walking now."

He fixed me with a gaze second only to an X-ray machine. "Are you sure you can make it? You look as if you
just lost your best friend in the world."

I chuckled, swallowing my bitterness. "I have, or just may very soon. I'll go now. Thanks for your concern." I managed a smile to be polite but it took every ounce of effort I had left.

He blinked, an expression of pure astonishment blazing across his features. "My apologies. I don't usually stare. It's just that you remind me of someone I used to know. I'm Wayne Ritch. And you are . . . ?"

I should have realized who he was right off the bat but I'd been so wrapped up in my problems that nothing else registered. He had the same obsidian eyes Jenky had mentioned, the same broad shoulders and short waist I remembered in the snapshot of my dad.

I repressed a sigh, thinking, Here we go again. "I'm Leigh Ann Warren. Your granddaughter."

The transformation was immediate. His expression had been polite before. Suddenly it was as if the sun had risen behind his face. "Of course, of course. Warren's baby girl." He took my hand, folding long slender fingers around mine. "I can't tell you how fervently I've prayed I'd meet you before I died."

It was my turn to react with astonishment. "You knew about me?"

"Warren got a message to me when you and your brother were born. Where is he?"

"Who? Dad?" My heart contracted. Ruth knew. Why didn't he?

"No, no, your brother. Will he be coming too?"

I almost hated to spoil the moment, but there was no way around it. "He died. I didn't even know about him until day before yesterday."

Sadness marred his broad smile. "I'm sorry to hear that. Life hasn't been kind to you, has it? First your twin, then your parents. I had private investigators trying to find you for years. No matter. You're here. You finally came." Suddenly an even deeper shadow settled across his face. "And the fact that you're out here means you've met your grandmother."

"Yes."

"And she turned you away?"

"Well," I said, trying for diplomacy, "I wasn't expecting a warm welcome. I'd been warned."

His brows arched. "By whom?"

"Ruth," I said, no compunction left.

He nodded. "I should have known. She's the younger by a few minutes, but it's always been Ruth who looked out for Liz." I guess my surprise must have shown because he grinned. "You didn't realize they're identical twins? Ruth never lost weight after each pregnancy. Six kids adds up to a lot of pounds. And twins run in our families. Ruth has two sets, all girls. So, she tried to run interference?"

"She tried to stop me from seeing . . . Mrs. Ritch. Forgive me, but I'm not comfortable calling her anything else. And I made certain your wife understood from the outset that claiming the family name was the farthest thing from my mind."

"I'm sorry to hear that," he said, his regret obvious.

"I came to ask for something of my father's I thought she might have. She doesn't. I'm sorry, Mr. Ritch—"

"Title-wise, it's doctor," he said, rocking from heel to toe. "As in M.D., retired. For you, I'd prefer it was Grandfather, or Granddad, if you can bring yourself to call me that."

If I'd been butter, I'd have melted all over those steps. "Thank you. Granddad." It felt good in my mouth, sounded right to my ears. Unfortunately, I couldn't hang around to savor it. "I've still got to go. I have until Saturday to save the lives of a couple of people I love very much."

He sobered. "That sounds serious. Is there something I can do to help?"

"Don't I wish." I said, then explained the hellish week in as few words as I could. "It never occurred to me that it wasn't my father's medal. I was praying the two of you had it and that you'd be willing to give it to me. Now——"

"Wayne!" The voice of my grandmother. She stood on the second-floor porch, disapproval all over her face. "I need you! This minute, please!"

He gazed up at her. "The light of my life calleth. She's not a bad person, Leigh. It's just that she counted on Warren for far more than she had a right to. She's also not well so I'd better go up and soothe her feathers. Listen, sweetheart, head for the gate. I'll be along to pick you up probably before you get there. If I'm delayed, please wait. I'll take you somewhere we can talk with no interruptions. And we do need to talk."

He still didn't understand. "Granddad, I don't have time. I've got to——"

He palmed my shoulder. "Trust me. I can help. Contrary to your grandmother's opinion, she doesn't know everything."

I looked up at him. "Are you saying——?"

"Wayne!" It was clear Elizabeth was not used to waiting.

"Coming, Liz!" To me, he said, "I'll cancel the cab and see you shortly." He extended a hand and we shook with almost comical formality before he bounded up the stairs.

I watched with admiration and more than a little envy. My grandfather could take the steps two at a time, something this granddaughter would never be able to do again. He gave me a thumbs-up, then went into the house. What a sweet man. Meanwhile, my grandmother glared down at me, bristling with anger. Turning my back on her, I walked away. I couldn't let her burst my balloon. I wasn't sure what my grandfather had up his sleeve, but I was certain he wouldn't have said what he had if he hadn't meant it. And his acceptance of me, something I thought wouldn't matter, did. It was icing on the cake.

I'd forgotten how far it was back to the gate. My knee began to mutter about halfway there, but I kept going, tortoise-style, chanting "slow and steady wins the race" under my breath. The temperature was in the forties, but it wasn't long before I realized that the new turtleneck was warmer than I'd expected and something had to go, in this case my stadium jacket.

I stepped off the road and stopped under a tree, my purse between my feet, and began to unbutton. The wind had died down, bathing the compound in a stillness so profound that I could even hear the swish of the bay. Which was the only reason I detected the crunch of stealthy footsteps through dead leaves and desiccated flora.

"Granddad?" I called, looking back the way I'd come.

The footsteps stopped.

"Grandfather?" I called again.

Nothing.

Immediately I went on full-scale alert. Something wasn't right here. It couldn't be my grandfather. If he'd been on foot, his tread on the driveway would have sounded as mine had, a soft squish-squish on the asphalt, not the crunch-crunch of dried pine needles and pine cones. Besides, he said he would pick me up, so obviously he'd be driving. Who then was out here with me?

"Hello?" I called. Nothing. I grabbed my purse and slipped further back into the trees. The wooded tracts between houses were thick and no doubt crawling with snakes and other wildlife, but if someone was trying to spook me, there was no point in making it easy for them. If I stayed on the road I'd be out in the open.

I began buttoning up again as fast as I could. The white turtleneck would be highly visible but the stadium jacket, a forest green with brown leather trim, would be more effective as camouflage. The palm of my right hand itched, screaming for the heft of a service revolver. I didn't often have reason to miss that thing, but I damned sure missed it now.

I made a visual survey of the immediate area but saw no one and nothing moving nearby. Then I heard a sound I couldn't identify, something between a buzz and a purr, mechanical in nature. Whatever it was, it seemed to be coming from back up the road toward my grandparents' house.

Peeking from behind a tree, I tried to see what it was. A golf cart, probably powered by electricity, my grandfather at the tiller. I started to move toward the asphalt, one arm raised to wave to him, when I was yanked backward by the hood of my jacket to a spot behind the tree again and pressed against it face front, a hand clamped over my nose and mouth.

"Wouldn't listen, would you?" a voice growled in my ear. "Couldn't leave things alone."

Panic arced across my chest. I couldn't breathe. The man leaned his full weight against me, constricting my lungs. Fortunately, he'd grabbed me just as I'd opened my mouth to call to my grandfather. The hand was gloved, but you take what you're given. It wasn't the first time I'd had to bite my way out of trouble. I clamped down with a vengeance, caught his finger next to the pinky between my teeth, and was rewarded with a bellow of pain.

"Leigh? Where are you? What's wrong? Leigh?"

I could barely hear him above the swearing going on behind me.

"Damn you, let *go*!"

Nothing doing. I held on with the determination of a pit bull.

He tried to yank the finger loose, in the process lessening the weight against my back and uncovering my nose. I tightened my jaw and, breathing through clenched teeth, filled my lungs while the filling was good. With my front squashed against the tree, that was about all I could do for the time being. I couldn't even elbow him in the gut.

Finally, in desperation, he jammed my forehead against the trunk with his free hand, the rough bark cutting into my skin like tiny knives. Stunned by the pain, I lost my grip on his finger. He jerked it free, then his hand, leaving the glove dangling from between my teeth. Then he was gone. Footsteps scrambled through the underbrush.

Blood oozing from my forehead, I staggered from behind the tree just as Granddad slowed to a stop.

"Leigh, you're hurt! Did you fall?" He set the brake and started to get off.

"I'm fine! Someone just grabbed me."

"What?"

I looked back over my shoulder in time to catch a glimpse of my assailant as he jumped from behind a spruce and raced off through the woods. "There he goes!"

My grandfather, his face transfigured by outrage, edged back onto the seat, released the brake, and veered off the roadway to give chase in the golf cart. Perhaps he knew something I didn't, but I couldn't see what he thought that would accomplish. He might be able to squeeze between the first three or four trees but beyond that would be impossible, unless he planned to abandon the golf cart and pursue my assailant on foot. I wasn't certain I liked that idea either. Just because he could bop up stairs two at a time didn't mean he was in any shape to run the hundred-yard dash.

"Grandfather, wait!"

I'd barely gotten it out when things went from bad to worse. The golf cart fishtailed, as if skidding on ice, Granddad struggling with the tiller. Before he could leap free, the little cart rolled over on its side like a beached whale.

I rushed toward him, skirting the vehicle, when, inexplicably, my feet went out from under me. Staying upright became a test of balance, my arms windmilling in a desperate attempt to remain vertical. I glanced down and saw the soft, slick mud exposed where the tires had lost purchase. All the deposits of fall blown down since last week's hard rain had hidden it but now my shoes were caked with the stuff. My grandfather lay half-in, half-out of the cart, his left leg pinned underneath it.

"Granddad?"

I probed for a pulse, watched the rise and fall of his chest. As far as I could tell he was having no trouble breathing but he was not responsive, his eyes half-closed. A smear of blood on the closest tree trunk supplied the reason. He'd whacked his head against it as the cart turned over.

I had dropped my purse when I'd been mugged. I picked my way back to it and used my cell phone to call for an ambulance, then hurried back to check on my grandfather. In that short time, his breathing had become more labored. I had to make a decision: stay with him or hotfoot it to the gate to unlock it. The gate won. Granddad's position made it impossible for me to administer CPR if he needed it, so it was imperative that the emergency crew be able to get in to him.

By the time I reached the brick enclosure, my lungs were on fire, and my forehead ached. I had one of those "I'm going to die" cramps in my side, but my knee had held up. The ambulance, a fire truck on its tail, arrived as I pulled the pin free of the hasp on the gate. A county cruiser brought up the rear.

The driver started to open his door. "What happened, lady? Did you fall?"

I'd forgotten about my forehead. "It's not me," I said, blocking the door. "My grandfather. About a quarter-mile along on the left." I jumped on his running board. Walking back was not an option. "He's pinned under his golf cart."

"Doc Ritch?" his attendant asked, leaning forward in his seat with alarm.

"Yes. He was unconscious when I left to come open the gate. His pulse was strong but his breathing was labored. Possible head wound; he hit it against a tree when the cart overturned."

"Shit," the driver muttered, and speeded up.

I tried to stay out of the way when we arrived, watching in awe as two of the rescue workers lifted the cart as if it weighed no more than a ten-speed. My grandfather's left leg had an additional bend in it, obviously broken. But there was more concern about whether he had suffered a closed head injury or might have broken his neck.

My stomach knotted in turmoil as they encased him in a cervical collar and brought out a backboard. What else could go wrong? Just as I was meeting a grandfather I hadn't known I had, a sweet man who'd not only welcomed me but who'd also hinted that he knew something about the coveted medal his wife did not, it appeared that fate had conspired to put him out of commission. Only in the deepest and darkest closets in my mind could I entertain the prospect that this man might not even survive, that there might be three funerals in the offing. In yet another closet a little easier to access, I felt responsible. All the while I explained what had happened to the county cop, and handed over the glove as evidence, another part of me had begun a litany of "if I hadn'ts."

If I hadn't waited until I was forced to find out more about my parents and their families, I needn't have wasted time in search of my grandparents after Jameson's call. I might have long since learned enough about my father from his father to have known immediately what Jameson had been talking about, what he wanted.

If I hadn't had to come to Ourland, I wouldn't have made someone desperate enough to assault me. And if I hadn't been assaulted, my grandfather would be fine, instead of being—

With a quick kick in my mental fanny, I called a halt to the list. Not only was it a waste of time, it was a means of procrastinating. Elizabeth Ritch had to be told.

The county cop, so young he made me feel antique, had completed his preliminary notes and contacted his dispatcher with a request for additional personnel to search the woods.

"And I'd better go alert his next of kin. How's he look, Gil?" he asked one of the medics.

"Not good. Gotta go." He got in the back and pulled the door closed.

I swallowed my panic as they left with lights flashing and siren blaring. I'd have given anything to ride with them but it wasn't my place to go. That belonged to my grandmother.

"Officer—," I said, and looked at his name tag for the first time. "Officer Mars, I realize that talking to his wife is part of your duties," I said, "but since I'm partly responsible for what happened, I'd feel better if I told her." Considering how Elizabeth felt about me, I had no doubt she'd be more than ready to shoot the messenger who delivered the bad news. Regardless, I felt it was something I should do.

"Sure," he responded, and made no attempt to hide his relief.

Amalie, in jeans and a bright orange sweater, answered the door, alarm shouting from her eyes when she saw the blood on my forehead and the uniform behind me. "What's wrong?" she asked, her voice a squeak. "What happened to you?"

"I'm fine, Amalie. It's your—" I hesitated, unable for the moment to work out what relation she was to my grandfather. "It's Dr. Ritch. He's had an accident. We need to speak to Mrs. Ritch."

"Uncle Wayne?" Her hand flew to her throat. "Come on. She's—"

"Who is it, Amalie?" Elizabeth stood at the top of the steps, Ruth, her chubby twin behind her. "You again?" She shot ice chips at me.

Mars stepped around me. "Which one of you is Mrs. Ritch?" he asked.

"We both are," they responded in unison.

Stumped for a second, he glanced at me.

"It's Dr. Ritch," I volunteered. "He's had an accident and is on his way to the hospital in an ambulance. It may be serious. You'll want to get there as soon as possible."

"I'll be glad to take you, ma'am," Mars said, looking from one to the other. He still wasn't sure which one he'd be ferrying.

"I won't be a minute," Elizabeth said, and hurried back toward her room.

"What happened to Wayne?" Ruth bustled down the stairs. "He was just here a few minutes ago."

"His golf cart overturned," Mars said tersely. "He has a broken leg and a possible head wound. I'm sorry, what relation are you to Dr. Ritch?"

"Sister-in-law," Ruth said, turning on her heel and starting back up. "Amalie, call Stu and W. Two and tell them to get over to the hospital. I'll go help Lizzie."

"Yes, ma'am." Fright had robbed the girl's face of all color.

"We'll wait outside in the cruiser," Mars said as Amalie headed for the old-fashioned phone on a table at the foot of the steps.

It was an inopportune time to ask, but the question hadn't occurred to me until I realized that Ruth and Elizabeth had the same last name. "Amalie, what relation is your grandfather to Dr. Ritch?"

She glanced up, mid-dial. "Was. Pop-pop died when I was eight. They were brothers. Twins."

Good grief. Granddad wasn't kidding when he said twins ran in the family. I glanced down at my engagement ring and wondered how Duck would react to that news. I thought I remembered that the incidence of twins tended to skip generations. Since I'd been one of two, I probably wouldn't have any. Of course that presupposed my getting out of Ourland in one piece. Considering the way things were going, that was definitely problematic.

I wound up finding my way to the hospital alone, since my grandmother took exception to my riding in the cruiser. This even before she'd been told what had led to her husband's accident.

"This young woman has nothing to do with our family," she said, as Mars held the passenger door open for her and her twin.

He looked from me to her, confused. "She isn't your granddaughter?"

Her jaw tightened. "Technically, she is. But I see no reason for her to accompany us to the hospital. Why is she with you anyway?"

The officer's eyes hardened. "If your husband survives, it'll be thanks to Ms. Warren here. She's the one who called for help and made sure we could get through your gate. Otherwise—"

"Never mind," I interrupted him. "You go ahead. I can take care of myself."

He gazed at me with sympathetic eyes. "Better have someone look at your forehead. You'll be around if we need you?"

"I don't know, but you can always get me on my cell phone. Thanks," I added, to let him know I appreciated his coming to my defense.

He smiled and for a moment I felt like a member of the brotherhood again. Then they were gone.

"Ms. Warren?" Amalie, halfway down the steps, resembled a frightened ten-year-old. "Was Uncle Wayne hurt really badly?"

I wasn't certain how to answer. "I'm no expert, Amalie. Broken bones mend. And with luck, the head wound will turn out to be a mild concussion. Would you mind calling a cab for me again?"

"Sure." She waffled for a second, then said, "Come on in. And let me get you a Band-Aid or something."

We went back in where she showed me to a bathroom straight out of yesteryear, the tank of the toilet up near the ceiling, flushed by pulling a chain. But the medicine cabinet was purely up-to-date.

She watched and winced while I picked bits of bark from the broken skin, swabbed it with peroxide, and smoothed a bandage over it.

"What happened?" she asked. "Did you fall?"

I debated whether or not to tell her, but figured she'd find out sooner or later. "Someone attacked me as I was walking to the gate."

She paled. "Inside the compound? How'd they get in?"

"I don't know, Amalie, but if it makes you feel any better, I'm pretty sure that whoever it was was after me in particular."

"Why?" she asked.

"I hope the point was to scare me enough so I'd go away. Apparently your great-aunt Elizabeth isn't the only one who isn't glad to see me."

She escorted me back to the front parlor and gestured toward a chair. "I don't understand what's going on," she said, biting her lip. "All my life, Gran and Aunt Liz have drummed into us the importance of family, of sticking together, helping each other. That's all you hear in Ourland. But if you're really Auntie's granddaughter—"

"I am," I said, taking a seat.

"—then how can she turn you away the way she did? That's so hypocritical. I mean, you're the only granddaughter she has!"

"It's a long, ugly story," I said, "and I think it would be better if you asked your aunt to explain it. I'm just grateful my grandfather feels differently. We only managed to talk for a few minutes. I just hope I get a chance to know him better. It's my fault he got hurt, Amalie. He saw my assailant running away and took off after him on the cart. If he hadn't, he'd be all right."

"But you might have been hurt worse. And you shouldn't feel guilty." A ghost of a smile crossed her face. "Everybody talks about the time Uncle Wayne chased a purse snatcher for four blocks and caught him. That's just Uncle Wayne."

Somehow I wasn't surprised. "Tell me about him, Amalie. He mentioned that he was a retired physician."

"An OB/GYN. He brought three-quarters of the babies born around here into the world, and never lost one. And it's a joke to call him retired; he volunteers at a couple of clinics. People in town still treat him as if he's their family doctor, calling him at all hours. He grabs his bag and off he goes. He keeps busy. He's even writing a book on the changes he's seen in gynecology and obstetrics since he got his license."

All this information made me even more anxious about him. I reminded Amalie that she hadn't called the cab yet. She used the phone, then drove me to the gate in a little black VW beetle.

"I really enjoyed talking to you," she said, as she closed the gate behind me. "Where are you going now, back to the city?"

"No, to my car and then to the hospital, whether my grandmother likes it or not. I have to find out how things are going."

"I'd take you," she said, "but I can't leave until I've gotten word to my dad." Seeming reluctant to see me leave, Amalie scribbled her phone number on the back of an envelope and made me promise to call her. "You're family," she said, chin jutting pugnaciously. "We have to keep in touch."

If she hadn't been on the other side of that gate, I'd have hugged her. We said goodbye and I hopped in the cab. It dropped me off in front of the exhibit hall, where I tossed my junk on the backseat and with the directions the cab-driver had given me, headed for the hospital and the con-frontation to come.

12

CERTAIN THAT MY GRANDFATHER WOULD STILL
be in the emergency room, I bypassed the main lobby and
drove around to the side entrance. I seemed to have become part of a parade, one of a line of cars turning into the
parking lot along with me. I used my handicapped tag and
found a spot near the door. In spite of that advantage, a
number of those who'd parked farther away managed to
beat me inside.

"Hey, Tee," one of them tossed over his shoulder as he
hurried by. "Glad you're okay. You comin' to see about
Doc Ritch? We rushed over as soon as we heard. This place
will be packed shortly."

The parade was explained. I'd forgotten about the Mach
2 speed of a small-town grapevine. And to my dismay, I
saw that the man who'd called me Tee was right. The small
waiting room was three-quarters full of people, few of
whom appeared to be potential patients. They stood,
milling around, with worried, anxious demeanors. Among
those nearest the doors to the treatment room were my
grandmother being comforted by her sister and a number
of others who in one way or another wore the imprint of
Ritch family genes. Besides Officer Mars on a telephone in
the corner, the only other face I recognized was that of Jon
Ritch, the manager-cum-maintenance man-cum bartender

at the Shores Inn. Seeing my determined approach, he shook his head as if to warn me off. I wasn't going for it.

"How is he?" I asked, elbowing my way through to Elizabeth. "Has he regained consciousness?"

"You!" She rounded on me. "It's your fault! You did this to him!"

"Aunt Liz," Jon said, and slipped an arm around her shoulder. "Come on, now. There's no call for that."

She shook him off. "Don't 'Aunt Liz' me! The policeman told me what happened. If it hadn't been for her, Wayne wouldn't be here. She caused this! I knew she was trouble the moment I laid eyes on her!"

"I don't get it," one of the Ritch clones said. "Who is she anyway, Liz?"

"Your cousin," I snapped, my temper fraying, "and her granddaughter, whether she likes it or not. At this point, I'm not all that happy about it either. All I want is whatever anyone can tell me about my grandfather's condition."

"Cousin? Grandfather?" Another from the Ritch contingent. "Just whose wild oats is she?"

Wild oats? I was about to explode when the doctor pushed through the swinging door from the rear, his lab coat streaked with blood. "Mrs. Ritch?" he asked, his gaze searching the faces of the older women.

"I'm Mrs. Ritch." Elizabeth rushed to him, chin lifted.

"Uh . . . would the rest of you please excuse us?" he asked.

I glanced back and saw that the waiting room was now crowded. And exiting an elevator, her face seamed with concern, was my Aunt Frances. Terrific. Another unfriendly country heard from.

"We're family," Ruth responded, more accurately than she could have imagined. "Please, how's Wayne?"

The doctor hesitated, then shrugged in resignation. It

was clear no one was moving. "Dr. Ritch is stable but his condition is critical. He has a broken left femur but all things considered, that's minor. We've done a CT scan. There's some swelling of his brain and an intracranial bleed. It's vital that we take him to surgery immediately. We'll need your permission."

"Do it, anything required. Will—" Elizabeth stopped, swallowed. "Will he be all right?"

You could have heard a feather hit the floor.

The doctor hedged. "A great deal depends on how his brain responds to the surgery. That's all I can say, at this point. If the surgery is successful and no other complications crop up, his chances are pretty good, considering his age. Rest assured we'll do the best we possibly can for him. I must get back. Please," he addressed the assemblage, "if you aren't members of the immediate family, I must ask you to wait outside or patients in need of care won't be able to get in. You might be more comfortable in the waiting room of the surgical wing, Mrs. Ritch. From surgery your husband will be taken to the critical care unit, but that'll be a while. We'll keep you posted. Try not to worry." He gave her a pat and a smile with the life span of a bolt of lightning, glanced at the mob, and hurried back inside.

"Critical," Elizabeth whispered. "Oh, my God."

"Leigh!"

I turned to locate the caller. Frances beckoned to me from the rear of the crowd. I maneuvered my way to her past curious eyes.

"I'll be damned," someone behind me said. "I could have sworn that was Tee."

"I couldn't hear what the doctor said. How's Wayne Senior? What happened?" Frances seemed genuinely alarmed.

Wayne Senior. Appropriate, but I guess I'd never thought of my father as Wayne Junior, perhaps because I had yet to hear anyone refer to him by his first name.

"He had an accident on his golf cart. He's in critical condition and they're taking him to surgery. How's Tracy?"

"Fine," she said, plainly distracted. "She's been discharged. Probably waiting for me out front."

"Uh . . . no, she's not." The elevator door had opened and the young woman being pushed out of it in a wheelchair by a nurse, my Aunt Bonita on her heels, was my cousin Tracy. She had to be. Her hair, a cap of glossy curls, was lighter than mine with blond highlights, but we shared the same burnt-almond coloring. I had a few years on her but we looked enough alike to be sisters. It was definitely creepy.

"Well, will you look at that," a raw-boned woman said. "Bonita, where you been hiding this one?"

"Told ya that wasn't Tee," another responded. "Didn't I tell ya?"

"Wow," the young woman with my and my mother's oval face and bowed lips said breathily when she reached us. She stared up at me, astonished. "And wow again. Mom was right. No wonder she passed out. What a hoot! Hi, I'm Tracy. What happened to your head?" Grinning, she stuck out a hand.

"Leigh Ann Warren. Had an argument with a tree." Her grin was infectious. I couldn't help but respond in kind. "Nice to meet you, cousin. Sorry about your accident. How's your ankle?"

"Hurts like hell," she said cheerily, "but it could have been worse." She sobered. "How's Doc Ritch? I didn't want to leave without finding out. Everybody in the place knows he's here."

I repeated what I'd told Frances, and as before, omitted details. I might as well have spilled it all. My grandmother was on the warpath again. Evidently she'd lost it while I'd been indulging in a mini–family reunion.

"I demand that you leave," she said, a-quiver with rage. "This is your fault, and you have no right to be here. No *right*!"

Around us, those unaware of what she meant glanced at one another curiously and at me with sudden suspicion. "Her fault? What did she do?"

"She caused it!" Her voice rose. "A bad seed from a bad seed! She has no right to be here!"

Granted, she was an old lady and, with the threat of losing her husband a real possibility, had every reason to be upset. But that bad seed business had pushed me too far.

"No right?" I parroted her, struggling to contain my own anger. "I have every right. That man is my grandfather !" A buzz of surprise rippled through the crowd. "I just met him and he, at least, greeted me with open arms. The thought that I may never get to know him better is devastating. But his accident was just that, an accident."

That stumped her but only momentarily. "Yes, but if you hadn't come, he wouldn't have been out there."

"I came because I had no other choice," I said, warning myself to keep my cool. It's not easy to talk with your teeth clenched. It hurts. "And I gather the golf cart was his usual mode of transportation in the compound," I added, "so he could have been out there any time. No?"

"Well, now, that's true enough," a Ritch volunteered. "He's a right demon on that thing. Drives the dogs crazy. But what's with this granddaddy-granddaughter business, Liz?" He stopped as the light dawned. "Wait a minute. She's Warren's daughter?"

Elizabeth swung around. "Shut your mouth, George.

The point is that Wayne would have been perfectly fine if he hadn't been trying to protect *her*!" She aimed an accusing finger at me.

"Protect her?" My Aunt Frances, who had edged her way out of sight at Elizabeth's approach, materialized at my side. "From what?" she demanded, slipping an arm around my shoulder. This from the woman who hours earlier had told me I wasn't welcome in her home. Go figure.

Jon nudged his way to center stage. "Something else happened, Ms. Warren?"

Elizabeth buttoned her lip, perhaps realizing that she'd said more than she'd meant to.

All eyes were glued on me, waiting for an explanation. I gave in with regret. "Someone attacked me."

"On the family grounds?" George asked, shocked. "That's the only place Wayne Senior uses that cart. Where were you exactly?"

"About halfway between their house and the gate."

Tracy pointed at my bandage. "He did that to you? The one who attacked you?"

"It's just a scratch," I assured her. "Honest. I bit him when he grabbed me. The only way he could get me to let go was to bang my head against a tree."

There was a smattering of laughter, more than a few stifled grins and "atta girls" of approval.

"Well, Uncle Wayne would have tried to intercede, no matter who you were," Jon said. "Did he recognize the man?"

"I don't know. He just took off after him on the cart," I explained. "He hit a patch of mud and the cart went into a skid and flipped over."

"See? That's what I meant," Elizabeth declared. "If she hadn't shown up, none of this would have happened."

"Wait a minute." Jon gazed at me in thought, glanced at

Tracy, then back at me. "Just why did you come to Our-land, Ms. Warren? What were you doing, tracing your roots or something?"

"No." I didn't appreciate his tone. "Until day before yes-terday, I didn't even know I had roots. I needed a combat medal that had been awarded to my father. I was told that he would have brought it home to his family. When I dis-covered who and where his parents were, I came to ask for it, the medal and nothing else. You will notice that I did *not* hit town with a brass band yesterday announcing who I was," I said, getting even hotter under the collar. "I got here around noon yesterday and in a little over thirty hours have had personal property stolen from my room, have lis-tened to an anonymous caller warn me to get out of town, and have been assaulted."

George, who didn't seem to know when to cut his losses, added, "On Ritch compound grounds, at that."

Elizabeth sent him a look hot enough to melt iron, then turned her glare on me. "You couldn't possibly mean someone in my family is responsible. Obviously an out-sider got past the gates. Ritch men do not attack women." She realized her error as soon as she'd made it.

"Oh?" Frances said, that one word colder than an Antarctic winter day. "Seems to me I remember one occa-sion when a Ritch man did just that and left my poor sister dead in a pool of her own blood. So would you care to re-phrase that last statement?"

The silence was, to use a cliché, deafening. Not a soul moved. It was clear a good many were hearing this story for the first time, while others listened with slowly dawn-ing comprehension and revived memories.

"It was never proved," Elizabeth spluttered. "If Warren had done it, he'd have been arrested, sent to jail."

"Kind of hard to find proof of anything in a pile of cinders." Bonita spoke up for the first time, Tracy watching with undisguised stupefaction. "And for somebody so certain Warren was innocent, you sure were quick to disown him and kick him out."

"He shamed us!" Elizabeth stood her ground. "He defied me and brought disgrace to the family name!"

"Disgrace to your family name?" Frances shrieked. "What about what he did to *our* family, to this town?"

"Stop it!" Tracy pleaded. "Both of you. There's no point in dredging up the past. It's over and done with."

"I'm not so sure about that." Jon spoke with surprising authority. Even Elizabeth closed her mouth. "And I apologize, Ms. Warren. I guess we really should have reported the break-in to the police."

"What break-in?" Mars, off the phone now, moved through to us. "What's going on here?" The bystanders around us backed up a step.

The puzzled visage of a doctor who peered out the door of the emergency room reminded me why we were here and I tuned out as Jon recounted my misadventures for the policeman's benefit. I wondered if my grandfather was in surgery yet, whether I'd lose him so soon after meeting him. And what if he failed to come around and was never able to give me a clue what he'd meant? The sands in my hourglass were down to the last inch or so of grains, with little or no time to recoup.

"Ma'am? Ms. Warren?"

"Sorry. Yes?" I wrestled my attention back to the moment and Officer Mars.

"I have to agree with Mr. Ritch here that you may be in danger. The first two incidents might not sound like much, but put them together with the assault today . . ."

"Newt," Tracy said, and squeezed her wheelchair between the officer and her mother.

He looked her way, surprised. "Tracy. Hi. Didn't see you down there. Sorry about your accident. Uh . . . where was I?"

"Newt," she said again. "I thought it was an accident too. Hit-and-run, sure, but still an accident. Now I'm having second thoughts, wondering if it wasn't deliberate."

"That makes two of us." Jon eyed me. "It occurs to me that whoever tried to run down Tracy might have thought she was Ms. Warren. There's a strong enough resemblance."

All right. I'd harbored the same suspicion even before I'd met Tracy, but I took no comfort in others thinking along the same lines. It lent validity to the notion and, in a convoluted way, made me harbor responsibility for her being hurt. And for all the lip I'd given Elizabeth, I still felt a measure of guilt over my grandfather's accident. I was beginning to long for a hair shirt.

Mars turned his head, scrutinizing us sidewise. "You're right, Mr. Ritch. They do look a lot alike. But thinking the hit-and-run was meant for Ms. Warren is reaching a bit."

Tracy thumped the toe of his shoe with a crutch. "Look, Newton Mars, I was there, you weren't. Read the report. I was in the crosswalk in the middle of the block, all by myself, wearing a white coat and clearly visible, even though it was dark. I'd checked for traffic from both directions before I stepped off the curb and there was nothing coming. The car pulled out from in front of the exhibit hall, no lights on, gunned the engine, roared right through the stop sign, and headed straight at me. He had to have seen me."

"She's right, Deputy." I recognized one of the salesladies from the dress shop. "I was outside taking a smoke break. I saw it all. And I thought it was Miss Warren there coming to pick up her sweat suit. Besides, everybody knows that Tee's almost never in town during the week since she moved. I've known her all my life, yet it never occurred to me it was her."

"Well," Mars said, retrieving his notepad from his pocket, "that might change the complexion of things. Perhaps today's assault wasn't a random occurrence or a crime of opportunity."

"Of course it wasn't," Frances said. "The Ritches-with-a-T strike again. I'd just like to know why."

"How—how dare you!" Ruth erupted. "How dare you smear our young men, our name!"

Frances squared her shoulders. "I didn't have to. Your sister just said it: Warren took care of that years ago by murdering *my* baby sister!"

It was the first time the word "murder" had been used and I wished it hadn't been. The crowd began to grumble and Mars, sensing that he was losing control, held up a hand. "That's enough. Simmer down. You heard the doc. Everyone who's not a member of the immediate family please leave. Now!" He waited until a few had gone outside. "My immediate concern is how we're going to protect you, Ms. Warren."

"Wait just a damn minute," a stocky, middle-aged man pushed his way to the front. "Just who is this lady, Frannie? How come she looks so much like Tee?"

"She's my niece, Peg's daughter. You remember Peg, Oscar."

"Gawd almighty," he rumbled. "I should have seen it. Well, in that case, Officer, don't you worry none about this little lady. She's a Rich, and the Rich, we take care of our own."

"Right," several voices responded. "No matter what it takes."

"Yeah," said another. "You Ritches better stay away from Peg's gal or you'll have us to answer to."

Things were getting ugly. How was it these people couldn't see how ridiculous they sounded? The Riches protecting me from the Ritches? I didn't have time for this.

"I can take care of myself," I said, freeing the arm Frances had hooked around mine.

"Not if you're staying at the inn." Frances reached for me again. "You're coming home with us."

More uproar ensued, Jon defending the motel, the Ritch contingent expressing outrage that they would harm anyone, and the homonyms dredging up slights real or imagined suffered over the years since. Suddenly it was Ourland versus Umber Shores with me stuck in the middle.

"Come on." I felt a tug on my hand. Tracy. "Wheel me out of here."

I freed myself from Frances's grasp again and slipped out of the waiting room pushing my cousin, leaving Mars to referee. Neither Rich nor Ritch even noticed.

13

"SORRY," TRACY SAID, A GRAVY-SOAKED FRENCH fry halfway between her plate and her mouth. "I know it's impolite to stare, but I can't help it. It's like I'm looking at myself a few years from now. How old are you anyway?"

"Thirty-two," I said, picking chunks of apple from my salad. I'd skipped lunch at the diner, in no mood to rejoin the cultural heritage bunch. I was in turmoil, past the point where I could decide what to do next. It was just as well Tracy had decided to assume the role of guardian angel for the time being.

We'd escaped the hospital in my car and, at my cousin's insistence, had left town to find a quiet place to eat and talk. Tracy decided on the Back Bay Café.

"The seafood's pretty good and their burgers and fries are even better," she'd declared. "And they don't bug you if you take more than fifteen minutes to eat."

She'd been right but perhaps the fact that we'd selected a table nearest the very noisy kitchen might have had something to do with no one caring how long we stayed.

I had to admit, however, that in the few stray moments when I wasn't wondering how my grandfather's surgery was going or trying to figure out what to do about getting the medal in the time remaining. I was enjoying my cousin's company. Bright, articulate, with a take-charge personality, Tracy had an offbeat sense of humor and philosophy of life to which I could relate. She worked in a branch of the local library, designed beaded jewelry as a hobby, and occasionally helped out at the exhibit hall. We'd fallen into an easy, comfortable rhythm in a very short time. I began to think that I might form some lasting relationships with my mother's side of the family anyhow.

She had done a masterful job of keeping the conversation light so far. She grinned. "It's nice to know what I'll look like at thirty. And let me tell you, the older I get, the younger thirty sounds. Now." Pushing her empty plate to one side, she wiped her hands, her demeanor becoming solemn. "I learned more about my family and my hometown in ten minutes back there at the hospital than I have in my twenty-three years as a resident. Typical kid, I guess, satisfied with the status quo and fed up to the ears with all the old folks' talk about Ourland and Umber Shores history. And family, family, family!"

"I'm beginning to understand perfectly," I said.

"I mean, I knew my mom had two younger sisters who had died but she didn't seem to want to talk about them and Aunt Fran flat-out wouldn't. I figured it was just too painful for them, so I didn't push. I had no idea Aunt Peg had married a Ritch-with-a-T. As for Aunt Fran, she never made a secret that she didn't like Miss Elizabeth, but I didn't think anything of it, since there aren't all that many people she likes anyway."

"I got the impression she has strong opinions," I said, as diplomatically as possible.

Tracy gave a hoot of laughter. "You can say that again. She takes some getting used to. But let's talk about you. What's this about needing a medal?"

I ran it all down for her, starting with the fire to explain why I'd been left with nothing and had known even less than nothing about my parents and their backgrounds.

"Like you," I said, "a typical kid, living in the moment, which happened to be Sunrise, North Carolina. So when this crazy man called demanding my dad's medal, I was starting from ground zero. It's been a roller-coaster week, one mind-blowing incident after another. After twenty-seven years of thinking of myself as an orphan, I find not one, but two branches of family, both within fifty miles of D.C. I go talk to my dad's folks and Elizabeth outright rejects me, and says my dad never received a medal. Five minutes later, her husband's eyes fill with joy at meeting me and he implies that I should pay Elizabeth no mind and that he might be able to help. Fifteen minutes later, he's unconscious, critically injured. And somewhere my foster mom and her new husband are prisoners, depending on me to save their lives by bringing this . . . this madman my father's medal. And here I sit wondering what the hell to do next."

I sighed and gave up on the Waldorf salad. Who was I kidding? I knew what I had to do. I had to get in that house again and search my grandfather's room. As there was no way Elizabeth was going to agree to that, I'd have to do it without her knowledge and permission. I'd hopped the fence before, I could do it again. I hadn't paid that much attention to whether or not there was an alarm system in the house. I'd cross that bridge when I came to it.

But what to do with myself until I could chance it? I'd checked out of the inn this morning. By the time I'd get back to the exhibit hall, the cultural heritage group would have disbanded, and I had no intention of staying in the hall alone. Perhaps the hospital's main waiting room or cafeteria.

"Exactly what did Doc Ritch say to you about your dad

and the medal?" Tracy asked. She'd been in a brown study of her own.

I repeated the conversation verbatim. "I'm not sure what to think. Jameson told Casper that he'd served with my father in Vietnam, yet Elizabeth says he never left the States. But since my father kept in touch with his dad after Elizabeth disowned him, and Granddad maintains she doesn't know as much as she thinks she does, she must have been wrong. Granddad knew why I needed the medal. I can't see him saying what he did to me if he didn't have it or know where it is."

"So you're hoping Doc regains consciousness and fills in what you need to know," she said.

"And soon," I admitted. "I was thinking about camping out at the hospital for a while, but it's a cinch I won't be able to get in to see him."

"Oh, don't worry about that." Tracy waved a hand of dismissal. "I've got a couple of buddies who are nurses over there. They'll tell me how he's doing and sneak you in, if I ask them to. But the question remains: who wants you out of the Shores? And why? I mean, none of us knew you existed before yesterday."

"That's not quite true," I said, as much for my benefit as hers. "I went to live with two different cousins of my mom's before I wound up with Nunna. The mother at the second place was named Andy. Maybe that was short for Andrea, I don't know."

Tracy screwed up her face, thinking. "We have family reunions alternate years and I don't remember a cousin named Andy. Mom will know who she is. And we'd better split and go home before Mom and Aunt Fran report you as a missing person. Just be prepared for them to fight over which one you'll be staying with."

"Oh." This was an unanticipated development, but it

might simplify matters. I'd have a base of operation, a place to think and plan. Elizabeth would probably remain at her husband's side until he was out of danger, knock wood. Hopefully that big old museum of hers would be empty.

Bonita's certainly was, the windows dark, the only light on the porch. Tracy directed me to Frances's house. Fortunately, all the fighting was over by the time we got there.

"Where have y'all been?" they demanded in concert. Bonita grabbed a chair for her daughter, but the question was directed at me.

"Chill, Ma, Auntie F.," Tracy said, leaning her crutches against the kitchen table. "I dragged Leigh off to lunch to get her away from all that craziness." The sisters flushed and she went on. "Park it, Leigh. I assume that since Mom's wearing the apron, she's doing the cooking."

"And so there's no misunderstanding, you, Leigh, will be staying here with me," Frances said, in an "argue at your own risk" tone of voice. "I was wrong this morning and I'm sorry. This is where your mother grew up and this is where you belong."

Tracy gaped at her openmouthed. "An apology? And they say the age of miracles has passed." Frances glowered at her, a complete waste of a frown since Tracy grinned back amiably. "I'm proud of you, Aunt Fran."

I glanced around while Fran, Tracy, and her mother bickered about other occasions when an apology would have been appropriate but hadn't been forthcoming. It was a comfortable house, warm, well cared for and well maintained, with a small room Tracy had called a parlor as we'd entered, and the remainder of the first floor one large room that was clearly the gathering place for eating and relaxing, a combined living/dining/family room and kitchen. Echoes of the past dominated the decor, every piece of furniture probably a cherished heirloom or a replica, yet with none of the untouched aura of the Ritch home. It was a nice old house but I felt no connection with my mother, perhaps because I saw no sign of her. Photos of Tracy and her brothers and their children crowded the mantel above the fireplaces and the wood-paneled walls, but I saw none of the sisters, neither old nor recent. I buried my disappointment and tried to look as if I were paying attention to the conversation. I tuned in just in time. Tracy had changed the subject.

"Now lookit, you two," she was saying. "We've got to figure out who's after Leigh. We didn't know about her until today. Neither did the Ritches, but somebody else must have. Her pictures were stolen yesterday and someone used me for target practice yesterday too."

"Wait a minute," I interrupted. "I did tell Mary Castle who I was right after dinner at the Eatery. I got the impression I could trust her."

"You can." Frances pulled a chair around and sat down. "She's family, too. Married a cousin of Bonita's husband."

"One of Dad's cousins?" Tracy asked. "How come I never knew that?"

"Probably because he was a no-account who drank himself to death years ago," Bonita said.

"Brother, the family dirt I've learned today. Uh—sorry. Poor choice of words." Tracy hooked a chair with her unencumbered foot. "Sit down, Mom. We've got a question for you. Leigh stayed with two sets of Aunt Peg's cousins after her parents died, but she doesn't remember their names."

"Our cousins?" Bonita said. "Where did they live?"

"The first place was in Baltimore somewhere, a middle-aged couple with no children."

"Jeremiah and Mildred," Frances said with no hesitation. "Never understood why she married him. Word was he'd lost some of his personal equipment in Korea and couldn't have babies."

"Frances!" Bonita looked scandalized for a second. Tracy dissolved with laughter.

"Oh, hush up! I put it as nicely as I could. Where else did you stay, Leigh?"

"I don't know where the place was, but there were four children in the family of the second. The mother's name was Andy. I've read a letter she wrote Nunna and she talks about someone named Sell." I wasn't ready to share the contents with them quite yet.

"Brady Sellers and Catherine," Frances said. "She and Millie were sisters." This was news. I hadn't known that. "They were Andersons, and there were two Catherines back then, so we called the youngest Andy. Sellers was career Army and they moved around a lot."

Bonita nodded. "I remember. In fact, Sellers sent us that beer stein from Germany that your dad used to like so much, Tracy. Never figured out why, since he didn't drink beer. But that was Wilson, always—"

"What I'm asking," Tracy broke in, I assume to head off a conversational detour by her mother, "is why they never told y'all about Leigh, especially if they couldn't keep her. Why didn't they send her here to one of you? And where are they now?"

"Well, dead, actually." Bonita sounded as if this was a bit of information she'd just remembered.

Her daughter turned a confused gaze on her. "Who? Which ones?"

"All of them, years ago. Let's see. Uncle Peakle, I think it was, saw Jerry and Mildred's obituary in a Baltimore paper and sent it to us. It's in the family scrapbook."

Frances got up and went out, returning moments later

with an enormous, jammed-packed album. She sat down and began thumbing through it. "Give me a minute. We may also have a Christmas card picture of Andy and her brood," she said, licking a finger as she turned the pages. "That was so sad, all those poor children."

"What do you mean?" I asked, vague pictures of them wafting through my mind. "What happened to them?"

"A fire. The whole family gone, just like that."

Bonita looked troubled. "That's quite a coincidence, isn't it? Guess I never thought about it, Jerry and Millie going the same way, I mean."

"Both families died?" I asked, reduced to a croak. "In fires?"

A stunned silence quieted the room, the only sound the hum of the refrigerator. Frances and Bonita seemed dazed.

"Yes," Bonita said, barely above a whisper. "Both families. In fires."

"I guess we never drew any parallels between the two because we didn't find out about Andy and the kids until so long after the fact," Frances said, her face a study in dismay. "Five or six years later, remember? Bunky found out when he was assigned to that place with all the cannons. East of Baltimore. That's where Sellers was stationed."

"Aberdeen Proving Ground?" I asked.

"Or Edgewood, maybe. They weren't living on base at the time. Lord, I feel just awful about this."

I'd have traded places with Frances in a heartbeat. Both families had taken me into their homes, the first couple for the remainder of the summer I was five, the second family for almost a year before Nunna came. And all had subsequently died in fires? Who was I, Molotov Mary? I felt sick.

"Aunt Frances," I said, "I need to see that obituary. And is this Bunky person still alive?"

The sisters exchanged a glance, then burst into giggles.

"He is," Bonita said. "We just hope his wife is, too. He's buried four. Seems to me number five would have had better sense. Why do you ask?"

"I'd like to find out the approximate date of the fire at Sellers and Andy's."

"Well, that's simple enough," Bonita said. "I'll call Bunky." She left the room.

"Nita," Frances called, rising with the book in her arms, "I need to borrow your glasses. I can't see a thing." She too left the kitchen.

Tracy sat up straight, suddenly intense. "We need to talk, but I'd prefer to do it when they're not around. I don't want to scare them, but if we're thinking the same thing about the fires. I'm not sure what we're up against here."

That had occurred to me as well. I may have put these people in danger. If anything happened to my aunts and Tracy, they'd have to consign me to a rubber room. "I'd better leave," I said. "Why take chances?"

"No way." She pointed at me for emphasis. "When Uncle Oscar said we take care of our own, he wasn't kidding. We don't aim to let anything happen to you. Besides, I've got three brothers and no sisters, so you're it. Mom's cooking dinner for you and Aunt Fran's letting you stay here, which means you're in with them too. We'll talk later," she finished, as Frances returned, granny glasses on her nose.

In the end, once Bunky had been consulted and Frances had found the obituary, the news was about as bad as it could get, as far as I was concerned. The Quintons, Jeremiah and Mildred, had died within a week after I'd been moved to Edgewood. Andy never told me, perhaps to spare me additional trauma. The Sellers' home had burned down approximately a month after I'd left with Nunna. Which explained why no one had ever responded to her letters letting them know how I was doing.

But as Tracy said later when we were alone again, we still had more questions than answers. We sat in front of the fireplace in the parlor, while the aunts prepared dinner and fought over whose recipe should be used for what.

"I'd think that someone was trying to wipe you out after your folks died," she ventured. "But why? I mean, anyone with that in mind would have scoped out the places beforehand. You weren't there any longer, so what was the point? Besides, nothing ever happened to you in Sunrise, so perhaps I'm wrong."

I had a theory about that, one that made me feel even worse than I had before. "Read this," I said, and handed her the letter Andy had written to Nunna.

She finished it quickly, read it a second time, then put it back in the envelope. "This is awful. You and your parents were in danger, even back then? From who? I mean, whom? And why did the cousins have to die? They weren't going to tell anyone where you were." She frowned. "Maybe I just answered my own question. They died so they wouldn't talk."

"Or maybe because they could," I suggested.

"Huh?"

"Suppose someone wanted to eliminate anyone who knew I had survived the fire? Tracy, there's something I should tell you. I didn't mention it before because I was so sure I'd imagined it. I thought I saw my father run from the building the day of the fire."

She did a double-take. "Say what?"

"The top floor where we lived was burning. I was outside on the lawn, bawling my head off because I'd tried to get upstairs to warn Mom and Dad but couldn't get past the smoke."

"Oh, you poor baby." Horrified, she stared at me.

"It was like a bad dream. I have this picture of my father hurrying out of the basement door at the side of the house. I called to him. He turned, saw me, then ran around the back of the house and through the back garden."

"But . . . but—"

"Exactly. Two bodies were found and a downstairs neighbor, a cop and a good friend of my father's, identified them as my parents on the basis of their jewelry. Until now I thought I had to have been hallucinating, but—" I swallowed, forced myself to continue. "Suppose I wasn't. Suppose it was my dad I saw."

"Leigh, you realize what you're saying?" Tracy asked.

"Yes. Andy's letter says my mom was frightened, but there's no mention of my father. What if it was my father she was afraid of? If the fire in our apartment was an accident, why did he run? I can't connect the fire at the cousins' with my father, but here in his hometown he's suspected of complicity in Faye's death and the fire in the church tower afterward."

"Yeah. Jesus," Tracy murmured.

"There's a part of me that rejects it all. It's just not the image of the man I remember living with, even though I don't remember much. But the former cop in me looks at all this and is forced to face the possibility that my father may have been an arsonist and a murderer. He may even have been on the run before. He wasn't using his real last name."

"So that's why you're Warren instead of Ritch-with-a-T. I wondered." Trace twirled a curl between her fingers in thought.

"It's all circumstantial, all supposition. But what else can I think?"

"Yeah." Tracy nodded. 'But if he is alive, where's he

been all this time? Not here, that's for sure. I wouldn't know him if I saw him, but you can bet your boots Mom and Aunt Frannie would. And no way would my aunt keep quiet about it. Everybody in town would know he was back."

I glanced at my watch. It was getting dark. I still felt that if there was even a remote chance that being in this house put these relatives in peril, I should leave, go back to D.C. The problem would be how to do it without causing an uproar. And I wanted to check on my grandfather before I left.

"My granddad said that my father got word to him after me and my brother were born," I said, back on track again.

"You have a brother?"

"Had. He must have died early on. That's something else I didn't know until this week. Anyway, I'm wondering if Granddad might have told someone else about me. Evidently not Elizabeth and Ruth. I was a complete surprise to them."

"Perhaps his brother," Tracy said. "After all, they were twins, and you know how twins are. But Mr. Stu's been dead for years. What are you getting at?"

"Just fiddling around with possibilities. Except for my grandfather, no one else here in town knew I existed. But by showing up, I've put someone's nose out of joint. Why? How am I a threat to anyone? I mean, it's not as if I came to claim some sort of inheritance."

Tracy jerked erect. "Hey-hey-hey! You may have hit the nail on the head. The way it works around here, you leave your land to your children, or grandchildren should your children die before you do. Doc Ritch and his wife own all that waterfront property. But there's only the one daughter left, your Aunt Rachel Ann, who's had one oar out of the water as long as I can remember."

"Really?" I asked.

"She has a small house in the compound, but everybody watches out for her because she's not exactly a candidate for independent living. You see where I'm going with this?"

"Uh, yes and no."

"You stand to inherit one helluva valuable stretch of sand some day. Doc and his wife are certain to have made some sort of provision for Miss Rachel, but they'd be as crazy as she is to leave all that property to her. It'll be yours!"

"No way." The prospect was too outlandish to consider. "I saw that waiting room full of Ritches. And there's Ruth's kids too. As close as she and Elizabeth are, twins who married twins, it's only logical she and my granddad would want to leave the land to Ruth's children."

Tracy shook her head adamantly. "You don't understand how things work around here. It's called the Ourland Covenant, drawn up in ought-one. It's not even legally binding, but the point of it is to prevent family squabbles and outsiders from winding up with our land. Our land, Leigh. It's preached at you from the time you learn to walk. Your children inherit, or your grandchildren. Or else."

"Or else what? You just said, it's not legally binding. What if you don't have any children or grandchildren?"

"If there are surviving siblings, it's split among them. If not, the property becomes part of the Ourland Trust and can be sold to the highest bidder, but only if they're descendants of the first families or are married to someone who is. As far as I know, no one has had the nerve to give the finger to the covenant and fight it in court, which is incredible when you stop to think about it. I guess we're all happily brainwashed. Our land. So before you showed up,

Miss Ruth would have inherited the property, assuming she outlived her sister. In fact—" Her eyes widened. "You'll get your mom's lot next door. Congratulations, cuz. You're a landowner!"

It was still too bizarre a notion to digest. And, considering something Mary Castle had said yesterday, I had to wonder why Elizabeth was lobbying to have her property designated a historical site. Wouldn't she prefer that Ruth inherit it? It didn't make sense, none of it. Unless, of course, I misread her reaction today and she did know I existed. As vindictive as she seemed to be, she might prefer that her land come under the aegis of the state rather than see it fall into the hands of her son's heir. In which case, she would definitely want me out of the way.

But would my own grandmother try to kill me? As much as I disliked what I'd seen of her, I found that hard to accept. Besides, she'd have had to enlist help. One thing was certain, Elizabeth Ritch was not the one whose finger bore my teeth marks, and the figure I'd seen was definitely male. Male or female, whatever his or her reason for seeing me as a threat, it made no difference. I had to get into the Ritch house and search my grandfather's room, and I couldn't let concern for my safety stop me.

Tracy regaled her mother and aunt with the saga of my search for the medal over dinner and ended it with "What can we do to help?"

Immediately, Frances said, "Regina."

Bonita looked blank for a moment before the light of understanding dawned in her eyes. "Of course! If anyone besides Doc knows if Warren got a Silver Star, it's her."

"Who's Regina?" I asked, determined not to get my hopes up. I'd been on this merry-go-round before.

"She was Doc's nurse for years. If Warren wrote to his father and didn't want Elizabeth to know, he'd have sent the letter to the office. Reggie opened all his mail. She and Glenda never blabbed about what went on in that office either. If Reggie knows, I can't guarantee she'll tell us even now. But we could ask."

"How far away is she?" I asked, reaching for my purse. "I can drive, if you like."

Frances stopped me. "It'll have to wait until tomorrow. Reggie's under hospice care. She can see visitors late morning, early afternoon, but she'd be in no shape to talk this late. We'll go tomorrow, I promise. I'll check with her aide first thing so they'll know we're coming."

Tomorrow. Thursday. Two days left. Inexplicably, I yawned, and barely managed to cover my mouth in time. "Sorry," I said. "That snuck up on me."

"You've had a long day." Frances got up. "It's my turn to stock up on coffee supplies for the exhibit hall, so I'd better get moving before the grocery store closes. Come on, Tracy. I can drop you off on the way. Bonita, take Leigh up to Peg and Faye's room. It's hers now anyway." With that, she swept out. I could swear there were tears in her eyes.

Tracy pushed herself to her uninjured foot and reached for her crutches. "Well, cousin, it's been interesting," she said. "I wish I could go with you to see Miss Reggie tomorrow, but there's a big deal meeting at the library and I have to be there. If you all think of anything I can do, give me a call at work, okay?"

I got up and walked with her to the door. "Thanks, Tracy. You've been super."

"Super enough that you won't disappear when all this is over? You've got to meet my brothers and their wives and crumb-snatchers. And I was serious about that sister shit."

"Tracy!" her mother said, admonishing her.

Her daughter grinned. "Sorry. It's not as if I didn't come by my potty mouth honestly. You should hear Mom when she's really steamed," she said to me. "But you know what I mean, right?"

"Right." I looped an arm around her shoulder. "I'll be back. That's a promise."

"Tracy!" Frances yelled from a SUV parked out front.

"The boss calleth," Tracy said. She leaned over and planted a quick peck on my cheek, gave me an embarrassed smile, and clunked down the steps.

"That child," Bonita said, shaking her head. "She's never forgiven me for not having another girl. Looks like she's appointed you a surrogate sister. I hope you don't mind. Sisters can be wonderful, but they can also be a giant pain in the ass." Her grin was a twin of her daughter's.

"I admit it'll be a new experience for me. I just hope I'm up to it. What kind of sister was my mother?" I asked.

She pointed toward the ceiling. "Come see for yourself."

14

IT WAS A BIG ROOM, ONE OF THREE ON THE SEC-
ond floor, and something told me that not much had
changed in it in years. There was a schizophrenic quality
about it, the personality of the former owners defiantly
shouting their differences. The left side of the room was
feminine in the extreme the opposite side displaying the
athletic inclination and interest in sports of its owner. To
my dismay, I had no inkling of which side reflected my
mother's personality.

One of the twin tester beds was covered with a white
chenille spread, a faded satin pillow embroidered with
"Deb Ball 1958" leaning against the headboard, the other
bed with a blue and green plaid coverlet, a pair of teddy
bears in Baltimore Colts and Orioles T-shirts resting on its
pillows. Faded pom-poms, pennants, and cheerleader paraphernalia dangled from tacks on the wall above it.

On one side of the room was a white dresser and matching desk, sprays of pansies across their drawer fronts. Atop
the dresser, vintage atomizers, and a silver comb, brush,
and mirror were carefully positioned on a silver filigreed
tray. The dresser on the opposite wall, a squat, unadorned
walnut monster on ball-clawed feet, wore a plain linen run-
ner, a tortoiseshell comb, a collection of thimbles and scis-
sors, and one small perfume bottle. I picked it up,

unscrewed the top, sniffed it and recoiled at the strong bite of alcohol. But underneath it, barely detectable, was the scent I'd pursued around the counters in Lord and Taylor years before. The label read "Apple Blossom." Now I knew.

"This one was Peg's." Bonita smoothed invisible wrinkles from the plaid spread and nestled the bear in her arms. "There wasn't a lot of fuss and frill about her," she said wistfully. "Peg didn't need that kind of thing to prove her femininity. She was smart and so creative, made her own clothes and most of ours and never used a pattern. And Lord, did she love the Baltimore Orioles and the Colts. It sounds terrible, but I was almost glad she didn't live to see them sold out from under the city."

Which brought up a question I'd been wondering about. "Aunt Bonita, how did you find out she was dead?"

She looked away. "You'll probably think this is silly, but I just knew. We were all tight, but Peg and I . . . It's hard to explain. Peg and I were really close, maybe because we were the two in the middle. I always knew what she was thinking and feeling and vice versa. And one day I realized I didn't have a sense of her here inside. That's when I knew."

"But nobody actually told you? You weren't officially notified?"

"No, but I wasn't surprised she was gone. Even then, there was no way to find out for certain, no matter how convinced I was, because I didn't know where she was or what she was calling herself?"

"You knew she and Dad weren't going by Ritch any longer?" I asked.

"Sit down, baby." She patted the space beside her. "There are things that only I know, things that might help you understand the ugliness you saw at the hospital."

I sat on the bed, at once wary and on edge, not at all certain I'd like what was coming. To my surprise and momentary relief, the subject was not my mother.

"I feel a little like a traitor doing this, but I owe it to Peg," she said, her discomfort obvious. "Faye was my baby sister and Fran's heart. She was smart, had twice the brains of the rest of us, but she was also a manipulative little bitch."

I gasped, then shut my mouth.

"The problem was that everybody liked Peg. If she and Faye were together, people were naturally drawn to Peg first. She just made you feel comfortable, fun to be around. Faye couldn't stand that. And anybody, male or female, that Peg considered a special friend, Faye would ingratiate herself with to sabotage the relationship. She put on a dynamite front. I never understood why folks around here never saw past it. Deep down Fran knew what Faye was like, but would never admit it, especially after Faye died. She hasn't exactly canonized her, just prefers to remember our baby sister through a filter, if you know what I mean. And she's done the opposite with Peg."

Uncertain why Bonita felt it necessary to tell me all this, I tried to digest the information. I also wondered why my grandmother had been so hot to trot to pair Faye with my father in holy wedlock.

"If Aunt Frances holds so much against my mother, why are her things still here?" I asked.

"Because I pitched a fit when I caught her tossing Peg's belongings in the trash. I told her if Faye's stuff stayed, so would Peg's or she could consider herself sisterless. And I meant it. What I want to explain," Bonita went on, "is that Peg and Warren didn't begin dating until they were in college. Faye was two years behind Peg and busy playing Miss Popularity over at Howard in D.C, so she didn't know that they were serious about each other and planned to be married once Peg got her master's. Then Warren asked Stu to stand in for him at a big dinner dance Peg had to attend."

"Who's Stu?" I asked.

"His cousin. Four or five of the Ritch boys were in the service then, and any of them would have been willing. It just happened that Stu was stationed at Fort Meade and was able to get leave. Warren was out West somewhere and couldn't make it."

"Who are all these Ritch boys?" I asked.

"Warren, Walter, Stuart, George, Freeman, Peter. They're cousins, sons of your grandparents' brothers and sisters. Couldn't be more than three or four years between the oldest and the youngest. They were like brothers themselves, hung out together, went sailing, to games, the kinds of things guys do." She patted my arm. "Let me finish now or I'll get sidetracked. So Stu takes Peg to the dinner dance. We figure that's when Faye found out about Warren and Peg."

"Don't tell me. Faye went after Dad?"

"Like a killer whale after a seal. I found her diary after she died, thank God, or I never would have guessed what she'd been up to. He came East for some sort of meeting at the Pentagon and managed to arrange a day here for a cousin's wedding. Faye was waiting for him. She met him at the bus station and told him Peg had been cheating on him. She got him drunk—everybody knows the Ritch boys have no head for alcohol—and got him into bed. And got pregnant."

So Ruth knew only part of the story. It was just as well. "She told you and Aunt Frances?"

"No. He had told her his unit was going to be shipped overseas before long, so she called him, told him, and wanted to know when they could get married."

Which put him between a rock and a hard place, I thought.

Bonita's eyes were focused somewhere beyond me, perhaps back through the years. "According to Faye's diary, he was very gentlemanly about it. He told her he'd support the child, pay all her medical expenses. If she didn't want to keep the baby he was certain one of his sisters would, and they would settle things before he was shipped out. The point is, that's not what Faye wanted to hear. From there, it's all supposition. We know he was expected home for two days before being shipped out, and Peg made a special arrangement with her professors so she'd be able to see him."

"He had told Mom about Faye?"

"I think he planned to as soon as she got in. Anyhow, several people saw Faye waiting outside the church that night and saw Warren drive up a few minutes later. Now, no one actually saw them go in together. But the next time anyone saw Faye she was dead, and the tower was on fire."

I wondered why Ruth hadn't mentioned the fire. The pattern was frightening. That made four incidents in which people had died and fire had been involved. "But if he was the only suspect, why was he never arrested?"

"Because Peg swore Warren had been with her. That was the night they drove to Elkton and got married."

"Ah." The legal ramifications were obvious. A wife could not be forced to testify against her husband.

"So nobody really knows what happened in that tower. But there's something else only Fran and I know. Faye had already had an abortion."

"What?" I thought back but couldn't remember. "Were abortions legal then?"

"No. This was 1963. The medical examiner told us.

That's when I searched until I found her diary. It was all in there, the whole, mean-spirited, sordid story, complete with little hearts decorating the I's. She cleaned out her savings account to pay for the abortion. The whole point was to trap him into marriage, to steal him from Peg. 'I've got him.' That's what she wrote. 'Wayne is *mine*!' "

The name startled me. "Wayne? Everyone else called Dad Warren. The only person I've heard called Wayne is my grandfather."

"Well, for pity's sake, she didn't mean Doc Ritch! You forget, I know how Faye's mind worked. That was her way of crowing that she'd landed Wayne Junior, an elder son of the community's favorite Ritch, and Peggy's Ritch at that. She was so sure she'd snagged the biggest fish in town."

Any way you looked at it, it wasn't a pretty picture. Faye's death solved a number of problems. With her out of the way, as far as Dad was concerned, no one would know about the baby until after he and Mom were married and Faye's body was found. And if Mom loved him so much that she'd stick with him in spite of the cloud of suspicion he was under, I had no doubt that she would refuse to testify against him. Perhaps Dad had no doubt either.

"I wonder if he ever told Mom about the pregnancy at all," I said.

"I really don't know." Bonita wrung her hands. "I never let on to Frannie, but I heard from Peg a few times after she left with Warren and she never mentioned Faye's pregnancy. It was the same situation as Warren writing his father; Peg had to send her letters to my job because Frannie would have ripped them up without ever opening them, even though they were addressed to me. I saved them, Leigh." Reaching down into the bodice of her blouse, she extracted several envelopes with a rubber band around them. "I was just going to let you read them, but now, knowing you don't have a single thing of hers, you should keep them. I thought about giving you one of her bears, and you can have one if you want it, but it wouldn't be the same. These are in her handwriting, a little piece of her. Besides, I have my memories of her. That will be enough."

Tears glistened on her lashes and I reacted instinctively, leaning over to wrap my arms around her. It wasn't just her generosity that touched me as much as the love she had for my mother even after all these years.

"I'd better finish loading the dishwasher," she said, wiping her eyes. She got up and smoothed her apron fussily.

"Aunt Bonita." I foiled her exit with a restraining hand. "You knew my father."

"All his life. We were the same age, went to the same schools until college."

That was good enough. "I have to know. Would you have thought him capable of murder?"

She dipped her head, then looked me in the eye. "No. A couple of others on that side of town, maybe, but they were questioned and had undisputed alibis. Warren was a good man, Leigh, one of those deep-down decent people who make this world a better place." She started for the door, but stopped and turned to face me. "I don't pretend to understand what happened. Even knowing what Faye did, how badly things looked when she died, I have never been able to bring myself to believe that Warren was responsible. To be honest, if he told her once and for all that he wouldn't marry her, I wouldn't put it past Faye to have jumped, just to make things look as bad as possible for him. She couldn't have guessed that he'd be suspected of killing her, but she was wily enough to know that sooner or later the abortion would come out, people would draw their own conclusions and Warren's name would be mud. She was just that single-minded when she set her heart on something, and just that malicious when she didn't get her way. And if I'd had the guts to tell Frannie that, I'd have felt a lot better about myself all these years. Read your letters." She turned and rushed from the room.

I sat for a moment and wondered what it had taken for my aunt to divulge what she had. Finally I moved from my mother's bed to the small roll-top desk on her side of the room, and opened it. All the cubbyholes were empty, which was disappointing, but I'd only raised the top for elbow room anyway. With my pulse throbbing, I removed the rubber band and looked for the first time at letters of the alphabet formed by my mother's hand. My mouth dropped open. If I hadn't known otherwise, I'd have thought I had addressed the envelope, our handwriting was that much alike.

After arranging the three in chronological order using the cancellations, I opened the first, dated September 17, 1966. There was no return address and the letter itself was short.

Dear Bonnie,

I just wanted you to know that we're fine. As you can tell from the envelope, we're living in Virginia on base. It's so painful being this close to Ourland and not being able to come home.

Warren swears he didn't kill Faye, Bon, and I believe him. I couldn't live with him or myself if I thought he did. We're still trying to work our way past the horror of that night, but it's so hard because we both miss our families. Miss Elizabeth re-

*fuses to take Warren's calls and Frannie made it
clear she would never forgive me for taking up for
him. But we'll muddle through together. I miss you
and Frannie, even Faye, so much. I'll try to write
again soon.*

Your loving sister,
Peg

I refolded the paper and slid it back in the envelope,
sharing her anguish. As I'd suspected, the wrench from the
bosom of her family had been hard for her. It pained me
that she had died without the reunion she longed for. And
if she missed Faye, it's a cinch she didn't know about the
pregnancy.

The second letter, dated months later, was disturbing.

Bonnie,

*Sorry it's been so long, but I've been working and
trying to get used to Warren being away. I don't even
know where he is, but he assured me the air force
isn't sending him to Vietnam. He writes when he can
but it's so hard not knowing anything. I do know
there's something else he isn't telling me. I try to be
a good military wife and accept that there are things
he's not allowed to talk about. I just hope I'm not
fooling myself thinking whatever he's keeping to
himself is related to that.*

*I'll be in touch. Kiss Frannie for me, just don't tell
her who it's from. I still miss you both.*

Love,
Peg

With the third letter dated July 6, 1967, I felt a chill.

Dear Bonnie,

Warren's back and has been discharged, but we'll be moving again soon for the second time since he got out. Someone's been harassing us for over a year. It's been horrible, Bonnie, the phone ringing in the middle of the night and no one's there, dead birds outside our door, books of burned matches in our mailbox. We've reported it but the police can't seem to stop it. I keep feeling Warren knows who's behind it but he says he doesn't and enough is enough. He worries about protecting me. So we're moving again and may even change our name. I'll get in touch as soon as I can. I'd give anything to be able to come home!

Love,
Peg

I returned the letter to the envelope, and sat, trying to shake off the despair that seemed to taint the ink she'd used. Much had been explained, and for the first time the pieces of the puzzle were beginning to mesh. I didn't have the whole picture by a long shot, but the little I had would be something to build on later. My major concern was how it might impact what I had to do here now. It was imperative that I be able to move around without having to worry about someone turning me into roadkill.

I was still working on that when the phone rang. Being nosy, I hurried downstairs, my precious letters in my purse, and tried to eavesdrop without being obvious about it. I needn't have bothered.

"Leigh?" Bonita came in from the kitchen. "That was Tee.

She wanted you to know she's called her friend, Harlette, who works at the hospital. Harlette's not on duty until the morning, but she says if you'll ask for her at the second floor nursing station, she'll take you up to critical care."

"That's wonderful," I said. "Was there any word about how my grandfather's doing?"

"I'm afraid not. Harlette knew he was out of surgery, but that's about all. Don't give up hope. Did . . . did the letters help you at all?" She lowered her voice as if her sister were within hearing. "I'll pull together a few pictures of her for you when I get home. A girl should have pictures of her mother."

I'd have thanked her, but was suddenly too choked up to speak. She patted my cheek and bustled back to the kitchen.

I followed. "I might be asking for trouble, Aunt Bonita, but I think I'll run over to the hospital now, just to see what I can find out."

"You'll be asking for trouble, that's for sure," she said, wrestling with an enormous cast-iron skillet. "But you should go anyway. And don't let Elizabeth bully you. She and Frannie are so much alike, so opinionated and convinced they're right all the time. Nobody's right all the time. You go on, baby. Oscar's parked out front. He'll follow you there."

"What?" I peered out the parlor window. "How long has he been there?"

"Since right after you and Tee arrived. Frannie called him. When he gets tired, his brother, Ken, will take over. One way or another, there'll be someone watching you until you leave town."

This would never do. When I jumped the Ritch fence, I wanted no witnesses. It was bad enough I'd have to break the law to begin with. I wasn't certain what to do, but I had to lose my tail.

"Aunt Bonita, I think it's best that I go back to D.C. when I leave the hospital. It's not that I don't appreciate the protection, I'm genuinely touched. But a round-the-clock bodyguard is too much to ask. I'm out of things to wear anyhow," I added to forestall her protest. "And I should check in with my friends and my fiancé."

Her face drooped. "I hate to see you go. And Frannie will be so disappointed."

I promised I'd be back tomorrow, asked her to thank Frances, and went while the going was good. If my aunt returned before I could escape, she might insist on going to the hospital with me. I got the impression she would jump at the chance to clash horns with Elizabeth and I would just as soon she not use me for an excuse for round two.

Oscar trailed me to the hospital in his twenty-year-old Caddy, becoming so intimate with my rear bumper that I checked it for dents when I got out. Fortunately, it was easy to convince him that there was no need for him to wait and escort me to the highway later. I'd caught him yawning when I'd left Fran's and I suspected his bedtime was fast approaching. He headed for home with a belch of smoke and a clatter of valves.

There was no sign of my grandparents' clan in emergency's waiting room, so I took an elevator to the second floor and was following the yellow arrow on the floor toward the critical care unit when a familiar voice called my name. I looked around and saw Amalie exiting an elevator from the far end of the hall, balancing several cups of coffee on a Styrofoam tray.

I waited for her, relieved to see a friendly face. "How's Granddad?" I asked, getting right to the point.

"A little better, according to the surgeon. The swelling in his brain is going down, they were able to stop the bleeding, and his vital signs are good. They're still waiting for him to wake up, though. He's still critical."

My spirits flagged. The longer he was unconscious, the bleaker the prognosis. He'd seemed so robust, so vibrant. The thought that he might not recover, might never be the same again, gouged a canyon in the pit of my stomach.

"Uh, Leigh, I wouldn't go back there if I were you," Amalie said, her manner apologetic. "For one thing, the whole family's there, a real mob scene. The staff is already stressed out because there are so many of us but they all know Uncle Wayne, so they're making allowances. Uncle Stu and Jon are trying to keep everybody quiet, but Aunt Liz practically foams at the mouth every time anyone mentions your name."

"Well, running into you solves my problem," I said. "All I wanted to know was how Granddad was doing."

Amalie had the look of a child who's just discovered that her hero is only human. "Aunt Liz is showing a side of herself I've never seen before. And I don't like it."

I found myself at a loss, uncertain how to respond. How could I excuse my grandmother's behavior? I tried for the high road, even though my heart wasn't in it.

"Try and cut her some slack, Amalie," I said. "Right or wrong, she lost a son and may lose her husband. She needs all the support she can get now. Besides, nobody's perfect. I'm sure she's a very nice person inside."

"Let's go over here a minute," she said, jerking her head toward a waiting area opposite the elevators.

We sat down and she was quiet for a moment. "What you said is right, but she's not being fair, Cousin Leigh." I was warmed by the appellation. "It's not as if you can choose your parents, and you're not responsible for what they may have done. If Uncle Wayne didn't hold it against you, how can she?" She squirmed uncomfortably. "Has the lady who raised you really been kidnapped?"

I nodded. She'd started the clock ticking in my head again. "I have her to thank for everything I've accomplished. She doesn't deserve this, damn it! If that man hurts her . . ." I couldn't finish.

Amalie moved over to sit beside me. "I wish I could help; I just don't know how."

If I hadn't been desperate, I would never have considered it. I had no choice. I had to take advantage of her offer.

"You might be able to help, Tracy. I need access to my grandparents' house."

That brought her up short. "Oh. Why?"

"Evidently my father kept in touch with my grandfather without Elizabeth's knowledge; he knew about me, knew he had a granddaughter somewhere. The way he responded when I explained about the medal made me think he might have it. If there's any chance that he does, I'm certain he would have given it to me. I need to look for it." I shut up. It was her decision to make.

Amalie looked thoughtful. "Wait here," she said finally. "I'll be right back." She picked up the tray of coffee cups and hurried toward the CCU waiting room. She was gone so long I began to worry, and was about to head for the waiting room myself when she reappeared with her coat and purse. "Sorry. I had to make sure how long Aunt Liz planned to stay. We're clear for a couple of hours anyway. Let's go."

I added another relative to the list of those I hoped to know better. "Amalie, I can't tell you how grateful I am."

Slipping her coat on, she looked me in the eye. "This is the first time I've ever gone against the family. But I'm not really, am I? Come on before I get cold feet."

* * *

Under the influence of night, my grandparents' home lost the feel of a museum and took on the aura of a haunted house. With sunshine flooding the windows, the signs that it was lived in were easily discernible. Darkness hid those signs and the first-floor rooms I could see from the center hall seemed to be infused with the spirits of those who had come before, to such an extent that I was damned glad I hadn't had to come alone.

There was an alarm system that Amalie disarmed, then flipped a switch that flooded the stairwell with light. "I doubt Uncle Wayne would keep anything he didn't want Aunt Liz to see in their bedroom," she said, closing the door. "His home office is on the third floor. We'll try there."

This would be a test. It was only recently that on good days I'd been able to take steps like an adult as opposed to a toddler. I might be able to handle one flight with dignity, but I wasn't as confident about two.

"We'll take the elevator," Amalie said, leading me to a door concealed behind the steps. Relieved, I expected a vintage model, but they'd opted for late-twentieth-century convenience, reliability and decor. The only thing missing was Muzak.

"I notice you limp sometimes," she added tentatively.

I explained how I'd injured it then went on a fishing expedition of my own. "Granddad mentioned that his wife isn't well."

"She had a stroke a couple of years ago. She hasn't been the same since." Pulling the elevator door shut, she pushed 3 and leaned in the corner while the car moved smoothly toward the top floor. "Then there's Gran." She sighed, her expression one of deep sadness. "You know, when you're a kid, you can't wait to grow up, but being an adult isn't all it's cracked up to be."

I'd have pursued that, since I had the impression that Amalie wanted to unburden, but when the elevator stopped she came erect, her moment of introspection seemingly forgotten.

The only light on the third floor spilled over from the stairwell. Amalie headed toward the end of the hall to a room directly above the one in which I'd met Elizabeth. It was smaller, due to the wedding cake construction, and entirely different in tone and feel. The walls were paneled from their midpoint down in a dark wood topped by a chair rail. Bookshelves filled two walls, crammed with medical tomes and, to my delight, several shelves of mysteries. This was a man after my own heart.

The furniture was heavily upholstered, the desk and matching credenza enormous, old, and well used. Behind it was a mile-long parade of wooden file cabinets. It would take longer than two hours to look through those drawers.

"All this came from his office," Amalie said. "The only thing new is the computer and printer. His patients pitched in and bought it for him."

Which simply reinforced the impression I'd gotten in the waiting room at the hospital. Wayne Ritch had made an indelible impression on this town.

Amalie pulled on the handle of one of the file cabinet drawers. It didn't budge. "Just checking. These are probably all locked. They're medical records. I know because I helped to get them in order when he moved up here. You start on that side of his desk and I'll do this side. If we don't find it in here, we'll check the credenza."

As many times as I'd assisted with search warrants, nothing would ever compare with the sense of invasion that accompanied every drawer I opened, every file I flipped through, every box and container I touched. I found it abhorrent. I'd have given anything to be somewhere else, doing something else. I had to remind myself constantly what this was for. It became a mantra: Nunna and Walter, Nunna and Walter.

But even as I searched, I became aware that something else was bugging me. I'd gone through several drawers when I stopped rifling the one at the bottom and just stood, trying to hear my inner voice.

"What?" Amalie asked, watching me.

I gestured for her to wait. "I'm working on it. Give me a minute."

I stepped from behind the desk, then moved slowly around the perimeter of the room, trying to identify the source of the itch at the base of my spine. It took the full minute I'd requested. When I flipped through the carousel of diskettes, I knew I was right. "We're wasting time. It's not here."

Amalie frowned. "How can you be sure?"

"Granddad said he'd be picking me up to take me somewhere we could talk undisturbed. With your Aunt Liz and your mother in the house, I doubt he intended to bring me back here. Tell me something. Is my grandfather a sentimental man, the type who holds on to things you give him?"

"Are you kidding?" She giggled. "He's one big ball of mush. He's always said you can't deliver babies for a living if you aren't."

"That's what I would have thought. Yet look around you. There's nothing personal up here, Amalie. It's all work-related. No family photos, no baby pictures, no knickknack-type things, nothing. And you said he was writing a book about changes in OB/GYN care. Have you come across anything that looks like the rough draft of a manuscript?"

Her frown deepened. "Uh-uh."

"The diskettes are labeled things like Letters-University,

Letters-AMA, E-mail, DBase 2 files, Excel files. Not one appears to have anything relating to research or medical history. He's got another office somewhere. He must have."

"Oh, my God." Amalie clapped her palm over her mouth. "The old home place. Walden Pond!"

"What?" It was my turn to frown. I decided not to do it again. It hurt. The Band-Aid on my forehead had stuck to the breaks in the skin. "I thought this was the home place."

"Well, it is, sort of," she said, with rising excitement. "I'm talking about the little place built by my double great-grandfather Wayne back in 1901 while this was going up. It's not much more than a two-room shack really, but I guess it was last year Uncle Wayne said he was thinking about renovating it. He said he needed a Walden Pond where he could work without hearing tours tramping up and down the steps and worrying about nieces and nephews—and Aunt Elizabeth—running in and out."

"Where is it?" I asked, my anticipation matching hers.

"Down on the edge of the compound." She closed her drawer. "But we'll have to wait until daylight. There's no road to it, just a path, and the last time I was there, it certainly didn't look like any work had been done on it. In fact it was barely visible because of the overgrowth."

"Too much overgrowth for him to use the golf cart? Because I'll bet that's where he planned to take me. Who was it, George, who said he only used the cart inside the compound?"

There was no doubt that Amalie did not like the idea of finding the place in the dark. "That's true, but there's still no point in our going back there tonight. It stays locked. And if that's where Uncle Wayne intended to go after he picked you up, he would have had the keys with him when he had the accident."

"In other words," I said, "my grandmother probably has

them now. They probably gave her his watch and ring and whatever he had in his pockets. Although—" I stopped to try to reconstruct the scene after the accident. "Amalie, what happened to the golf cart? I don't remember seeing it when I followed you here. Where is it?"

She looked blank. "Got me. Why?"

"Because the key might still be in it. And it might be on a key ring with all his others"

Her face cleared. "It is, on one my brother bought for him. It sort of looks like that dancing baby on the Web. Let's check and see if the cart's under the house."

It wasn't.

"I bet it's at W. Two's," Amalie said, with an air of certainty as we stood outside at the foot of the steps.

"Where?"

"My cousin, Wayne Walter—we call him W. Two— owns the service station. He takes care of all our cars."

"How many Waynes are there, for crying out loud?" I asked, frustrated at confronting yet another obstacle.

"I forget." She began counting on her fingers. "Eight or nine, I guess. It's a family name. One of the founders was named Wayne and there have been several in every generation since. The oldest boy in a given generation gets to be called Wayne if he wants. Another one of those family things. The rest of them use their other name to avoid confusion."

Which explains why my father was called Warren. That being the case, why would Faye have referred to him as Wayne?

"Leigh?"

I tucked the question away to ask Bonita when I could. "Sorry. What did you say?"

"I've got to go home and hit the books. I have an early class."

I had no choice but to give in with as much grace as I could. Amalie had already done more than I had any right to expect.

"But," she added, proving me wrong, "I can check with W. Two to be sure and if he has the keys, I'll get them to you as soon as I can."

It was pushing it, but I had to try. "Would it be asking too much for you to check before you go home? I'll follow you to the service station, if that will help."

She pulled me into the amber glow from the porch lights. "You aren't still talking about trying to get into that place tonight, are you?"

"I'm running out of time, Amalie," I said. "If your cousin has the keys, yes, I'll come back tonight. Just give me directions from here."

She examined my face, saw my determination. "Okay. You know those gothic novels where the heroine goes up to the attic or down to the basement of a big old house when nobody else with one tinch of sense would do it? The one where you know good and well she's walking into trouble? Well, that's how I feel about this."

I wasn't exactly looking forward to it either. But I asked myself, Were Nunna and Walter worth it? There was only one answer. Damn straight.

15

THE LIGHTS IN OURLAND SHORES AUTO SERVICE
were out except for a dim glow for security inside. The
golf cart was barely visible, parked in one of the bays.

Amalie got out of her car and trotted back to me wearing
a sheepish expression. "I forgot. This is Wednesday. W.
Two's over at the exhibit hall in a town council meeting."
She checked her watch. "Although by now, it may have
disintegrated into their weekly poker game. No sense in us
playing follow the leader. I'll leave the beetle here and ride
with you."

"How's W. Two going to feel about coming back to open
up again?" I asked as I maneuvered through the Shores'
dimly lit streets.

"Wayne leave the poker table?" She snorted. "All he's
gonna do is give me the keys to the station."

"He'd trust you with them?"

"Why not? I'm family." That apparently was sufficient
reason in this town.

But the exhibit hall was dark too. I exhaled in disappointment. "Well, we tried."

Amalie released her seat belt and opened the door. "We
haven't even started yet. Come on. They're in back."

I found that hard to picture. There was barely space
enough to turn around in the kitchen, much less room for a

poker table. "How do they manage that?" I asked. "Sit at the countertop?"

"Good grief, no." She was halfway to the door. "They use a small room on the opposite side. The womenfolk didn't feel they should be playing cards in the sanctuary, since the Presbyterians have their Sunday services in here. Never mind that there's bingo in it once a month. You coming?"

I grabbed my purse and tagged along behind her, wishing I had half her energy.

The front door was unlocked. Amalie went in, trotting through the foyer into the main room with easy familiarity and flipping on the lights. "The tables won't be full tonight," she said as she headed toward the far side of the dais. "Half of them are over at the hospital." A roar of masculine laughter filtered toward us. She looked back over her shoulder and grinned. "Ready to meet more cousins?"

That stopped me. "Perhaps I should wait out here. And if I were you, I wouldn't let on that I'm with you or why you want the keys."

She took a moment to process that. "You're right. In fact, I'll tell W. Two that I'll leave the one for the cart and take the rest. Be right back." She disappeared into the dimness on the far side of the dais, a shaft of light slicing across the floor as she opened the door.

"Hey, Ammie," someone said. "What's the latest on Wayne Senior?"

She closed the door, muffling her response.

But the question tickled a thought percolating on a back burner in my mind and I drifted over to the family trees to peer at the Ritch panels. Amalie had been off by two in her count of present-day Waynes. There were eleven, seven of whom might be considered contemporaries of my father. Not all surnamed Ritch but still twigs on the family branches. George Wayne, Wayne Freeman, Wayne Stuart, William Wayne and Wayne Walter. A Victor Wayne had died in childhood and a Carlton Wayne fairly recently.

The door of the back room opened and Amalie said, "Thanks, cuz. I'll drop this off on the way to class in the morning. Tell Carrie hello for me." She rounded the dais and dangled keys at me, a pleased smile lighting her face. "Great minds. He'd already removed the key to the golf cart and had these on him. Or y we'll still have to go back to get my car."

"No problem. Wait, Amalie," I said, as she headed for the light switches. "Are all these Waynes still around?"

She came back. "You mean, living in Ourland? Uh-uh. George and W. Two are. Freeman lives in Philly, Uncle Stu lives in Annapolis, and Uncle Bill just moved from Baltimore to Atlanta. Why?"

"Just wondered," I said, since there was no way to check the theory I was hatching until I talked to Bonita again.

All the way to the service station and back to the compound, I had the feeling there were other questions I should have asked, but promptly forgot it as I followed Amalie past my grandparents' home. Immediately, the road narrowed and we were swallowed by the night. We crept along at ten miles an hour, Amalie's high beams cutting a path through inky darkness unrelieved by moon and stars. The trees closed in on us and I began to understand why my young cousin had been so hesitant about doing this after dark. It was damned scary back here.

I was both relieved when her brake lights glared a bloody crimson and appalled when I saw the building illuminated by those high beams. This was my grandfather's Walden Pond, this shack with no sign that it had been touched by other than wind and weather for decades? He'd be better off razing it and starting over. Paint flaked from its outer shell, plank siding hung askew. I couldn't see the roof and shuddered to imagine the condition it was in.

Opening her door, Amalie leaned out and called back to me. "Park as close to me as you can. There's not a lot of room to turn around. I'll leave my lights on until we get the door open."

She was right. There was a walkway of sorts consisting of stone or concrete pavers but that was all. Where my grandfather parked his golf cart was beyond me. I pulled up beside her Volkswagen, leaving barely enough room to get out of my car. By the time I'd squeezed past her front fenders, calf-high weeds snatching at the fabric of my slacks, Amalie was at the door, trying various keys.

"I swear, this will take all night," she muttered. "Half the relatives have given Uncle Wayne keys to their houses. And I still can't half see what I'm doing."

I found my penlight and held it on the lock, which gleamed brightly, obviously recently installed. It was an incongruous note, considering the condition of the rest of the place. Gaps in the siding exposed what looked like newspaper used as insulation. It was perhaps large enough for two rooms, with a pair of boarded-up windows on our side. The step Amalie stood on as she swore her way through a good dozen keys looked as if it might collapse under her if she breathed too hard.

"Got it!" she said finally, pushing the door open. "Leigh, this is dumb, and probably dangerous. I gotta tell you, I really, really don't want to go in here."

I directed the beam on the floor just inside the door. The surface gleamed, the reflection momentarily blinding me.

"Why don't I go in first," I said, and waited until she was on solid ground before taking her place on the step, having no faith that it would hold both of us. I stuck a hand inside, patted the wall gingerly, and felt light switches under my fingers. I flipped one and winced as a bright, fluorescent glow flared overhead.

Amalie gasped. "That sneaky old man! Look at this! How'd you guess?"

"I didn't," I admitted, moving into the room. "But once I saw that the floor was hardwood parquet, it was just logical that he'd had the place wired, too." Not only had it been brought up to code, it was precisely the kind of space that suited what little I'd learned of my grandfather—warm, cozy and comfortable, with none of the formality of the office in the house. "Don't forget your headlights," I reminded Amalie. "Or do you have to leave?"

"Leave? Are you nuts?" She flashed an impish expression. "No way would I miss a chance to look around in here. Don't touch a thing before I come back. I don't want you to get a head start."

She returned in less than thirty seconds, practically quivering with anticipation. "What did I tell you about him?" she crowed, pointing at the wall just inside the door. "Wayne Warren Ritch, M.D. One big ball of mush."

The top half was papered with row upon row of photos of babies taken soon after birth, each hand-labeled with the infant's name. The bottom half of the wall contained shelves crammed with thank-you gifts, knickknacks, childish drawings, stuffed animals. "I bet this is everything anybody's ever given him or made for him," Amalie said. "I can't believe he kept all this."

I gave it only a cursory glance, since this was clearly not the place he would keep something he wanted to hide. And as ramshackle as the exterior was, no expense had been spared in the interior. If there had been more than one room before, the walls had been removed to leave a single open, airy space. A pair of doors on one side revealed a bathroom complete with shower, and, adjacent to it, a walk-in storage closet containing a pair of file cabinets. Overhead were rough-hewn beams, a fan, and skylights that appeared to open. The windows we'd seen on the outside were hidden behind the wall with the baby pictures, but directly opposite it was an expanse of plate glass that spanned the width of the cabin.

"What's the view from here?" I asked Amalie, who was still perusing the collection on the shelves.

"Hmmm?" She turned. "Oh, wow. The bay. This sits right up next to the Ritch property line. There's nothing out there but undeveloped land until you get to Chesland Beach. I see why he calls it his Walden Pond. It's about as private as it can get. I wonder why he hasn't fixed up the outside?"

"Probably," I said, "so it'll stay as private as it can get. If it looks as bad in daylight as it does at night, anybody with sense will think it's too close to collapse to even poke around."

I left her to ooh and ahh over the hidden refrigerator and two-burner range top masked by redwood cabinets, which also contained storage shelves and lateral files. The room was large enough to hold an arrangement of easy chairs with a matching loveseat in front of a massive stone fireplace and, positioned where he could look out on the bay as he worked, a redwood desk with computer, printer, and a collection of miniature toys on one corner. This, I was sure, was where he did his writing. And playing.

"Where should we start?" Amalie asked, wiggling her fingers.

I suggested she tackle the desk and I'd begin with the file cabinet in the walk-in closet, still uneasy with this invasion of my grandfather's privacy. As I moved past the fireplace to the closet door, I glanced at the row of framed pictures on the mantel and suffered a moment of wistfulness. These were all family portraits, my family, I reminded myself again, the formal one of my grandparents holding an honored site dead center.

There were photos of a young Ruth and her husband, and one or two others of him and my grandfather, mirror images of one another. The two were an obvious catch, a handsome, drop-dead pair.

A number of faces matched those I'd seen in the waiting room earlier, although my grandparents, George, Jon, and Ruth were the only relatives whose names I knew. Belatedly, I recognized the face of the idiot who had almost collided with me yesterday. I should have realized he was a Ritch. The portrait of Amalie in cap and gown was charming, showing a gap between her front teeth that must have been closed by braces since then. Several generations were represented, all members of the Ritch clan. I experienced an unreasonable pinch of resentment that photos of me and mine were missing. On the end, however, partially hidden by an old snapshot of my grandmother and her twin, was the one that made me send a mental apology in my grandfather's direction. And I'd almost missed it.

The portrait, formally posed, showed two smiling young servicemen in uniform. Though clearly not twins, the resemblance between them left no doubt they were closely related. Both shared a milk-chocolate coloring, broad foreheads, straight noses, full lips with trim mustaches. The face of one was not quite as narrow as the other, the jawline slightly more pugnacious, the expression around the lips faintly petulant. One had dark eyes, the other far lighter, somewhere between brown and gray. I knew them both. I'd seen them both.

Lightheaded, I closed my eyes. Finally, finally I remembered the whole man, the tall, laughing figure who held my hand as we walked to the playground beside the church. I remembered the dark eyes that gleamed as brightly as the patent-leather Mary Janes I wore on Sundays, remembered the delighted grin as my father tickled me into submission. And he was dead. There was no longer any doubt. An agonizing moment of loss overwhelmed me as I grieved anew. Then I opened my eyes and looked again at the hazel ones that had glared at me with such malevolence that day.

"Amalie, who's this?" I asked, my voice sounding unfamiliar in my ears.

I'd caught her fiddling with a miniature crossbow on the desk. She flushed with an embarrassed smile. "Sorry. I couldn't resist. These may be little, but they're expensive and they really work, so we weren't allowed to touch them. They disappeared from the house after Uncle Wayne caught my brother playing darts with this. Who's who?" She joined me in front of the hearth.

"This one."

"I'm not sure about him," she said, a finger on my father's neatly knotted tie, "but that's Uncle Stu, my mom's big brother. Geez, he was a hunk, huh? You wouldn't know him now."

Hoping to appear a normal functioning adult in spite of what was going on in my head, I said, "The other man is my father, so this picture was taken almost thirty-five years ago. Your uncle's bound to have changed in that time."

"Well, he has, in spades. There's probably another of him somewhere," she said, scanning the other photographs. "Yeah. Here." She removed a family grouping in a silver frame, parents with one boy and three girls. Again, I knew him, the careless driver of the Land Rover. Much heavier, his face lined and far fleshier, his hair completely gray, he bore no resemblance to the earlier picture. Comparing the two, Amalie shook her head and put the portrait back with a thump. "Who'd have thought it? From hunk to hulk."

"You don't like him," I said, my mouth engaging before my brain could stop it.

She flushed again, then shrugged. "Hey, I can't stand Freeman either. And five minutes around my Aunt Jo and I'm ready to shoot myself. But with Uncle Stu . . . It's hard to explain. I mean, I like him and I don't. He's so . . . so intense about everything he can be scary. He's always worrying about what other people think, know what I mean?"

Remembering my friend Sheryl's mother back in Sunrise, I knew exactly what she meant.

"To give him credit, though," Amalie continued, as if in apology to her uncle in absentia, "he's made a mint in real estate, owns a couple of classy restaurants in Annapolis. And he's done a lot for the town, even though he doesn't live here. Plus he's footing the bill for all Gran's medical expenses, the specialists and stuff."

"Gran," I said, trying to remember who was what to whom. "You mean Ruth? She's sick too?"

"Terminal." A sudden dampness glistened in the corners of her eyes, apparently taking her off guard. She wiped them away. "Breast cancer. She had surgery a long time ago, but it's back and she found out too late. The doctors advised her to get her affairs in order. Isn't that a hell of a way to tell someone they're dying? Anyhow," she said, gazing at the old portrait again, "Uncle Stu's been terrific with Gran, so I guess I shouldn't be so hard on him. He needs to take better care of himself. Jon's always nagging him to go on a diet."

"The manager of the motel Jon?" I asked.

"Yeah. Uncle Stu's his dad. Yours was cute too." She stepped back and squinted at them. "They really look a lot alike, don't they? I guess they would, being sons of identical twins. I'd better get back to work. It's getting late."

I managed to pull myself away and went into the closet, but I found it difficult to concentrate on the matter at hand. My dad was dead, and the man I'd seen fleeing our basement was his cousin Stuart.

I stepped into the doorway. "Amalie, does your uncle Stuart smoke a pipe?"

She looked up. "Yeah. How'd you know?"

"A lucky guess." I returned to the file cabinet, my brain hurling questions like a pitcher warming up. Why had Stuart been there the day of the fire? Why had he run?

Negligent handling of smoking material. My head snapped up in shock. The fire had been his fault? It made sense. My parents were nonsmokers. But how could Stuart flee without trying to get help for my parents? And why hadn't he acknowledged me when he saw me in the yard? Why had he left me? He had to be the phantom who'd been dogging me since my arrival in Ourland. I was the only person who knew what a coward he'd been. If what people thought was that important to him, what I knew could ruin him.

I opened a drawer, impelled by a new urgency. If my father's medal was here, I had to find it and get the hell out of Dodge. I had no interest in confronting Stuart or accusing him of anything at the moment. I could always do that later. Nunna and Walter came first.

The file drawers contained everything from the plans used for the renovation to receipts, travel brochures, letters, insurance policies, and inventories. I had little faith that I'd find what I was looking for here. The drawers were unlocked, their contents too accessible. Then I tugged at the bottom one and found it locked.

"Amalie, have you come across a smallish key in the desk?" I stepped into the room. "For a file cabinet."

She marked her place in the drawer she'd been going through and opened the center one. "Nope. Just regular office stuff, staples and paperclips and stamps. Guess this is a paperweight, maybe." She extracted a small, highly polished wooden cube.

My interest peaking, I took it, examined it closely. "It's a puzzle box. One side slides open, perhaps others, too. Duck loves these things."

"Who's Duck?"

"My fiancé. That's his nickname. Lord, I don't have time for this," I grumbled, pushing each side in one direction, then the other. At the third, I felt something give, just as elsewhere something chirped. Startled, I jumped.

"My cell phone," Amalie said, reaching for her purse, and taking out a phone the size of a credit card.

I kept nudging at the cube as she answered.

"I'm fine, Mom," she said, rolling her eyes. "What's the problem? I'm in the compound. I'll be home soon." She fingered the crossbow again, unable to resist the forbidden toy.

The side panel of the cube slid about the length of a fingernail. I tuned out Amalie's conversation to concentrate on what I was doing. By the time she'd finished, I'd managed to dislodge the second side. Pushing against the third, I exhaled with relief. It slid back to reveal a small open space inside. Nestled in the niche was a silver key.

"I'm gonna have to leave," Amalie said, dropping the phone back into her purse. "Everybody's been looking for me when all they had to do was call. You did it? You think that's it?"

"I'd make book on it," I said, and hurried back to the

locked drawer. The key fit, the cylinder turned smoothly and I opened the drawer. Its only contents were an old Nike shoe box and one solitary file beneath it labeled Cranshaw Investigative Agency.

I removed them and took them out to the desk. "Cross your fingers," I said, taking the top off the box. It was full of paper of one sort or another, among them envelopes addressed to Dr. Wayne W. Ritch, most with no return address. But the handwriting was the same on all of them, firm, squared printing. I opened one, saw "Dear Dad," and squeezed my eyes closed for a three-word prayer of thanksgiving.

"You found it." Amalie's voice was soft.

"Not quite yet," I said, groping through the remainder. There were other mementoes my father had sent, including several baby pictures. A closer look at them sent my heart into overdrive, photos of me and my brother, Lee, taken soon after birth. My brother.

We, I thought to myself, were two plug-ugly babies. Faces that looked like Silly Putty. Cheeks and hair enough for yet another set of twins. There were a few more of us perhaps a year old, and yet another of us as bow-legged novice walkers still holding on to adult hands as a hedge against gravity. We were considerably better-looking by then, in fact, downright cute. Lee had Dad's very dark eyes, alight with intelligence and hail fellow well met. I put them aside to examine more closely later and began rooting through the mass of papers again.

It was on the very bottom in a slender box tucked into a brown envelope. I lifted the top. A Silver Star. Red, white, and blue ribbon from which dangled a five-pointed star, leaves encircling a smaller star in its center. Gently, I turned it over. "For gallantry in action," and in a space below, my father's name.

"So that's it," Amalie said. "Your Holy Grail."

I lowered myself into the chair, my legs unable to support me any longer. I couldn't breathe. "No, Amalie. This isn't it. The one I need was damaged in an accident and one of its legs was bent. These are perfect. This isn't the one. Oh, God." Pain, real or imagined, radiated from my stomach straight back to my spine. I bent over, laid my head on the desk. "Oh, God, Amalie, what am I going to do?"

16

I'M NOT SURE HOW LONG I SAT, INCONSOLABLE, with Amalie doing her best to comfort me. But there was nothing to be said, and after a while, my cousin's presence became yet another burden. She seemed oddly distracted even as she tried to concentrate on me and I remembered her concern about getting home. With the last remnants of control I could muster, I let her off the hook.

"Why don't you go, Amalie, before your mom calls out the Mounties. I'm fine now, just need a few more minutes, but there's no need for you to hang around. You go on."

"You're sure you'll be okay?" she asked, shouldering her purse. "Wait. Considering how much Uncle Wayne believes in catnaps . . ." She darted to the loveseat and lifted the cushions. "Thought so. This is a sleeper, so there's no reason you couldn't crash right here tonight. Who'd know? If anyone sees you driving through the compound tomorrow morning, they'll assume you're coming from Uncle Wayne's. Please stay, Leigh. I don't think you're in any shape to drive."

"A good idea," I said, urging her to the door to speed her departure. "I'll do that. And thanks for everything, Amalie. You've been terrific."

She hesitated, something I couldn't read in her eyes,

then turned to hug me. "Don't give up yet, cousin," she said. "Just don't give up yet. Okay?"

I nodded, fatigue thickening my tongue. "Okay. Now, git."

I watched her leave, waiting outside on the step until she'd carefully turned around and headed out. She flashed her high beams in farewell and was gone, the trees closing in on her so I couldn't even see her taillights as she neared the road.

Finally, gratefully, alone, I was sorry I'd misled her, but I had no intention of staying overnight. I simply needed some time to myself. I wanted to read my father's letters in solitude, get a better sense of the man I'd never gotten to know. I had to do it here and now. I didn't feel free to take them with me to D.C., not without my grandfather's permission, and I wasn't sure when or if I'd ever get that.

I checked to be sure I'd locked the car and had just stepped into the doorway when I detected it, unfortunately a second too late: the sickening stench of Dutch Treasure. Before I could react, a vicious shove from behind propelled me into the room and onto my knees.

Stunned, my right knee howling with insult, I remained on all fours for a minute before rolling to one side and swiveling around to face the bogeyman who had haunted my nightmares in the weeks after the fire.

Amalie was right; except for the pale, soulless eyes, I would not have recognized him. Portly, jowly, dew-lapped and broad of beam, he was nevertheless a frightening figure as he gazed down at me, made even more threatening by the lethal-looking double action revolver in his pudgy hand.

"You Rich women," he said softly. "Just couldn't leave well enough alone, could you?"

It was a second before I realized I should delete the T in the name. "Who are you and what do you want?" I asked, playing for time.

"Oh, you know me. And I know you, recognized you the moment I saw you yesterday. It was like seeing a ghost. If I didn't know better, I'd swear you were Faye's child instead of Peg's. Inherited her genes too, or you wouldn't be here ruining everything I've worked toward. A troublemaker, just like Faye."

"What," I asked, "are you talking about?" I pushed myself to my feet, testing my weight. And flunked. Damm it, every time the knee felt about as well as it ever would, something happened to put it out of commission again. As Duck said on occasion, I was now in deep shit. I had to think fast.

"Imaginative too," he added, with a wisp of a smile. "That ridiculous story about coming here to get Warren's medal."

Anger nudged my fear aside for a moment. "That ridiculous story just happens to be true. And I found it." Taking a chance that I could walk without support, I moved to the desk. "See?" I held up the box containing the Silver Star. "My foster mother and her husband are being held hostage until I give their kidnapper this stupid medal. Why in God's name would I make up a story like that?"

He waggled the gun, gesturing for me to sit down behind the desk. "Why not? As inane as it is, it was all the excuse you needed to turn up in Ourland, wasn't it? And of course, you had no intention of ruining my reputation on top of staking your claim to your inheritance, none at all. Between Peg's lot, and your grandparents', which includes Warren's huge tract, you'd own a prime stretch of waterfront property, land I've had plans for as long as I can remember."

So that's what this was all about? Real estate, for God's sake? I concentrated on keeping cool as I tried to compartmentalize what was going on in my head. He was far too big for me to overpower, the gun affording him an advantage he didn't even need. I had to keep him talking while I tried to figure out how the hell I was going to leave here alive. If I died, so would Nunna and Walter. I glanced at the clock but suddenly couldn't figure out what day it was.

"Listen, Mr. Whoever You Are," I said, focused again.

He stiffened, squared his shoulders. "The name is Ritch. Wayne Stuart Ritch."

"All right, Mr. Wayne Stuart Ritch. Until Sunday, I didn't know I had grandparents, didn't know I had any relatives at all. And I want nothing from any of them. I found what I came for." I put the lid on the box containing the Silver Star I'd blown several days trying to find for nothing. But he didn't know that. I had to be convincing. "It's the only thing I'll take with me when I leave. This is what the man wants to save my mom's life."

"Your mom?" His forehead wrinkled.

"My foster mother," I amended. "For all practical purposes, she's the only mother I've known."

His expression cleared, became cagey. "Oh, yes. The fire. I was really sorry about that. But it was his fault, you know."

"His who?"

"Warren's. My offer was more than reasonable, tit for tat. All he had to do was leave things alone. He owed me. But no, not Warren. Not everyone's golden boy. Mr. Perfect. It just wasn't fair." Sounding like a petulant child, he sat down in the chair at the corner of the desk, holding the revolver rather carelessly on his left knee. A southpaw, something to remember.

"What wasn't fair?" I asked, wondering if there was

anything on the desk I could use as a weapon if I could get close enough to him. The letter opener? Not sharp enough. The cannon? The best it could shoot would be BBs.

"I was supposed to be the oldest, you know."

"Uh . . . really?" This man jumped from one subject to another with the agility of a grasshopper.

He made himself comfortable, seeming anxious to explain. "My dad was older than Uncle Wayne by seven minutes so it was only right that when Mama and Aunt Liz got pregnant about the same time, I should be born first. I'd have been the son *most* entitled to be called Wayne. Only Aunt Liz started having problems and the next thing you know, there's Warren, six weeks premature. He beat me by six weeks. He *stole* my *name!*"

I massaged my forehead, carefully avoiding the bandage. I hadn't realized that the Wayne thing was so important around here. "But everyone says my father always used his middle name," I reminded him.

"Just to rub it in, since he could claim the title any time he wanted. And from the very beginning he was always first at everything. First to walk and talk, first in athletics, first in our graduating class, and first in the heart of every girl in town. When I was in the service, that's where they called me Wayne. It felt *good*. But all I had to do was hit town and I was Stuart again. Plain old second-place Stuey. As hard as I tried, I could never quite catch up."

This was stupid, a man his age carping about stuff that was forty years behind him. But he was the one with the gun. I'd be wise to keep him talking.

"From what I've heard, you've more than caught up," I said. "Not half an hour ago Amalie was bragging about the things you've done for the family, how successful you've become."

He allowed himself the first genuine smile I'd seen.

"Amalie said that? I'm surprised. Somehow I thought she didn't like me. But everything I've done so far is peanuts. The plans I have . . ." He laughed, suddenly animated. "If my cousins only knew who really holds their mortgages. And just as soon as I've gotten my hands on the last three lots, they're all in for a surprise. Let's see them laugh at me then. That waterfront property's going to be mine, from here all the way over to the southern edge of town. And to hell with the Ourland Covenant and the trust. They don't have a legal leg to stand on. Nobody's going to tell me what I can do with my land. Nobody! It'll be Wayne's Waterland, with shops and rides and restaurants. Classy, though, not cheesy like the usual boardwalk trash."

He'd warmed to a favorite subject, so I listened with half an ear as he described ideas he'd been chewing on for thirty years. It sounded like a cross between Colonial Williamsburg in Virginia and Ocean City, Maryland, the underlying theme that of African-American history and culture. He dreamed of visitors in the hundreds of thousands, this in a town the size of a truck stop. I let him ramble on, while I proposed this plan of action and that and discarded them all. He'd been spouting off for a good fifteen minutes before he suddenly stopped, his expression sheepish. "Sorry. I'm boring you."

"Not at all," I said, feigning interest. "It sounds exciting, just the kind of thing this area needs. I hope it works out for you."

"It will. I've come too far to let anyone stand in my way. You chose an inopportune time to show up, little Leigh-Leigh."

It was also an unfortunate choice of words, because suddenly I remembered, more a sliver of a moment than anything else, and I must have been very young when it happened. But I could still see him insisting that I come "give him some sugar." All he wanted was a peck on the cheek, but somehow I knew that he was responsible for the tears in my mother's eyes and the taut set of my father's mouth. I didn't like this stranger who looked like my dad in so many ways but didn't in so many others. I didn't like the way he smelled and he paid no attention to me when I insisted my name was just plain Leigh, not Leigh-Leigh. And even though they hadn't said a word, I had sensed that my parents wanted me to kiss him. So I had. And promptly threw up.

That's all there was of it, but it was enough to explain my reaction to the pipe tobacco. I filed that away. It wasn't important any longer. I had to convince this man that I was no danger to him.

"Look," I said. "I'm thirty-two years old. I have a life, a fiancé, friends. I'm perfectly content with what I have. Nothing in Ourland interests me, least of all any property I stand to inherit. If you want me to sign something swearing to that, fine. All I want is this Silver Star so I can save my foster mother's life."

He shook his head, his features resembling a hound's look of melancholia. "Please. Don't insult my intelligence. How can I believe you, considering the things you've done? You're no better than I am. At least I've tried to atone for the sins of my youth and prayed for forgiveness. You, on the other hand, haven't changed. You're still a scheming, conniving bitch and a murderess."

"Excuse me?" My compartmentalizing went out the window.

"You killed my son!" he shouted, slamming a fist onto the desktop with such force that everything on it danced a jig. So did my heart. "You had no reason to see a butcher and kill my son." He leaned forward as he spoke and I saw

for the first time the madness in those pale, brown-gray eyes. "I *told* you I'd take care of you, Faye. I *told* you I'd see that our child would be brought up in a good home. There was no need for you to have an abortion."

He'd been scary before. It was nothing to what he was now. The skin on the nape of my neck pebbled with goose bumps. "My name is Leigh, Mr. Ritch. Little Leigh-Leigh, remember?"

"Oh, I remember," he said, rising. He began to pace. I eased the drawer open and leaned forward over the desk, hoping it would hide the hand groping inside it. "Warren's little girl. And that's what you wanted when you were coming on to me so hard. Warren. Found out too late that it was Warren Peg planned to marry, not me. So my child was expendable. Well, you paid for that, didn't you? It just didn't occur to me you'd jump. And I felt cheated at first. But it worked out okay. I still remember the look on your face when you came to and saw me standing in the door, waiting for that look so I could close the door and lock you in and listen to you scream as the fire ate you alive."

I gave an involuntary shiver and willed myself still. This was one sick man.

"And they thought Warren had been with you. Isn't that funny? Everyone knew he was coming that weekend, but I wasn't expected. It was pure luck I saw you waiting outside the church. But you paid for your treachery. And so did good old Warren. He took my son, I took his."

"What?" I was so shocked that I almost missed the sound that didn't belong. I had become super-sensitive to the ambience of this room, to the tick of the clock on the wall above the fireplace, the occasional hum of the refrigerator, the muted murmur of the bay. I wasn't even sure if what I'd heard had actually come from somewhere outside or from within my skull, since with his last admission, I felt as if the top of my head was coming off. "You *kidnapped* my brother? My twin?"

"I couldn't believe how easy it was," he said, and chuckled, still pacing, slapping the little revolver against his thigh. "They'd just moved. The baby-sitter had probably never seen Warren, so all I had to do was show up and say I had to take the boy to the doctor. The sitter went into that room full of squalling brats and brought him out and placed him in his daddy's arms. Mine! It had taken me months to find dear old Warren and Peg. They'd tried to evade payback, moving and using different names but I tracked them down, thanks to sweet, dumb Glenda. She worked in Uncle Wayne's office back then, remember? One roll between the sheets and she kept me posted about mail from Warren for the longest. Regina never guessed. I even married Glenda in gratitude. No regrets. It guaranteed her silence and she's been well rewarded. And I got my son back. I'm very proud of him."

He gave me a smile full of parental pride. "You met him at the inn. A good-looking boy, isn't he? I felt badly about swiping his master key to get into your room, but I had to be certain who you were."

I felt as if my brain was full of fizzy water, with bubbles caroming along the convolutions of my gray matter, tiny explosive charges bursting as the magnitude of each of this insane man's acts began to register. Jon Ritch, who I'd regarded last night with a semblance of a roving eye, the dimpled manager of the Shores Inn, was my brother?

"You sick, evil son of a bitch!" I yelled, past controlling myself. "How could you? He was a baby! My twin! Didn't my parents suspect it was you?"

He looked around, seemed to remember where he was and to whom he was talking. "Of course, but pay someone enough money and they'll swear you were somewhere else, in this case, Jamaica. They put two and two together, once they got wind of the illegitimate son I'd decided to raise out of the goodness of my heart. And I tried to reason with them that day, I really did," he said, with deadly earnest. "They had you. It was only fair that I keep the boy. But they wouldn't listen. They said they were coming home to get him. I couldn't let them do that. Jon should have been my son! Mine! And you, you should have paid attention to my warnings. But then, you're a Rich, aren't you?"

"And my mother's cousins?" I demanded. "The Quintons, the Sellers? Are you responsible for what happened to them too?" I figured, what the hell. In for a penny, in for a pound. Or dollar.

He glared, full of indignation, and pointed at me. I wouldn't have minded except that the pistol served as the accusing finger. I'd begun to doubt he remembered he had it.

"Now, you just wait a minute there, missy," he said. "That was your grandfather's fault, not mine. He hired a private detective to find you all, and the man kept getting too close. I couldn't chance him talking to those people. Once Uncle Wayne found out that Warren and Peg were dead and you were still alive, he'd have wanted you to come to live with him and Aunt Liz. You had seen me that day. You'd have told on me. And things were going too well by then. I had Jon, a family, don't you see? I didn't even know those people were Peg's cousins. But I had a family to protect. Family's important, the be-all and end-all. Without family, you're nothing."

"But it didn't matter that that's what you'd left me with, nothing," I said softly, my fury at this insane man making me rash.

"But you weren't," he reminded me, all sweet reason. "You wound up with someone who did very well by you. You must love her, or you wouldn't be here. And I can't tell you how sorry I am about her," he said. "Because I can't let you leave here. You see that, don't you? I'm the oldest son. I'm Wayne. I have to protect my family."

"Even though I'm a part of it," I said, stroking the shaft of the projectile of the miniature crossbow. It was the only thing to hand. The little arrow was on it but I didn't know whether the bow was cocked. I couldn't afford to look at it openly. Stuart might be crazy but he wasn't stupid.

"You are sort of family, aren't you?" He gazed at me with immense sadness. "A first cousin once removed, or a second cousin. I've never been able to keep that straight. Warren's daughter. It always comes back to Warren. Are you religious?"

The question came from so far out of left field that it distracted my surreptitious scrutiny of the crossbow. "That's an odd thing to ask. What do you care?"

He seemed hurt by my attitude. "I just thought that if you are a churchgoing woman, you might like a moment to pray, that's all. It seemed the decent thing to do. Well, if you aren't—"

His arm began an upward arc when the door slammed open with such a loud retort, I thought he had fired. Jon stepped into the room, one hand pushing Amalie behind him with a protective gesture. He looked first at Stuart, his face devoid of expression, then at me. In that moment, I was more afraid of his rejection than of the weapon in Stuart's hand. And in the next, because it lasted no longer than that, I saw I had no need for concern. Perhaps it was in his eyes, perhaps behind them, I don't know. All I do know is that in that split second exchange of glances, I sensed his acknowledgment and acceptance of the relationship between us.

He turned to his father. "Dad, what are you doing?" I heard no reproach or disapproval in the words, only curiosity.

Stuart did not respond in kind. "Get out of here, son, and take Ammie with you. This has nothing to do with you."

"Now, Dad," Jon said gently, "it has everything to do with me. I can't let you shoot my sister."

I felt as if I'd ingested some sort of psychogenic drug that affected my senses. I seemed to expand, becoming somehow taller, larger, stronger. Jon had called me his sister. To an only child, the words seemed infused with some sort of magic. I was no longer alone.

"She's *not* your sister!" Stuart erupted, facing him. "She's just Warren and Peg's brat. She's nothing to us!"

"Perhaps yesterday she wasn't," Jon said, his voice low and even. "Today she is." He hadn't moved from the doorway. He stood, his weight balanced evenly on feet spread shoulder-width apart, his hands at his sides. I recognized the stance. Jon clearly knew some form of martial arts. "Put the gun down, Dad."

"Now you see there," Stuart said. "You called me Dad. How can she be your sister if I'm your dad? She's trouble, Jon, a threat to my plans, everything I'm building for our future. She's a danger to the family, to us."

Jon moved a few, casual steps closer, his manner still calm, reasonable, unthreatening. "But don't you understand that if you kill her, you'll have to kill me too?"

"And me," Amalie said, popping through the doorway. Her eyes were the size of Oreo cookies and I could see her trembling from across the room. But her chin was elevated in a pose that reminded me of my grandmother. She was obviously terrified, but that was not going to stop her. Then she tore her gaze from her uncle to look at me. Her eyes flicked to the crossbow under my hand and away again. I expanded even more. Message received.

Stuart was shaking his head. "I could never hurt you, son. Or Amalie. You're blood, family. No, just her."

"You didn't understand what I meant," Jon said, eyes narrowed. "If you plan to shoot my sister, you'll have to shoot me first."

Amalie cleared her throat and edged up to Jon, plastering herself against his side as if they'd been joined at the hip.

"Me, too, Uncle Stu," she said again, so frightened she sounded like Minnie Mouse.

Stuart stood, the revolver at hip level as he stared into the eyes of the man he'd raised as his own. "You're taking her side?" he asked, his voice a croak.

Jon nodded. "You're forcing me to. She's family, my sister."

"And you're just like everybody else," Stuart snarled. "Taking up for Warren against me, after all I've done for you. Well, to hell with you, then!"

Time became maple syrup–slow. I saw his shoulder move, saw his arm seem to float upward, the pistol steady in his hand. And in that snail's pace moment, I also saw something else. Jon would not be able to move efficiently. Frozen in terror, Amalie was in his way. No matter what he did, the bullet would hit him.

I reached for the crossbow and Jon reacted at the same time, his leg whipping out to kick the weapon from Stuart's hand. If Amalie hadn't been sticking to him like Krazy Glue, it might have worked. As it was, the best he managed was to knock Stuart's arm toward the ceiling. From that point, a scuffle for control of the gun began, which I'd like to think Jon could have won, even though his opponent had a good fifty pounds on him. But there was still his young cousin to factor into the equation.

Amalie, who'd been knocked off balance when Jon moved, toppled toward the desk, her left foot striking him hard behind the right knee, which buckled. He began to fall toward her, still holding fast to Stuart's arm, his descent pulling the arm downward in the same direction. If the gun went off, only a flip of a coin would determine which of them it would hit, Jon or Amalie.

I didn't think, I simply acted, aimed the crossbow and fired, praying that the bullet-shaped head of the arrow would hit hard enough to hurt or distract, praying that it wouldn't cause the man to fire in reflex, praying that what I'd done hadn't made things worse.

A bellow of pain shattered the silence, I wasn't certain from whom. Then I saw it, the three-inch long missile embedded to its feather tip in Stuart's neck. Blood arced toward me, spraying across my chest. A heartbeat passed and another arc spurted from Stuart's thick neck. I'd hit a carotid artery. He dropped the revolver to claw at his collar, a roar of pain and rage emitting from his throat with each gush of blood.

I darted around the desk to get the gun, but Amalie, on all fours, had regained enough composure to kick it out of the way.

Stuart sank to his knees, gurgling.

"Dad!" Jon cried, wrapping his arms around him and lowering him to the floor.

I hesitated, but to my credit, for only a second. If I'd lived some other life, had been some other person, I'd have done nothing and watch this murderer of my parents and a host of others bleed to death. But I hadn't and I wasn't. I had to do the right thing.

"Amalie, call nine-one-one," I said, stepping past the

man's body. "Pressure, Jon. We need pressure against it."
With fingers that felt like cooked spaghetti, I yanked Stuart's tie loose and ripped at the buttons of his collar, pulling it free of his neck. I pressed my hand against the wound, the feathered tip protruding between my fingers. I didn't dare pull it out, but if I could at least stem the flow, that might be enough to prevent his bleeding out before the minute hand reached twelve.

"Let me do it," Jon said, cradling Stuart in his arms. "My hands are larger."

"No." Stuart reached up and pried my fingers away. "No point." His voice was weakening. Blood still pulsed from the wound in rhythmic spurts but with ever lessening velocity, saturating his collar, oozing onto the highly polished floor.

"Dad, please." Jon tried to ease his hand into position, but once again Stuart pulled it free.

"Better this way," he said. "You understand why I did it, don't you, son? It was my place to do it. I was the oldest. It was my birthright. My name is . . . Wayne."

Then, as we watched, the light went out behind those pale brownish-gray eyes. The blood continued to gush, but at a slower pace, until it stopped altogether.

Jon lowered his head, his forehead against his father's, tears coursing down his cheeks.

"Jon, I'm sorry." I couldn't think of anything else to say.

He nodded, his head causing Stuart's to bob as well, as if he too understood.

I got up and went to wait outside with Amalie, leaving father and son alone together.

17

IT WAS A LONG, LONG NIGHT. BETWEEN POLICE reports and the news leaking out faster than the speed of sound, and every Ritch in creation showing up and clamoring for explanation, by the time things had quieted down I was operating on automatic pilot. The fact that I had been responsible for the death of another person hovered way back behind my subconscious, its ugly head emerging to leer at me at odd moments. It was something to grapple with later. I just hoped I wouldn't have to grapple with Nunna's and Walter's death as well.

Around three in the morning, an ice pack on my knee, I found myself in the comfortable living room of Jon's home, surrounded by family still trying to shake off the numbing impact of the events of the night. Family on this occasion included Jon; his wife, Melissa; Amalie; my grandmother; my aunts Frances and Bonita; and Tracy. Jon's sisters—"I guess they're actually cousins," he'd said earlier, as he'd struggled with the newness of it—were with Ruth, who had collapsed under the weight of her son's revelations. Before we'd barely taken seats, someone banged on the door.

"Open up!" a familiar voice bellowed. "This damned thing's heavy!" Mary Castle and her nephew with a vat of coffee and trays of sandwiches. "Don't care what's happened," she said, heading for the kitchen as if she knew the way. "Folks got to eat. You stay here, Melissa. I can find whatever I need."

Other than that boisterous interruption, it was a somber gathering, with no one certain what to say. Bonita was in shock, muttering repeatedly under her breath, "I never dreamed she meant Stu. *Nobody* ever called him Wayne."

In the end, it was my grandmother, Elizabeth, who decided to take the floor. She cleared her throat and seven pairs of eyes snapped in her direction. I lowered mine, too tired to hold them level.

"Well," she said, her voice cracking with strain, "it looks as if we seniors have all acted like a bunch of fools, and I guess I should be the first to apologize for both Ruth and myself. The only problem is who to apologize to first. You, Frances, Bonita? Or you there, Leigh. You lost so much. No parents, a life without blood kin, my rejection of you once you'd found us. Or you, Jon. In a sense you've been lucky, because I always considered Stuart and Glenda loving parents. And you've had your sisters around you." He nodded, but didn't speak.

"But as a twin," she continued, "I'm the only one here who knows what you were cheated out of, that unique bond twins share. So I'm reduced to simply apologizing all around. I am so, so sorry. I can't tell you . . ." She ran down, tears welling in eyes already bloodshot from crying.

"We've all lost loved ones," Frances said softly, strain adding years to her face. "And did things that will always haunt us. I'm doubly guilty because I knew how flawed my baby sister was. I knew it. It was easier to turn on Peg than admit how miserably I'd failed with Faye." She glanced at her sister, then at Jon and me. "But I might as well own up now and hope you won't hate me for it. I knew about you two."

Bonita jerked in her chair. "What?"

"There was one letter from Peg you never saw. You were out on maternity leave and Jennie gave it to me to give to you. I read it. It was sent right after Jon had disappeared. I—I tore it up. I'm so sorry, all of you."

"Lordy, two apologies in one night," Tracy said. She might have meant to be flippant but I, for one, heard her anger.

Elizabeth shook her head rapidly. "Please. She isn't alone. Ruth and I, we refused to acknowledge how troubled Stuart was, from the time he was a little thing. More than one teacher suggested counseling. We didn't listen. As for Warren . . ." She swallowed. "What I did to my son— and Peg? That's something I'll have to live with, my own personal little hell. We have a lot to make up for."

"Elizabeth." Bonita spoke to her for the first time. "No one ever notified us. Who told you Peg and Warren were dead?"

My grandmother gazed at her in dismay. "Oh, my Lord. Bonita, I had no idea. Stuart told us several years after they died. He said Warren and Peg hadn't been getting along, that a violent argument had erupted and Warren had killed her, then their child, their son. Then he'd set their home on fire and hadn't been able to get out himself. To my everlasting shame, I believed him. Wayne never did."

"And Leigh?" Tracy asked. "What did he say about her?"

"He never mentioned her. We had no idea they'd had a second child."

My eyes and Jon's met in unspoken agreement. He'd seen the contents of the shoe box and knew that my grandfather had searched for the two of us for years before giving up. It would be up to him to tell her that, if he lived.

"Well." Tracy looked around. "This is encouraging.

Leigh, we'll understand if you'd prefer to have nothing to do with us, but welcome to the family anyway."

It was a struggle, but I managed a smile. "Thanks."

"Thank you," Melissa said, slipping an arm around her husband's shoulder, "for saving my Jon's life." She reminded me of Duck's sister, not all that much to look at, but one smile in your direction and you were reduced to puppy dog adoration.

"And for saving mine too," Amalie said. She'd seemed the one most affected by what had happened, admitting earlier to being so scared, she'd wet her pants. She also felt guilty for having gotten in the way.

"Don't forget I was saving my hide as well," I said. "Which reminds me. I never got a chance to ask. What made you come back tonight?"

"Oh!" Inexplicably, she regained her usual perkiness. "I couldn't say anything at the time, because I had to be sure."

"About what, Amalie?" I hoped this wouldn't take long. I was beginning to fade.

"The Silver Star. I was sure I'd seen the one you described. You know, with the bent leg? I was hauling ass—"

"Amalie!" My grandmother looked scandalized.

"Sorry. I called here as soon as I got back out to the road. Melissa said Jon was on his way to Aunt Liz's for something or other, so I intercepted him and told him what you'd said about the medal. He confirmed what I'd thought—he used to work at the gas station—and we were coming to tell you when we heard Uncle Stuart through the door." She shuddered, momentarily off track.

"To tell me what, Amalie?" I asked, fully alert now.

"That the Silver Star the man wants is W. Two's. It's in the service station, on a wall with all his public service citations."

I wasn't sure whether to kiss her or throttle her. "You mean I was ten feet from it tonight?"

"Well, yeah. You said the medal had been in an accident, right? And that's how one leg had gotten bent. Well, W. Two's practically the only teetotaler in town. Give him the least excuse and he'll tell you about the time he got shit-faced—his description, not mine, Aunt Liz," Ammie forestalled her. "He was drunk and drove a Jeep into a ravine. He was trying to back up onto the road when he felt a bump. He had backed over his duffel bag. The Jeep had no top and the bag had bounced out. Anyhow, that's how it was damaged."

"In other words," I said, nearing outright hysteria, "Jameson tracked down the wrong Lieutenant Ritch? Oh, my God." I slumped, overcome by the irony of it all.

"I'll go by the station and get it first thing in the morning," Jon said. "Look at it this way, Leigh." He left his wife's side and knelt in front of me. "If that crazy dude hadn't screwed up, we would never have met. I would never have found out that I have another sister, much less a twin. And there's a whole town waiting to embrace you as part of the family."

"Amen," Bonita said.

"I make no excuses for my father," Jon added, pain emanating from his eyes. "I never saw the man I met tonight. He really was a good father. And the rest, they're good people, Leigh. When this is all over, I hope you'll feel that the hell you've gone through was worth it. Think about it," he said, pulling me into his arms. "Melissa, Leigh's dead on her feet. Put her to bed. See you in a few hours, sis."

Sis. That supplied enough fuel to help me up the stairs. I fell asleep and dreamed of a row of bow-legged Silver Stars high-kicking their way across a stage like the Rockettes. I awoke disoriented, my head full of oatmeal. But on the whole, I felt terrific. The nightmare was almost over. Yeah, right.

"Whoa! Just wait a minute here!" Wayne Walter Ritch, a twig off a shorter, stockier branch on the family tree, stared popeyed at Jon. We'd arrived at the service station just as W. Two had unlocked the doors. And there it was on the wall adjacent to the counter in a glass-fronted frame, his Silver Star, the tip of the bottom right leg curved up as if someone had taken a curling iron to it. "What the hell you mean, she needs my star? I mean, I thought it was Warren's she was after. And I felt real bad for her since as far as I know he never got one."

"He did," I said, swallowing my annoyance at being discussed as if I wasn't there. I opened the box to show it to him. "I guess my grandfather's the only person who knows why it was given to him. And I know it won't be the same, but I'll let you keep his in exchange. Please, Mr. Ritch, you'll be saving the lives of two very good, decent people caught in the middle through no fault of their own."

"The name's Wayne," he said, and squinted at me, a frown decorating his forehead. "Or, since you're family, W. Two. You're gonna have to explain that to me. I mean, I heard this and that, but none of it made any sense. Jon." He scowled, and leaned to look past me to the outdoors. "Go take the air hose away from that jackass. Comes in here every Monday for the past thirty years and still can't fill his tires without help. You got some flat-out idiots in your family, young lady. Gives me no comfort that they're my family too." He waited until Jon had spoken to the man at the air pump, then focused on me again. "Sorry. Now what's this all about?"

Hoping I had his full attention, I explained about last Saturday's phone call and my efforts since. About halfway through, I sensed a change in his attitude, an alertness he hadn't exhibited before.

"Back up a minute," he said, when I'd finished. "Tell me again what he said. Lieutenant what?"

"I thought he was saying 'lieutenant rich college-boy,' only now I figure he meant Ritch-with-a-T."

He nodded, his head bobbing slowly, his gaze somewhere between me and Vietnam. "Uh-huh," he said, wagging a finger. "I remember that racist son of a bitch. Dropped the Warbler on the way to the copter and took off running. Here I am, bleeding like a stuck pig, carrying Skinny over one shoulder and a chunk out of the other and incoming exploding all around us. I couldn't leave that boy there. If incoming didn't get him, they'd have flayed him alive before the sun set. Besides, he was one of my men! So I went back and got him. He died anyway, but at least he died in the arms of his buddies. That's why they gave me my Silver Star. What was that asshole's name? Something to do with working girls. Hooker! Jimmy Gee Hooker. Everybody called him Gee."

Exhilarated at having a name to give the FBI, I began scrambling in my bag for my phone.

"Yeah, that's what Hooker used to call me behind my back: Lieutenant Ritch Boy. Know why? Because my old man had a boat. He was a waterman, for God's sake! That's how he earned his living. And I worked my way through college. But as far as Hooker was concerned, a boat meant we had money." Wayne snorted. "It's him. Gotta be. Crazy fool."

"Little Walt's here." Jon stepped in, wiping his hands with a paper towel. "He's filling Chet's tires."

Jon's return had interrupted my search for Pinky's business card. I'd finally located it when I realized I'd missed something. "I'm sorry, Wayne. What did you say?"

"I can't do it." His eyes pleaded with me. "That bunged-up star and this no-account shoulder are all I have to show for the hell of Vietnam. That star says the man who runs this service station, the one who pumps your gas when it's cold and rainy and you don't want to get out of your car, that man is courageous. That man is a patriot. I need that, Leigh, especially on mornings when I get up and can't move this arm until Carrie's spent a half hour massaging my shoulder. I need it after one of my screaming nightmares. I really, really need it."

I looked away, unable to bear the anguish I saw. It was very nearly on a par with mine.

"What I can do," he said, "if you want me to, that is, is to take one of my tools and try to make Warren's match mine. What do you say?"

I couldn't speak, simply handed him the box and slumped into a folding chair with relief.

"What about the back?" Jon asked. "Warren's name is on it."

My relief shriveled like a pricked balloon. "I forgot that."

Wayne turned it over and grinned. "What's the big deal? It says Lt. Wayne W. Ritch, same as mine. All I need to do is get rid of the last letter of USAF. Hooker will never know the difference. You two might as well go get a cup of coffee or something. No telling how long it'll take if I'm interrupted. It should be ready when you get back."

I searched for words to convey how grateful I was. "You can't know how much this means," I said finally.

"Hey." It was amazing what a smile did for his craggy features. "You're family. And Warren's kid. See you in a while." He left for the service bay.

"That's what family means around here." Jon opened the outer door and escorted me toward my car. "And I'll tell you. I've taken a lot of teasing over the years," he said with a chuckle, "but for the first time in my life, I'm beginning to appreciate being named Wayne."

I stopped. "You're kidding. Not Jon Wayne Ritch?"

"You got it." But as he neared the driver's side to open the door for me, he looked back at me in thought. "I just realized something. That's probably not my real name, is it?"

I debated whether to tell him, but considering all the misinformation we'd grown up with, it was time he heard the truth. What he did with it was his decision. "Your first name is Lee, your middle name is Anderson. But I guess I'll always think of you as Jon."

"Brother Jon," he amended, and perhaps on a whim, folded his arms around me. "My sister," he said into my hair. "Have mercy, my twin. I still can't get over it."

"Well, now isn't this sweet?" a familiar voice said behind me.

I whirled around. "Duck!" In a nanosecond, I was out of Jon's arms and into Duck's. "I found it! It was the wrong one, but it'll work. One of my cousins is fixing it right now."

"Terrific! That's great news." He pushed me at arm's length and gazed down at me. "Now. One of your cousins? Would it be too much to hope that this dude whose front you were glued to is another one of them?"

I turned around to see Jon wearing a grin the width of the Chesapeake Bay bridge. "Dillon Kennedy, meet my brother, Jon Wayne Ritch."

Duck's pupils flared open like a cat's. "You're kidding."

I howled. "That's exactly what I said not one minute ago."

Jon stepped forward, hand extended. "And you must be The Man. Hey, bro. Nice to meet you."

They shook, then went through that brotherhood thing

with curled fingers gripped and fists bopped, one atop the other. There followed a moment of embarrassed silence, both grinning like idiots, before Duck grabbed Jon in a bear hug. "Hey, bro yourself," he said. There ensued a lot of back pounding before they separated. Men are so strange.

"You been taking good care of my lady?" Duck asked, the ritual and male bonding completed.

Jon sobered. "If I said yes, I'd be lying. She's had a rough few days in this town, thanks to . . . my father."

I shut down, shunting the images of last night aside.

"Your dad?" Duck looked from Jon to me and, perhaps sensing my withdrawal, turned back to him for an answer.

Jon had evidently picked up on it too. "It's a long story. We're on our way to get a cup of coffee. Come with us. I'll fill you in."

"Okay, but before we do anything else, Leigh, something's wrong with your phone. When's the last time you used it? I've been trying to reach you since night before last."

"Oh, God." I panicked, digging it out of the pocket I'd dropped it in a few minutes before. "It can't be the battery. I charged it at the motel. It was plugged in all night."

Duck took it and turned it on. The warning light glowed dimly. "Must not be holding a charge. Where's the adapter?"

I scrounged around in the bottom of my bag until I found it. Duck examined it and made a face. "Here's the problem. One of the contact points has broken off. And mine's a different model. Past time you got a new phone anyway."

"But what if Jameson's been trying to call me?" I asked, conjuring up an image of the enraged kidnapper taking out his frustration on Nunna. "And his name's Hooker. W. Two remembered him. James Gee Hooker. I've got to let the FBI know."

"Use mine," Jon said. "It's in the car. You can call them on the way to the Eatery."

Neither Pinky nor Grayson answered his cell phone, however, and I was reduced to passing on my bonanza about Jameson's real name and the fact that I had found the medal to someone else at the Bureau who promised to relay the message. It was such a letdown that I felt cheated. That on top of the emotional fallout from the night before reduced me to a blue funk.

Duck, in the backseat, palmed my shoulder. "You okay, babe?" he asked.

"She's fine." Jon, driving, reached over to give my arm a reassuring squeeze.

"No, I'm not," I admitted, forcing the words past the taste of bile on my tongue. "I killed his father, Duck. Killed him. Almost eight years with the department when I might have expected something like this to happen, it didn't. Three months after I turn in my badge, I have to take a man's life."

"In the process saving mine. our cousin's, and her own," Jon said tightly. "Make no mistake, Duck, he was my father and I loved him, but he left her no choice."

Duck sat back. "How far is this place? Looks like I've got a lot of catching up to do."

Mary Castle took to Duck as if he were a long-lost duckling, so Jon was forced to relate my misadventures with Mary popping out of the kitchen every few minutes to bring Duck something else. Home fries to go with the ham and eggs she'd insisted on making, then grits. "Just a spoonful or two. Gotta have grits." Then flapjacks. I lost count after that.

"I gotta say," Duck said to Jon around mouthfuls, "you're taking the death of your father awfully well."

Jon's eyes lost focus for a moment. "You had to be there to understand. I mean, over the years I'd seen him lose it, show a side of himself that was downright manic. And I'd overheard things when I was growing up, like how troubled he'd been as a kid, setting fires, acting out. I guess we all assumed that for the most part he'd finally conquered his demons. But the man I heard talking last night had crossed over into a whole 'nother country. When I opened that door and saw him holding the gun, I knew that there was a distinct possibility I might have to kill him."

"Could you have done it?" Duck asked with a curious intensity.

Jon studied his empty cup. "That's what scared me the most, Duck, the fact that I was absolutely prepared to do it. It was like listening to one of those madmen on a documentary about serial killers. Only it was my father's voice. I couldn't let him take any more lives. I just couldn't."

Duck nodded, apparently satisfied with the answer. "Sometimes you have no other options. I'm sorry I couldn't be here for you, babe."

I couldn't even summon enough energy to bristle at his slip. But the next time he called me that, I'd kick him.

We'd just finished coffee when Duck's cell phone chirped. After answering it, he grinned and handed it to me.

Janeece screamed into the phone. "Hey, girlfriend, where the hell have you been? The senior citizen wing of Investigators Anonymous has been trying to get you. They found the Airstream!"

"Where?" I shouted. Mary stuck her head out of the kitchen, a warning scowl in place. I waved at her in apology.

"On a parking lot for RVs on Hilton Head. And bless their hearts, they lied their fannies off to get the information, but they know where Miss Nunna and Mr. Walter are staying! I called Pinky and told him. He and Grayson are on their way down there now to meet agents from the field office."

I wasn't happy about that. The whole scenario changed with Pinky and Grayson in the act. They'd alert the local police and by the time all the various elements of law enforcement were in place, there'd be a stakeout and SWAT teams and snipers up the wazoo. And since James Gee Hooker had nothing to lose, a shootout. At the end of it, Nunna and Walter would be toast.

"How long ago did Mrs. Franklin call you about finding the Airstream?" I asked.

"Hell, I don't know. An hour, hour and a half ago. They did try to reach you and finally called here. You were smart to leave my number. When I couldn't get through to you either—what's the matter with your damned phone?—Duck was the only other person I could think of to contact. It took me half an hour of working my way down the Kennedys in the phone book before I got his mother and convinced her to give me the number for his cell phone. You want the address in Hilton Head or what?" she demanded.

"You have to ask? What is it?"

Duck scribbled as I repeated the information Janeece rattled off. "I gave the FBI guys Duck's cell phone number, so y'all should be hearing from them as soon as they know something."

"You think I'm gonna wait? Thanks, honey. Bye!" Rising, I handed the phone back to Duck. "Come on. We've gotta go to BWI and catch the next flight down to Hilton Head."

Jon tossed a twenty onto the table. "They've found your folks? Terrific! But . . . I'm not sure how the police will feel about your leaving town."

"Tell 'em I'll be back," I growled. Nothing would stop me short of arrest and even then, they'd be wise to check me for a sharp-edged spoon. I would tunnel my way from here to South Carolina if I had to.

Jon must have seen the glint in my eyes because he backed off. "Okay, but don't forget, you've got to stop by the gas station to pick up the medal."

"God! Thanks for reminding me." I wasn't even sure I still needed it, but if nothing else, it was a bargaining chip.

The chaos of the next couple of hours subtracted ten years off my life. With the Silver Star and its new bent leg in hand, we drove my car to Baltimore-Washington International Airport, blew half a century finding a parking space, took a shuttle bus to the terminal, and spent another half century trying to get a flight to points south. There were no direct ones to the island and those from various hubs were small planes already fully booked.

We could fly to Savannah, the next nearest airport, get a rental, and drive to Hilton Head, roughly forty minutes away.

"I'll never get there in time," I fretted. "I wish Janeece hadn't called the feds. I could have gone down, given the man the medal, and that would be the end of it."

Duck turned to face me. "You don't really believe that, do you?" he asked, his voice gentle. "Hooker's nuts. He's held two people against their will, crossed state lines, threatened their lives. You'd let him get away with all that?"

"If Nunna and Walter are safe? Damned straight, I would."

"Well, that's not gonna happen. The FBI will do everything they can to avoid placing their lives in further jeopardy, but there's no way Hooker's gonna get away scot-free, no matter when we get there. Now, settle down while I make a couple of calls."

He was right, but I didn't have to like it. I perched on a bench, stewing, while he spent the next sixteen minutes on his phone. By the time he finished, I was ready to kill him.

And he knew it. "Let's go," he said, before I could erupt. "Waco's brother will fly us down in his private plane. We've got twenty minutes to meet him."

As simple as that. At least on the surface. I didn't have the heart to ask how much it was costing him. Perhaps we could skip the honeymoon, even though we hadn't decided where to go. I felt rotten. The only times I'd thought about Duck the last couple of days had been to figure out how to avoid talking to him so he wouldn't try to talk me out of what I felt I had to do. Yet here he was, coming through for me, no questions asked.

"Duck," I said, as we hurried back through the terminal. "I love you." The effect I'd had in mind was lost, since I was out of breath.

He stopped in his tracks and stared at me. "Are you all right, babe?"

I sighed, giving up. What the hell, as long as no one else called me that. "I'm fine. I'm with you, aren't I?"

His responding smile was slow in coming, the kiss he planted on me even slower, and it succeeded in wiping out any remaining breath I had. If Duck could patent his kissing technique, we'd be rich enough to have our own private plane. But he couldn't and we weren't and didn't, so we finally aborted the smooching and ran the rest of the way to meet our transportation to Al's hangar.

* * *

I wish I could say I enjoyed the flight. It was a neat little jet, and we certainly didn't want for creature comforts on the way, but I simply couldn't relax. I had no sense of how fast we were going once we were aloft, but time seemed to crawl, and all I could think of was the possibility of arriving just in time to witness everything going to hell—unless I could reach Pinky to let him know I was en route with the ransom that might save Nunna's and Walter's lives.

The jet was equipped with a phone, and I grabbed it. It took jumping through a few electronic hoops before I convinced my contact at the Bureau to put me through to Pinky, wherever he was.

He answered, sounding harried. "Pinkleton."

"Pinky, this is Leigh Ann. Janeece called me. Where are you? Did you get my message?"

"No. We've been a little busy and I haven't—what is that noise I hear? Where are you?"

"On the way to Hilton Head. We should be landing shortly," I added, feeling the plane beginning to descend.

"How'd you manage that?" he asked, sounding slightly peeved. "We just got here ourselves."

"Friends in high places. Listen, Pinky, the kidnapper's name is James Gee Hooker." I spelled the middle name so there'd be no mistake. "And I have the medal he wants. Please, please, don't do anything until I get there."

He hesitated. "Well, since you're that close . . . We need to bring you up-to-date anyway, so why don't you meet us at the police station. We—"

"No way, José," I interrupted him. "I'm headed directly to the villa, wherever it is. I'm going to give that man his medal and walk out of there with Nunna and Walter. What you do afterward is your business."

"Leigh—" It was the first time he'd called me that.

"I don't want to hear it," I shouted. "That woman raised

me, Pinky! You guys show up there with your SWAT teams and hostage negotiators and you'll get her killed! And I swear to you, as God is my witness, if anything happens to her because you guys fuck up, I will *kill* you and gladly spend the rest of my life in jail! *You have been warned!*"

"Give me that," Duck said, and wrestled the phone from me. He was too late. I'd already terminated the connection. "Now you listen to me." He held my jaw firmly, and glared at me nose-to-nose. "I love you, but if you think I'm gonna marry a woman whose bed is in a federal pen somewhere, you've got another think coming. A man has his needs, you know."

"What?" The statement was so patently unfeeling and un-Duck-like that it was like a knife through the heart. "How could you say—?' A slow, calculating grin tugged at his lips and I considered belting him. "You bastard."

"Made you think, didn't I? Now, you calm down, babe. The feds know what's at stake. They're trained to handle this kind of situation and we're gonna let them do just that. You take one step out of line and I will put your lights out, do you understand me? I have never hit a woman before but if you jeopardize their setup, you're gonna be my first. Can you imagine how you'd feel if something stupid you did got Miss Nunna and her husband killed?"

I hadn't been entirely convinced until that last question. And I could admit to being as close to out of control as I'd ever been. Being personally involved had short-circuited every bit of training and experience I had.

"Okay," I said, and pulled into my shell. It was the only way I'd be able to survive whatever was to come.

Holding up my end of the bargain, I held my peace and listened to my pulse thud in my ears as Duck arranged for a rental, bought a map, and found his way to the police station, only to be told that Pinky and Grayson et al. were waiting for me at the villa. I ground my molars in frustration, which effectively kept my mouth closed. Whatever works.

Hilton Head was warm and green, traffic moving along the main highway at forty-five mph, no faster, no slower. I couldn't see it somewhere off to our left, but the scent of the ocean perfumed the air. It might be early November and chilly north of here, but I'd shed my jacket as soon as we'd landed, and wondered how long I could survive in my turtleneck.

"This might be a nice place for a honeymoon," Duck said as we drove to the villa. "Or a visit someday," he added, hedging his bets. "Relax, Leigh. Everything will be all right."

"One of your hunches?" I asked, with only a hint of sarcasm, since I had great respect for the man's intuition.

"Right. One of my hunches."

As idiotic as it was, for the first time in six days, I felt a glimmer of optimism.

I'm not sure what I expected, but the villa was one of dozens of apartments in a complex of five-storied brick buildings nestled on the bank of a lake, or perhaps a lagoon, I wasn't certain which. Aside from a pair of cruisers parked near the entrance to the main building of the complex, there was no other sign of a police presence or unusual activity. A tennis game was in progress on one of the courts off to the side, and a couple of shorts-clad teenagers shot hoops on a cement-covered surface nearby. A family with a pair of toddlers and an infant in bathing suits appeared ready for a trip to a pool or a beach.

"Are you sure this is the right place?" I asked as Duck wound his way between cars in search of an empty slot.

"Must be. There's Grayson." He jerked his head toward

my right, where Special Agent Grayson was climbing from under the wheel of an innocuous beige sedan. A second later, Pinky stepped out from the passenger side and waved, pointing downward. They'd saved a spot for us.

Duck parked. I was onto the asphalt before he'd cut the engine. "Have you located them yet? Which unit are they in?"

"Their villa's in building three over there," Grayson said, locking his door. "But at the moment, they're in the lobby of the administration building."

"They're barricaded in a lobby?" Duck asked, peering at them sidewise. Pinky's expression was grim.

"Come on." Grayson shoved his hands in his pockets and started walking toward the entrance. "One of the local boys went in with us so we could explain the problem and ask their cooperation in vacating building three. Turns out there was no need. Mr. and Mrs. Sturgis were in the lobby waiting for a tour bus."

"A what?" I yelped, trying to keep up with legs a darn sight healthier than mine.

"There's a tour of wildlife areas or something," Pinky volunteered. "Another fifteen minutes and we'd have missed them."

"So they're all right? Where's Hooker?" I asked.

"We don't know." Grayson held the door for me.

The spacious lobby was cool and dim compared to the noon sunlight and it was a moment before my eyes adjusted. The rear wall afforded an unobstructed view of a lush green lawn and beyond it, the serene silver-hued water I'd glimpsed before. Several people sat on the thickly upholstered sofas and chairs positioned to take advantage of the vista. Some read newspapers or magazines from the rack near the check-in counter. One man dozed, head back, mouth open.

"Where are they?" I demanded, searching for the face I'd feared I'd never see alive again.

Pinky, his somber expression unchanged, nodded toward a far corner, where a uniformed cop knelt beside a couple on a sofa that faced a television mounted near the ceiling.

The uniform saw us coming and rose. "Miz Warren?" he asked.

I nodded at him, my eyes glued to the snow-white hair of the woman. It was short, thinning, wrong. Slowly she turned to confront me with frightened eyes.

My heart shattered. Somehow I got the words out. "This is *not* my foster mother. This is *not* Nunnally Layton Sturgis."

18

"WELL, I RECKON I CAN KISS MY FOOT AND THE farm goodbye," the man sitting next to the imposter muttered. Leaning over, he reached down to pick up a pair of crutches lying on the floor in front of him.

I wasn't sure I got the meaning of the last part of that and at this point, didn't really care, but the first part became clear. His right pants leg was empty, the cuff folded and pinned close below the knee. Now I understood the comment of the Georgia trooper who'd stopped them about how well "Walter" handled his disability. Appreciably shorter, his complexion a muddy brown, he looked nothing like Nunna's husband. He wore hard times across his face like a second skin.

Out of deference to his handicap, I assume, the feds and the policeman asked the manager if there was somewhere close and private we could use to talk to the couple. I was in no mood for concessions. As far as I was concerned, we should be headed for the closest interrogation room.

"We did it because we were desperate," the woman said, once we'd been seated in a lounge where employees took their breaks. "We were trying to save our farm." Her chin quivered and tears dribbled down seams in a face the color of pumpernickel.

"To bring you up to speed, Ms. Warren," Grayson said,

"this is Clayton and Mariah Beardsley from Taubrey, North Carolina."

"Ma'am," Mr. Beardsley said mournfully, touching his forehead as if tipping a hat.

"Can I speak, please, sir?" Mrs. Beardsley asked, already speaking volumes with her manner and body language.

Grayson glanced at the uniform, who nodded. Perhaps Grayson had more savvy than I'd given him credit for.

"It's like this, sir. Things have been real hard for us since Clay lost his leg." She twisted a handkerchief between grossly deformed fingers. "The children helped work the farm while they were growin' up, but they got their own families to worry about now. I'm the one to do it these last ten years or so, with Clay helpin' out as best he can. But now that I've got the rheumatoid arthritis, I ain't worth poot." Her husband reached for her hand and patted it. "It's been harder and harder to keep up, and the taxes . . ." She shook her head, then looked up at each of us, settling finally on me. "It ain't much, the farm, but it's all we got. So when Mr. Hooker come to us with his offer, it seemed like a gift straight from heaven."

"Back up a minute, Mrs. Beardsley." Pinky sat down at the table. Behind us, the refrigerator clunked on, making us jump. "Tell us about Mr. Hooker. How is it you know him?"

"He and his boy run the only game in town," Mr. Beardsley said. "In the next town, actually, over the line in Tennessee. Never met him until we were in the VA hospital together. His boy, Gee Junior, is right smart, a born tinkerer. And when his daddy came home all messed up with those hook things, Gee Junior set out to make him some better ones."

Several sets of antennas went on alert. "Wait." Pinky said. "Hooker has artificial arms?"

"Yes, sir. Only to look at him you wouldn't know it. That's what I was tellin' you. His boy made him some that worked better, and then another set that worked better still and look like proper hands. Next thing you know, the boy's in business. Mostly the inner workings, computerized gears and things, don't ya know. Made himself a mint."

Pinky leaned back, his eyes closed, and shook his head, with no explanation needed. Now we knew the reason for the absence of any other fingerprints in Nunna's house.

"Go on, Mr. Beardsley." Pinky sat erect again. "I didn't mean to interrupt."

"It was like this. Mr. Hooker, he shows up one day about a month back and says he has an offer to put before us. He says he will see that I get one of those fancy pro—"

"Prosthesis," his wife pronounced carefully.

"Whatever. He'll see that I get one so that I can go back to working the farm if me and the missus will deliver this trailer thing to a lot here on Hilton Head. He says we can even stay in his son's villa rent-free for a week. Turns out a villa's nothing but an apartment," he added sheepishly. "I was looking for a whole house. The villa's nice, though. I told the old lady all we needed was groceries and our clothes and a body could move right in. It's got furniture and towels and everything."

Even Grayson chuckled.

"Anyhow," Mr. Beardsley continued, "I tell him that sounds right nice but a new pros—foot ain't gonna do me a bit of good if I lose the farm and if we don't pay the back taxes, sure as shootin,' we're gonna lose it. So he says if we agree, he'll take care of that too. So I says, you do and we'll deliver that trailer to West Hell if he wants. Reckon I can have one of those Coca-Colas? I'm right parched."

Duck moved quickly to the soft drinks machine. Mr.

Beardsley downed half the bottle in one swallow, smacked his lips, then cleared his throat.

"Well, he leaves and after a day or so and nothing happens, I figure he's changed his mind. Then the tax assessor's office calls to let us know that the back taxes have been paid. He's sorta like an old friend, after all these years, so I wasn't surprised he called. But I sure was relieved to know we were caught up."

"For the first time in three years," his wife said softly.

"The next thing you know, a car pulls up to take me over to Abbottsville to be fitted for the foot, and I know we're in business. We pack and ask our youngest to take care of things while we're gone. And late Saturday, Mr. Hooker, he shows up pulling this big old silver trailer behind a pretty silver Taurus. He carries our bags out and everything. And he gives us a map with roads we should take marked on it and this envelope with spending money and the documents we'll need. He says if we're stopped, show the documents to the police. And, bless Patty, we did get stopped. So I whip out the envelope and the next thing we know they're callin' us by some other names. Turns out Mr. Hooker pulled a fast one on us. He had us put our licenses in the envelope, said we might as well keep everything together. Then he asked for it back to check something and must have switched them, because the ones in there damn sure wasn't ours."

"Why didn't you speak up then?" Grayson asked.

"You ever had your finger caught in a car door, mister?"

Thrown by the question, Grayson frowned. "Can't say I have."

"It don't feel good at all. And that's the way we felt. If we opened the door and told the truth, I figured Mr. Hooker would cancel the order for the foot they're makin' for me, and maybe get the bank to stop the check for the tax money. We'd lose everything."

"We were between a rock and a hard place." Mrs. Beardsley dabbed at her eyes. "We tried calling Mr. Hooker to find out why he'd done what he did, but all we got was his answering machine. So we kept going."

I was buying only so much. "But you must have understood how serious things were when the trooper told you that I hadn't heard from you and thought you had been abducted."

"He meant *you*?" Mrs. Beardsley covered her mouth, stunned. "He said our daughter. I thought he was talking about our Billie Jean."

"And," the officer said wryly, "there's some question whether they know what abducted' means."

"Oh, my God," I whispered.

"Clay and me talked about it after the trooper left," Mrs. Beardsley went on, "and we figured nothing we did was gonna make things any worse. Sooner or later we were gonna get caught and have to go to jail. The kind of luck we've had, it was almost guaranteed. We'd lose the farm anyways. So once we got here, it was so pretty and nice, we decided we might as well enjoy ourselves, make the most of what time we had left together, because there ain't no coed jails." Leaning to the side, she pecked her husband's cheek.

"So that's what happened," he said, his voice gruff with emotion. "Are we under arrest now?"

I couldn't handle it. I left the room, left the building by the doors that opened onto the water. By the time Duck caught up with me, I had trotted beyond the boundaries of the complex, headed for the one adjacent. I hurt like hell all over, the pain in my knee nothing compared to the one mangling my heart. I knew those people, knew precisely the kind of life they had. There were a number of people in Sunrise in the same straits. If they'd been offered a way out from under, they'd have taken it, too. And I couldn't blame them.

"Babe?" Duck said, wrapping his arms around me.

I plastered my front against his and cried for the second time in less than a week, a record for me. I'm not by nature a blubberer, but the scene in that lounge had been too much for me.

"What's going to happen to them?" I asked, when I'd dried up.

"I don't know. Whatever the feds do, we have no control over it. Those poor people were duped, but the bottom line is that they should have 'fessed up when they were stopped and they didn't. It's clear they had no idea what Hooker was up to. Perhaps that'll count for something. We'd better get on back."

Arms entwined, we were approaching the patio outside the administration building when I stopped. "They're in Sunrise."

Duck eyed me, brows hoisted. "Miss Nunna and Mr. Walter? I don't think so. They're probably at the Beardsley's farm."

"Not with their youngest taking care of the place for them. And Hooker wouldn't jeopardize his family or his son's business by taking them back to Tennessee."

"Probably not," Duck agreed, "but there's a hell of a lot of country between there and Sunrise where he could hold them. And a place as small as your hometown where everybody knows everyone else's business? He'd never get away with it."

"I need to think about this." I plunked down on a redwood Adirondack chair on the patio.

The only way Hooker might be able to pull it off in Sunrise is if he somehow rendered himself invisible, just another strand in the fabric of the community. Even though I'd been home for a month back in late August to help Nunna prepare for her wedding, I'd been so engrossed in that process, and in getting over my split with Duck, that I hadn't paid much attention to what was going on beyond Sunset Road. Besides, since Nunna lived east of Main Street on the dark side of town, as my neighbors called the black community, I might be there for weeks before I'd become aware of a newcomer on the west side.

But he'd been a stranger to Mrs. Elias. Mrs. E. was a notorious gossip and nosy to a fault, but would even she know about someone new beyond Main Street? Not necessarily. The west side was considerably larger and more populous than ours. Hooker might be there for quite a while before Mrs. Elias caught sight of him.

"Let me borrow your phone," I said. I had tried to check in with Chief Sheriff a couple of times and hadn't been able to reach him. No answer. He was probably at the hospital with his wife.

Clearing my mind with effort, I dredged up another number from the past, hoping that it hadn't changed.

"Fred's," Maudine shouted above Dolly Parton singing "Nine to Five." "What'll you have?"

"Maudine, this is Leigh Ann. Can you hear me?"

"Are you kidding? Hold on a minute." After a second or two of rustling noises and a considerable lessening of the volume of the music, she came back on. "Okay. Who's this again?"

"Leigh Ann. Listen, the man you said came in for coffee that night, the one with the bad cough. Was that the first time you'd seen him?"

"No, just the first time he'd been in here. In fact, I've

been trying to find the chief to tell him it turns out that fellow was looking around for property to buy a while back. Cecelia Nickleby's kicked the habit after forty years of two packs a day, and he's the reason. She says he stopped in her agency to ask what was available."

"Did he buy a place?" I asked, on the edge of my seat.

"Not from her, but she's pretty sure he found something."

"How long ago did he stop by to see her?" I asked.

"Don't know, but she says she had her last cigarette six weeks ago. Does that help?"

I assured her it did, and asked that she keep trying to reach the chief. "If you get him, tell him I'll be there as soon as I can."

"This is about Miss Nunna, right?" she asked softly. "I've been praying for her and Mr. Walter."

"Pray harder. Every little bit helps. Thanks, Maudine." I popped the end button and returned the phone to Duck. "He's there somewhere. I've got to get a flight home." I extended a hand and he pulled me to my feet.

"Not a problem. Al said he'd wait for us. We'd better let the suits know what's up."

I rolled my eyes at him. "Do we have to?"

I guess he decided not to dignify that with a response, since I didn't get one. He towed me back into the lounge. The Beardsleys were gone. I took a deep breath, figuring I'd need every bit of lung power I had to bring the suits around to my way of thinking. They fooled me. They bit immediately.

By the time we drove into Sunrise, I could say with conviction that my government was working for me. Pinky and Grayson had pulled out all the stops, including squaring my absence with the Anne Arundel County deputies back in Maryland, procuring a new cell phone for me with the same number, as well as picking up the cost of the use of Al's Learjet.

"Duck," I whispered as we flew from Hilton Head to a private field I'd never heard of near Asheville, "what the heck does Al do? I mean, a brother with his own private jet?"

He chuckled. "He used to fly for United and threw in with two other retired pilots to go into the charter business. They do pretty well. We're just lucky the plane was free today. It's booked for a flight to Orlando on Sunday."

Sunday. God willing, Nunna and Walter would be home again by then. Which reminded me of their stand-ins.

"Duck, what happened to Mr. and Mrs. Beardsley?"

He glanced back to where Pinky and Grayson sat a few seats away. "Well, they're in big trouble, make no mistake about that," he said quietly. "Whether they were aware of their role in the kidnapping or not, and the feds seem to be convinced they weren't, they presented false driver's licenses as their own. The irony is if they hadn't been stopped, they probably wouldn't have noticed that it wasn't their licenses. Hooker found somebody who did a damned good job. It's their photos with Miss Nunna's and Mr. Walter's vital statistics. But once the state trooper addressed them as Mr. and Mrs. Sturgis and they made no attempt to correct the situation, they were criminally liable. Al says he'll call a lawyer friend and see if he can help out."

"But the bottom line is that they'll lose their farm."

"Maybe, maybe not. You can't solve everybody's problems, honey. Let's concentrate on getting your folks out of their bind, okay?"

I knew he was right and I hadn't forgotten about Nunna and Walter for a moment. I just felt badly that the Beardsleys had been victimized too.

Pinky and Grayson had their heads together going over

the data they'd received on James Gee Hooker. From the little I could hear, they knew everything there was to know about him short of the color of his underwear. They were waiting impatiently for a report on recent property sales within a hundred miles of Sunrise. I had tried to tell them they'd get faster results by asking Cece Nickleby or Raney Kirkpatrick who between them knew everybody's business when it came to local real estate, but Grayson didn't seem to take me seriously. I got the impression, however, that Pinky understood perfectly. Considering the size of the town in which he and Janeece had grown up, I was not surprised.

Field agents from the Charlotte office were waiting when we landed, and introduced themselves as Roberts and Milton. They bore little physical resemblance to Grayson and Pinky, but their demeanors were indistinguishable from the two I'd come to know. They had little to add to what we'd already learned, since they'd just arrived themselves.

"We've arranged for three cars," Milton said. "If we stagger our arrivals by ten or fifteen minutes, I figured we'll attract less attention that way."

I laughed, resulting in looks of consternation from the agents. "Sorry. You grew up in a big city, didn't you?"

He glanced at Roberts with uncertainty. "Chicago."

"It figures. You have to understand how things work in my neck of the woods. There's only one road into Sunrise and the first place we'll pass will be Mrs. Youngman's. By the time we hit Main Street, thanks to her, three-quarters of the population will know that two cars with two respectably dressed white men in each are in Sunrise, and oh, by the way, Leigh Ann and her intended are back too, isn't that nice? And about half a dozen women and two men will begin baking cakes to bring to Nunna's to find out what's going on."

Roberts exuded a superior air. "If that's the case, how has Hooker managed to slip in and out of town without attracting attention?"

"He wouldn't have, the first time. Talk to enough people and someone will be able to give you the exact date he arrived. But from what the Beardsleys said, Hooker's from a one-stoplight town just like Sunrise. He'd know that all he'd have to do is to keep coming back and appear to have a legitimate reason for it. By his third appearance, he's no longer a stranger, he's part of the woodwork. As simple as that. I'm willing to bet you Hooker's been setting this up for weeks."

Three of the four agents seemed exasperated. Pinky just grinned. "So two cars will do it," he said, struggling to recover some semblance of a professional air. "We need to go over how we're going to handle this anyway. Ms. Warren and Mr. Kennedy might as well lead the way."

His cohorts nodded and we followed them to the black sedans we'd be using.

It was a sober, anxiety-riddled drive. Even my old familiar mountains, the sight of which would normally lower my blood pressure by a good ten or fifteen points, had little effect. I'd begun to think we should delay our arrival until we'd heard from Hooker. He might not necessarily be in on the town's grapevine, but if he was out and about, he'd hear of our arrival before dusk. There was no way to tell how he'd react. Were we putting Nunna and Walter in even more danger?

We'd just turned from the highway onto the road into town when my new cell phone burped, an unfamiliar and unexpected sound. My fingers seemed numb as I fumbled to answer it.

"Leigh Ann?"

I could breathe again. "Hey, Mr. Sheriff. We're on the

way, about a quarter mile from Mrs. Youngman's. The FBI's with us. Is everything all right?"

"Yes, ma'am. I just got in from Asheville. Finally brought the missus home."

"How is she?" I asked, to acknowledge his concerns.

"Right as rain. Kidney stones was all. They poked one of those scopes in her and got 'em out. Looka here, Maudine just called and I'm feeling like six kinds of fool. I think I seen that feller several times. If she'd said something about his artificial hands instead of yammerin' on about how much sugar he used in his coffee, I'd have realized it right off. I do know he was asking about different places that might be for sale. Y'all come on by here. I'm about to call Raney Kirkpatrick, find out what he knows. See y'all directly."

"Make the second right," I said to Duck.

"To Nehemiah's?" Trust him to remember the way. He and the chief had become bosom buddies in record time last summer. There weren't many who called Mr. Sheriff by his first name. "Think we should stop and tell the others where we're going?"

"No way. Either they follow us or they're on their own."

The suits honked at us as we negotiated the turn, so I stuck my arm out of the window and gave them a "wagon's ho!"

Phone to his ear, the chief stood waiting for us on the porch of his slate-gray farmhouse. He waved us on, directing parking with his free hand. Five hounds, the older ones siblings of Nunna's dog, Hannibal, loped around from the side yard baying as if they'd treed a raccoon.

"Hush up!" Mr. Sheriff bellowed, and they quieted, swarming around the cars like sharks on the scent of blood, the younger ones, still in the puppy stage, fairly quivering with excitement.

The feds didn't budge, eyeing the dogs with open suspicion. I took a moment to greet them and was rewarded with swishing tails, which the suits took to be an encouraging sign. A rear door opened and Pinky was the first to get out as the chief ended his call.

Pinky crossed immediately to shake the old man's hand and introduce himself with the deference due a lawman of the chief's age and experience. I liked him for that. Janeece's former schoolmate had just ratcheted himself up a couple of notches in my book.

Grayson followed suit. The chief acknowledged the agents from the field office, then turned to Duck with a wide, welcoming grin. "Well, if it ain't my old buddy, Duck. Thought Leigh Ann here had thrown you over for some other feller."

"I don't give up that easily." Duck extended a hand, and they engaged in a round of back-pounding. "I hear Mrs. Sheriff's home and doing well."

"Just fine," he said, opening the door to usher us in. "She's catnapping. I won't wake her or she'll be down here trying to fix y'all something to eat. Have a seat."

The room hadn't changed since the last time I'd seen it, the same well-worn and well-loved furniture, lamps, and prints. The chief's recliner looked slightly more disreputable, dog turd–brown vinyl splitting in a few more places. He settled in it, and took a moment to scratch the wisps of white hair around his bald spot. "That was Raney Kirkpatrick I was talking to. He's checking his files. Says this feller, Haley—"

"If it's our man," Grayson interrupted, "his real name is Hooker."

Mr. Sheriff's pale eyes took Grayson's measure, and it was clear what he thought of the agent's manners. "Hooker, then. Seems he was looking for commercial property, not residential. Raney says Hooker talked about bringing in some light industry, but he was vague about what kind. Nothing Raney showed him seemed to fit the bill. But he does have a phone number for him. He's looking for it. Should hear from him directly."

I chomped at the bit and fidgeted while the agents double-checked to be certain that Hooker was in fact the person Mr. Sheriff had seen.

"Gotta be. How many fellers you figure are walking around town with two artificial arms? Raney picked up on it right off. Said if it was quiet enough in the office, you could hear the gears whenever he bent his elbows. And—"

He broke off as his portable phone rang, and reached for a pad and pencil on the end table as he answered. "Raney? You find it?" He nodded at us as he jotted it down. "I thank you. What?" Frowning, he locked eyes with me. "That's right interesting. You take care, hear?" He deposited the phone with exaggerated care. "Seems Mr. Hooker found himself a place. Raney's girl, Stella, just told him when he asked her to find the number. Hooker left the message, only she forgot to tell anybody. The bulbs ain't too bright in Stella's family," he said for the agents' benefits. "Anyhow, here's the number. Can't say I recognize the exchange."

Milton, using his cell phone, set a search in motion. The speed in which we had an answer was both astonishing and a little frightening. I began to suspect that the numbers game had eliminated any privacy a person thought he had.

"A cell phone," Milton reported. "If we can reach him and keep him talking long enough, we can trace him. His phone company's waiting to help."

"Since he's been searching for property," Duck said, fingers steepled under his chin, "why not use that, call him with a new property that's become available?"

"Two's better," Roberts said.

"Right. Make them sound so attractive that even if he says he's already found something, convince him that he'd be wise to at least check them out. What do you think, Nehemiah?"

"It's worth a try."

Milton began to pace, his immaculate dark suit and muscular physique slightly incongruous in this environment of worn and warm, country comfort. "Appeal to his ego, massage whatever business sense he has, make him feel like a big shot. That's probably the only way I'll be able to keep him on the line."

It was time for my two cents. "It won't work unless the chief does it," I said firmly. "Hooker's got to hear essence of Sunrise in the voice of whoever calls him and you can't fake that. Besides, Hooker knows the territory now. The chief can pick a place on Main in case Hooker expressed interest in something close in, and another further out on the fringes and describe them with conviction."

Roberts bobbed his blond head. "She's right. Are you willing, sir?"

" 'Course." The chief seemed intrigued by his role. "Let me think about this here, work on a good lie."

I tuned out, trusting Mr. Sheriff's instincts to come up with a believable tale. My concern was what would happen after the suits knew Hooker's whereabouts. One of the calls Milton had made after arranging the phone trace was to the county police. Once again I envisioned a stakeout and cops bellowing into bullhorns and all hell breaking loose. I closed my eyes, rubbed my temples and prayed. I'd never felt quite as helpless.

I wasn't even aware that Mr. Sheriff had dialed the number until Duck came to kneel beside me and grabbed my hand. I looked up just as the chief hit the button to engage the speakerphone. There was a ring, a click, then a voice.

"Hook—" He coughed, caught himself. "Haley here. Who's this?"

I almost jumped out of my skin. It was the same hoarse growl that had launched this nightmare six long days ago. At my reaction, the special agents exchanged glances rife with triumph.

"Mr. Haley," the chief said, "this is Nehemiah Lucas, Bluenose Mountain Realtors. Raney Kirkpatrick suggested I call you about a couple of commercial properties that have become available." Mr. Sheriff glanced at the agents, who nodded encouragement.

"Uh—too late. I found a place that'll do just fine," Hooker responded.

I sat up straight, frowning. I'd heard something.

"Well, wait now." The chief settled into his spiel. "Before you commit yourself, you might want to hear about these. Raney described you as an astute businessman. He was sure someone with your foresight would be able to see the potential in both these properties. It would help, though, if I had a better idea of how you'd put them to use. What business are you in now?"

There was a two second hesitation. "Prosthetics. Computer-driven arms, hands, legs, feet. Mostly the inner workings, anyway."

"You don't say!" The chief appeared to be enjoying himself. "I've got a nephew who lost an arm to a thresher. He's got a hook, more like pincers, and he's damned sure not happy with it. He just might be interested in your product. What can you tell me about it?"

It was a smart move. Roberts and Grayson actually grinned. Pinky gave him a thumbs up.

"Above or below the elbow?" Hooker asked.

"Uh—above."

"He needs to see what we have to offer. Our latest model

is the most versatile on the market." With an occasional pause for a labored breath, Hooker launched into a polished spiel I would have thought beyond the capability of the person who'd called me. We'd considered him wily. Now we knew he was also damned smart, as in intelligent.

But that acknowledgment was on one level while on quite another, my ears were working overtime. Leaving my chair, I stood beside the phone, straining to identify a sound in the background. Somewhere between an irritating squeal and a groan, it was faint enough to be heard only when Hooker paused to gather lung power. I knew that sound! Working hard to ignore the intrusiveness of Hooker's sales pitch, I concentrated with every ounce of gray matter at my disposal.

"That sounds like just what that nephew of mine needs," the chief said, "but what kind of money are we talking about?"

"Well, now, let me think a minute."

That was yet another excuse to move the phone away as he coughed. In between them, I heard it again and the synapses controlling memory arced like lightning during a July storm. Hoping I hadn't given myself away, I covered my face as if I couldn't stand to listen any longer and moved quickly outside.

Duck was half a step behind me. Pinky stood in the open door, concern pleated his brow.

"What's up, babe?"

"I know where he is," I said, my voice low. "Give me the keys to the car."

"The hell I will. If you know, *tell* them!"

Pinky eased out onto the porch. "Are you sure?"

"Yes."

"You wait right here," he said, opened the door and beckoned for Roberts. I seethed while they indulged in an

animated, whispered discussion. Roberts popped back inside, pulled Milton into a corner for yet another round of
gesture-packed conversation, during which Milton kept
shaking his head.

"Give me the goddamned keys!" I growled, anger flow-
ing through my veins.

Roberts moved quickly back out to us. "Milton prefers to
rely on the results of the phone company's triangulation."

"Fine. Y'all can stay here," I snapped. "I'm leaving. I'll
walk if I have to. It's not that far away. When the chief gets
off the phone, tell him I heard the windmill in the background. He'll know what I mean. Are you driving me or
what?" I snapped at Duck.

"Windmill," Roberts repeated. "You all go on. Ride with
them, Pinkleton." He whipped a business card from his
breast pocket. "Here's my beeper number. Size up the situation. If it looks like she's right, give me a call. Not one of
you," he said, clearly issuing an order, "makes a move
without backup. Is that understood?"

"Understood," Pinky said. "If the trace indicates otherwise, you have my numbers."

Roberts nodded, looked from Duck to me, his special
agent face in place, then slipped back inside.

"Let's hit it," Duck said, and with a hand on my elbow,
hurried to our car.

19

"SUNRISE USED TO BE A ONE-INDUSTRY TOWN," I said, as we left the chief's property. "Everybody worked for Sundler's Mill. When it folded, the effect was devastating. It was years before the town got on its feet again. Even now it's tipping lightly. But Sundler's has been vacant ever since, slowly rotting away. It's dangerous! My God, when I think of Nunna and Walter in there . . ." I shuddered, my foot pressing against a nonexistent accelerator to make us go faster.

"Tell me about the windmill," Pinky said from the backseat.

"There used to be three of them, but only one has any vanes on it now. The next right and slow down as soon as you make the turn," I directed, "or you'll gut the undercarriage. The road in has got to be in rotten shape."

My crystal ball was in apple-pie working order. Fifty feet past the turn only Duck's instant reflexes prevented our going nose down into a pothole the size of Wisconsin. "I guess we walk," he said, reversed out to the road again and parked on the shoulder "If Hooker's here, I don't want our backup to make the same mistake we did. How far?"

"Maybe a third of a mile."

It felt a lot farther, what with the ruts, craters and waist-high weeds protruding from gaps in the gravel. Brambles ripped at our slacks. A snarl of roots from an ancient oak sent Duck sprawling ass over teakettle. He swore and brushed himself off. "Hooker had damned sure better be here, babe."

"Come on," I prodded him. "The sun's going down."

"All the more reason to wait to hear from Roberts," Pinky said. But I had already glimpsed some weather-worn siding at the end of the road.

"Good Lord," Pinky breathed when we'd reached the clearing. We stopped behind the billboard-sized Sundler's Mill sign and peered around it. "This is pretty awful."

Nestled at the foot of the mountains, two long, dilapidated buildings sat perpendicular to us and parallel to each other, windows shattered, siding curled from the exterior like wood shavings, whole sections of the corrugated roof missing.

"Nobody could stay in this hellhole," Pinky said.

"Move two steps this way." I tugged him toward the left end of the billboard. "Look there, in the distance between the two buildings."

"Be damned. The windmill." Duck looked at me with suspicion. "How is it you knew how it sounds?"

"There used to be an overlook up there before a rockfall wiped it out. A great spot for necking. Nice and quiet except for the squeal of the windmills."

I could tell it was pure torture but Duck managed not to pursue the subject further.

"What's that?" Pinky sidled toward me, squinting. "A reflection off something at the far end of the shed on the right."

He had good eyes. All I could see were mauve bits of the setting sun bouncing off shards of broken glass on the ground.

I switched places with him and finally relinquished the

camouflage the billboard afforded, stooping as I edged from behind it. Considering the height of the weeds, I don't know what I was worried about. And Pinky had hit the jackpot.

I scurried back to them, my voice a squeak. "It's the bumper of some sort of SUV! I *knew* it!"

At that moment, thanks to a short-lived breeze, the windmill moved, its irritating squeak an explanation point at the end of my sentence. And, supplying additional confirmation, a stocky figure in white from head to toe stepped from a door difficult to see from our vantage point. He hawked, spat, then disappeared from view. To our astonishment, he had a phone to his ear.

Duck chuckled. "Nehemiah's still at it."

"Did you see what he was wearing?" I asked, poking him. "The kind of uniform they wear in clean rooms where they manufacture sensitive instruments! No wonder there was no trace of him at Nunna's."

No response from Pinky, frantically preoccupied with trying to make out the numbers on Roberts's business card. I found the penlight on my key ring and he ducked behind the sign to shield its glow as he made the call.

"Tell them to hurry!" I whispered, and darted from the security of the sign again, to take up a position at the end of the building closest to us.

Behind me, Duck swore and followed. "Get back there! He'll spot you."

"How the hell can he spot me if he's inside? Has Pinky gotten through yet?"

"I don't know. Look!" He knelt, pulling me down.

On hands and knees, I peeked around the corner just as Nunna emerged, cradling a large pot in her arms, her posture suggesting that it was heavy. Hooker stepped into view, watching as she picked her way through underbrush and hurled the contents of the pot as far as she could. Even from a distance, I could see her shudder, and in a moment of stunned comprehension, I understood what I had seen.

"That was a slop jar!"

"A what?"

With great dignity, she made her way out of the underbrush and returned to the building. Hooker followed and I heard the door slam behind him.

"That son of a bitch has them using that thing as a chamber pot!" I lowered my head at the thought of my foster mother, one of the most modest women I knew, reduced to hovering over that thing to answer calls of nature. She looked all right, although her hair was a bit disheveled, in itself a clue to the primitive nature of her accommodations. And where was Walter?

Just then, a shriek reverberated through the dusk, the piercing sound playing catch me if you can against the mountain behind the building. It was Nunna.

I took off, darting to the side opposite the door from which the two had emerged, keeping as low as I could. I heard Duck hiss at me and ignored him. If Hooker had laid one single finger on her . . . Remembering that, technically, he had no fingers was no consolation.

Windows paraded the length of the mill, the unbroken ones too encrusted with dirt and grime to see through. The shattered glass from the remainder littered the ground and I moved farther out to avoid stepping on them. A crunch startled me and I looked back to see Duck beckoning frantically for me to return. Ignoring him, I kept going, slowing as I reached the last window. It was no cleaner than the others, but I thought I detected a dim glow from beyond it.

Absent any glass shards to worry about, I crouched under it and slowly came erect, peering in to find myself confronted with the back of Walter's head. What illumination there was emanated from a hurricane lantern on a crate in a small room outfitted with army cots. I assumed Walter was sitting on one, a second positioned perpendicular to it along the wall. The offensive stock pot was in the far corner nearest a door that opened onto the interior.

Nunna stood, her back against it, clutching a blanket to her chest, her eyes wide with terror. Having seen her in this state only once before, I could guess the source of her panic. My beloved Nunna had once outbluffed a mountain lion that had invaded our backyard, but let a rat within spitting distance and she came undone.

I heard the pounding of footsteps before the door burst open, hitting Nunna in the back.

"What the hell's going on in here?" Hooker panted. "A man can't even take a leak in peace."

"Another rat," Walter said. "Bigger than the last one. I tried to get him with my cane, but he ran under Nunnally's cot."

"Goddamned pain in the neck. Give me that."

Hoping that Hooker would be too busy searching for the rat to notice, I peeked in again. Hooker's rear end mooned me as he knelt to look under the cot.

Wincing, Nunna was rubbing her back, her bottom lip between her teeth. Her eyes locked with her husband's, as if calculating whether to run, and then, naked astonishment blazing across her face, with mine. I was surprised she could see me. I ducked and hurried around the end of the building past the dark sports utility vehicle looming in the dusk.

Somewhere in the distance, the roar of supercharged engines cut through the silence. The cavalry was on the way. But if I could hear them, there was a good chance Hooker might too. Pulling up short at the edge of the building, I stuck my head around the corner. The door from which

Hooker and Nunna had emerged earlier was perhaps six feet away, a pile of trash between me and it. Skirting the trash, I edged toward the door. The early evening was silent again. I assumed our backup had arrived and had stopped where we had left our car.

I was debating the wisdom of slipping inside when a ruckus from the interior made me freeze in place.

"I killed him, you get rid of him," Hooker said. "Outside, lady! Don't you move, old man!"

Footsteps scuffed toward the door. They were too close. There was no way I could get back around the end of the building before they came out. I was empty-handed, with nothing to use as a weapon. Frantic, I looked behind me. If there was something in the trash I could use . . .

Stooping, I groped the pile. My fingers closed on something that pricked the skin, a thin triangular blade of some sort of hand saw.

The door flew open and slammed against the wall, missing me by inches. Nunna came lurching out, obviously propelled from behind. The building was one step up and she fell, hard, the rat she carried arcing into the dusk.

Hooker stepped down onto the ground, a Saturday night special in his artificial right hand. I hadn't counted on that.

"Get up, old lady." He drew back a stocky leg to kick her, and pure, white-hot rage became my rocket launcher. With a roar of primeval origins, I hurtled toward him. He toppled sideways with a bellow, the arm on which he'd fallen emitting the sound of grinding gears, the other flailing under me. He was heavier, but fury gave me the advantage.

I yanked him over onto his stomach, snatched the hood of his uniform off, and planted both knees dead center of his back. I couldn't see the revolver. With my left hand entwined in his hair, I yanked his head toward me and pressed the point of the rusty blade against his exposed neck.

"Babe, don't!" Duck's voice penetrated a bloodred haze, my pulse so loud in my ears that he sounded miles away. "Don't do it!"

"He hurt Nunna! And he's carrying!"

"No, he's not." Nunna, still on all fours, rolled over into a sitting position, the gun under her hand. "See. I've got it and I'm fine." She frowned. "What happened to your forehead? And your hand's bleeding, honey. Put that thing down."

"Let it go, babe." Duck knelt at my side, his fingers a vice around my wrist. "You've got him, Leigh. Now, let it go."

Slowly the haze dissipated. The rage took a bit longer. It was even money as to which of us was breathing harder, Hooker or me. His was noisier, however, phlegm-filled, rattling. He began to cough, his body bucking with each expulsion of air. He was helpless. And as much as I hated him, as much as I wanted to send him to hell, I was still Leigh Ann Warren. I couldn't do it.

I dropped the blade, only now aware of the stabbing pain and the series of tiny punctures across my palm. Tetanus City. I scrambled to my feet to help Nunna to hers, grabbed her to hang on for dear, dear life. "He hurt you! I couldn't stand it."

"Nothing a soak in epsom salts won't cure," she murmured, rocking me. "I'm so sorry to put you through this. Walter, are you all right?"

I released her and turned to see the chief helping Nunna's husband negotiate the step to the ground. Walter glanced around, taking in the assemblage of agents and county cops. "I'm fine, sweetheart," he said. "Looks like I missed something."

Hooker was being handcuffed.

"What good you figure that's gonna do?" Mr. Sheriff asked. "If he can get those arms of his off, y'all will be holding air."

The uniforms looked embarrassed and began reconsidering their options.

"Where do you figure I'm going?" Hooker wheezed. "I wouldn't have hurt them, anyway, not seriously. All I wanted was my medal."

Devoid of any sympathy for him, I said, "Well, I have it, and you aren't going to get it." If I hadn't seen his mistreatment of Nunna, I might have considered it. But I had. And there were the Beardsleys and what he'd done to them. Uh-uh. No way would I give him my father's Silver Star.

20

TEN DAYS LATER, SURROUNDED BY PEOPLE named Rich and Ritch from everywhere imaginable, I was back in the exhibit hall in Ourland at a surprise family reunion held in my honor. It was a bittersweet occasion, with Stuart's death still fresh on everyone's mind, but the reunion had been Elizabeth's idea and no one had had the nerve to suggest she wait. Considering how frail her twin appeared, I suspected that my grandmother wanted to be sure that Ruth would be around to attend.

The family had blown a mint to do this. We sat at linen-covered tables being served by caterers in formal wear, with Mary Castle overseeing them. I'd met so many cousins on both sides of the family that I'd long since lost track of their names.

"I've got a question," Duck said to Bonita. "Explain the different spellings of Rich, please."

Frances butted in. "Our ancestors were slaves on a plantation owned by a family originally from the French West Indies named Ritchelieu. Once our folks were freed, they decided on the surname Ritch-with-a-T. But most of them were illiterate. When others wrote the name for them, they spelled it without the T. It wasn't until all the cousins were reunited and moved here a couple of generations later that they discovered the mistake. By then it was too much trouble to change."

"And you're both," Duck said to me, his gaze a caress. "For another three weeks, that is."

My grandparents and aunts had pushed to help pay for a big wedding, but I'd stonewalled. I wanted to keep things as simple as possible.

My grandfather, still a little pale and yet to regain his former vigor, sat between Nunna and Walter, chatting with them like an old friend, his eyes meeting mine every now and then. There was a unique bond between us which I suspected we'd be well advised to downplay. Elizabeth was still upset that when he'd finally regained consciousness, the first person he'd asked for had been me.

It was nearing ten when the affair wound down. I was tired, anxious to leave, if only for some quiet time to become accustomed to being a part of such a big, demonstrative family. Duck was helping me into my coat when W. Two and Jon approached us.

"Hey, sis," Jon said, "I've been meaning to ask you, what's happened to the couple Hooker used as stand-ins for your folks?"

"They're in good hands," I said. "Hooker's son has hired a dynamite lawyer to defend them. Hooker Junior's determined to make up for what his father did."

"Well, you'll understand why I sympathize with him," Jon said. "I guess he and I are in the same boat, hoping we can atone for the sins of our fathers—which has nothing to do with the offer we'd like you to consider, sis. After you've talked it over with Duck, of course. Give us an answer when you get back from your honeymoon."

"Sure. What's up?" I wiggled my fingers into my gloves, itching to head for home.

"We need us a police force," W. Two said gruffly.

"There's no reason for us to keep relying on the county when we're entitled to have a law enforcement presence of our own."

I stopped my finger wiggling. "You are?"

"Sure. I thought about asking Duck here, but we can't give him the kind of money he's making now. And he'd probably keel over from boredom. Appearances to the contrary," he said, lowering his voice, "we don't go in much for murder around here." Jon winced, but kept still. "We do have our share of cutups and dustups, rowdy behavior, especially during the summer when outsiders are visiting residents. And every now and again, somebody hits on our stores. So the need is there. if you're interested."

I was in shock at being asked. "But my knee."

"It's not like you'll have any pursuits on foot." Jon grinned. "Besides, we've got Uncle Wayne for that. Seriously, sis, we wouldn't ask if we didn't think you could handle it. Hire a couple of men to work for you. You have the experience, maybe not much administrative, but that'll come. And you have a stake in this town since you're a landowner."

That shook me. I guess I hadn t taken that seriously. I glanced back at Duck.

"Don't look at me," he said, palms up in surrender. "It's up to you. No reason you couldn't commute. I don't know where this property of yours is—"

"On the waterfront," Jon supplied.

Duck's eyes saucered. "You're kidding! On the bay? We are getting married tonight!"

"Stop fooling around," I said, in no mood for jocularity. "I want to know how you feel about this."

He sobered. "What's the problem, babe? You want to be a cop, right? Out among the people instead of sitting on your can behind a desk. It might get a little tricky when the people are members of your family, but hey, if they break the law, you throw their asses in jail and worry about hurt feelings later. If you've got property, we'll build on it, live both places. Now are there any other monkey wrenches you can think of?"

I'd known Dillon Kennedy for just short of ten years and didn't think I'd ever love him more than this moment. I had him, and Nunna and Walter back. I had grandparents, a twin brother, and more family than I knew what to do with. Now this.

I let out a whoop. "Hot *damn*! I've got me a *J-O-B!!*"